Whitewood House

To my dear friend, Tamzin Lodge, who gave me the inspiration for this story.

Prologue

As twilight descended on the Close, electric lights blinked on in the houses, in a variety of rooms, the lives of the occupants momentarily framed by windows until such time as drapes or blinds were closed to shut out the night. Only one house stood alone and silent in the midst of all this illumination.

The darkened windows of Whitewood House stared out in vacant desolation across the grassed area before it, as if lonely and dreaming of a time when its rooms had also been filled by music and conversation, with the love and laughter of a family. Yet this was no ordinary residence. Whitewood House refused to fall into disrepair or allow for the vague rumour of ghosts to linger within its walls. It certainly had its own secrets, yet these were more than a source of intrigue. It was as though the house knew daylight would return, after the long night, the bright sunlight witnessing to the fact that the neighbouring buildings were mere copies of a handsome, cleverly-designed and well-built original house. Anyone entering immediately felt they had come home, for the house seemed to promise comfort during difficult times, and always hope for the future. Very soon a new, young family would arrive and Whitewood House would welcome its members and win their hearts.

In the meantime, the house refused to be excluded from this festivity of lights, this electrical show of human life-force. With a faint murmur of pleasure, a window high up to the side of the house, barely visible through the branches of a tree, faintly glowed in the darkness.

Clack, clack, ching. The writer examined the typewritten page on the roller of the old black Imperial typewriter, ideas for the new novel still fresh. The story commenced.

Chapter One
2015

The office chair creaked as Clive Acton leaned forward, steepling his fingers and blowing gently on them as he surveyed the papers scattered across the surface of his desk. The investigation, which had taken some months, had been extensive, his research thorough, and he now felt he was at last in a position to make a start on the detailed report he'd been hired to provide.

His wealthy client had stipulated complete confidentiality and that he not only personally manage the job, but also do the necessary leg-work and write up himself. The task had so far proved challenging and time-consuming, as he'd known it would. However, the pay-off would mean a desperately needed reprieve for his struggling new agency, buying valuable time to build up its reputation. Still, he couldn't help but wonder – with some cynicism – why all the secrecy? What were his client's motives in acquiring such in-depth information concerning land which had long been protected by law from further development?

Acton had visited the location of his subject matter, and taking care to be discreet, had explored the lie of the land and taken photographs. He had printed these off for reference purposes and used the internet to put together a demographic area profile. He now read through his notes for the physical description of the place, comparing them to the pictures:

'Whitewood Close is located on the outskirts of the rural village of Bushwell, approximately seven miles from the town of Rainham in the Medway area of the county of Kent. The road leading to and beyond Whitewood Close, and the land upon which the small housing estate is built, together with the acres surrounding it, is known as Darrington Way. The Close is secluded, access being gained via a turn-off from the lane

through Darrington Way onto a private road. It consists of a cluster of five detached houses built in a semi-circle around a wide green, hedged on the far side with trees.

'The original building, formerly known as Whitewood House, is positioned in the middle of the semi-circle of houses. It was built in the early sixties and reflects the fashion during that period for spacious accommodation. The structure is of red brick with a part-tiled, part white wooden fascia, and large windows, now double-glazed. There is a garage at the rear of the property, to one side. The other four houses, built in the early seventies, were constructed in a similar style in keeping with the original property.'

Acton had discovered that this first house, and thereafter the Close, had been named for the white butterflies which had once frequented the woods and meadows beyond the houses. However, neighbouring land to Darrington Way had long since been urbanised, and much of the natural habitat had disappeared beneath a sprawling housing development attached to Bushwell Village. As a result, the delicate white butterflies had gradually disappeared and were now the mere whisper of a memory, despite the thin belt of protected woodland to the rear, and relatively small fields of agricultural land to the other three sides of Whitewood Close.

The next document Acton picked up was a Photostat copy of a faded newspaper article dated 13th January, 1895 reporting the mysterious disappearance of a promising young scientist, Albert Edward Henry Darrington. According to the article the police suspected foul play, although further research by Acton revealed that Darrington's body had never been found and, with no obvious suspects, the case had been left open, the mystery remaining unsolved. The missing scientist was the person for whom Darrington Way was named and copies had been made of the deeds showing his ownership of the land. Intrigued, the private investigator had been able to discover very little about the man, except that he had been born an only child to Edna Harriet Darrington and Sir George Alfred Felix Darrington on 26th June 1863, and he was baptised at St. Luke's Church in Bushwell two months later. He was educated at Cambridge and was well-respected in his field of expertise, having contributed to a number of scientific journals. These days, Acton thought, Albert would have been called a physicist, for matter and energy appeared to be of principal interest to him.

Darrington's land had been in his family for generations, as far back as the reign of the Tudors and Acton had wondered why the family had never had a stately home constructed. After further research, he discovered that the Darringtons had been a merchant family, living much of the time abroad, travelling to and from London or residing there. The land in Kent was therefore put to agricultural use, with rents collected and profit reaped by the family. Thus, the land had passed down the Darrington line through the centuries and Albert had automatically inherited it when he came of age.

Albert hadn't known either of his parents as they had died while he was a baby, and he had apparently never found the time to marry. Since he had left no close family when he disappeared, the property had eventually passed to his third cousin, Jonathon Edward Fisherton in 1903.

Information about Fisherton had been reasonably easy to come by. Not only were there detailed public records concerning his business ventures, but copies of personal correspondence still survived and were exhibited in a local museum. Fisherton was famous because he was already, by the Edwardian era, a wealthy industrialist. However, by his own admission, his one weakness at the time of acquiring the land had been his young, heavily pregnant wife. When he took her to view the pretty meadow, fields and woodland, she apparently fell in love with the place and made her husband promise to leave it exactly as they'd found it. Jonathon was a man of his word, and left a letter with his last Will and Testament to explain why he had retained Darrington Way, even though he had been unfortunate enough in later years to lose a large portion of his wealth due to poor overseas investments. His young wife had died in childbirth shortly after their visit and the baby, a girl, died three days later. In his letter, he declared himself heartbroken and confessed that he had never once returned to look at the land again.

Happily, records reveal that Jonathon remarried later in life, having sold off his remaining shares in factories and a mill, and he had retired to the West Country. His second wife, the daughter of a vicar, gave him three children to comfort him in his declining years, the first being a son, Nathaniel Joseph Fisherton, born in the winter of 1910.

Clive Acton sighed as he perused the documents and his notes; by this point, he had become so engrossed in the family history that if his wealthy client had withdrawn his business, Acton might have considered continuing his research in his own free time purely out of interest. Fortunately, that eventuality had not occurred.

Acton discovered that by the time Nathaniel Fisherton came into his inheritance, he'd already taken the cloth, and he donated most of the money and property he'd been left to a charity involved in missionary work in Africa. However, he kept Darrington Way out of respect for his late father's wishes and so, upon Nathaniel's early demise from pneumonia at the age of 50 in 1960, it was bequeathed to his only son, Henry Mark Fisherton, then aged 21.

Henry had studied theology probably (Acton believed) to please his parents since his real passion had obviously been the writing of fiction – science fiction to be exact. His work in this respect revealed an avid interest in engineering and technology, and by the time he'd finished his theological degree, he'd also managed to write and find a publisher for his debut novel which was about space explorers and was set in the distant future. The advance cheque he had received from his second novel about time travel, and the royalties that quickly accrued, helped finance the building of Whitewood House in 1962 as a home for himself and his new wife. This subsequently became number 3 Whitewood Close due to its central position in the Close.

Acton was curious as to how and why Henry had somehow later come to sell the small meadow immediately surrounding Whitewood House. His early novels had quickly become bestsellers and he'd written and sold a whole series of books based on the same characters from his second novel in the years that followed. These were taken on by one of the most prominent publishing houses and the novels continued to be popular today, so it seemed unlikely he would have needed the money.

As a result of the sale of the portion of land, the houses on either side of the original house were added eight years later, very much against Henry's wishes. This was evidenced by the vast amount of legal documentation which existed showing he had fought hard to prevent the building work and, although he failed to halt the development of the Close around his home, he was successful in ensuring the land immediately surrounding the Close was protected for the future. Having done this, he had shut up the house and emigrated with his young daughter to America in December of 1974. There was no record of his wife having accompanied them.

In time, Henry's daughter, Melody-Aria, had returned as an adult to live in the house with her husband, Roger Stockman, a man much older than herself who had been one of her father's associates in the States. Henry remained in America, having remarried. He suffered a fatal heart attack in 1987 aged just 48.

Number 3 Whitewood house was sold in 2007 to the present owners, a Mr. Sean Miles and his wife, Imogen. Acton had been unable to trace the present whereabouts of the Stockmans, so their reasons for selling and anything else appertaining to their lives remained unknown. This, of course, would have to be rectified through further enquiries along with certain other aspects of the report, for he had no doubt whatsoever that his client would be dissatisfied with incomplete information.

Acton shuffled the notes and documents he'd been examining to one side and picked up the final bundle of papers. These contained details and history of ownership of the other four houses on the site and of the tenancy agreements for the farmland and woodland. He glanced through them briefly before using his intercom to instruct his assistant to order in food from a local Chinese restaurant. He knew he was going to be busy for some time.

Chapter Two

Music, pierced with melancholy, began to play and then the shuffling of shoes informed Imogen that people were getting to their feet as she walked arm in arm with her father, following her mother's coffin into the chapel. They were met with the sweet, slightly musky smell of chrysanthemums – her mum's favourite flowers – and the warmth of melting candlewax. As a funeral director's wife, her mother had planned her own funeral meticulously to spare her family the burden. Imogen watched as the coffin was placed on pedestals between two flower stands, the autumnal colours of the blooms reflected on the dark polished wood, then her brother, Simon, bowed with the rest of the poll bearers and took his place in the pew by her side.

Imogen waited for the music to come to an end yet it continued on; something wasn't quite right. She was overwhelmed by fatigue and felt herself falling. She reached for the pew in front of her in a vain attempt to keep from fainting and with a jerk of panic, woke up. The dream, an aching memory, faded, unlike the sorrowful melody which refused to dissipate, drifting softly up the stairs from the room below.

Sean must be home, she thought, mildly surprised by his choice of music. She dragged herself from bed, wrapping her dressing gown about her and pushing her feet into the comfortable warmth of slippers. It wasn't yet morning, she surmised, though dawn wasn't far off. It was as good a time as any to confront him. She made her way down the stairs and as she reached the lounge door, the track finished, although it immediately began again. The door was ajar and she pushed it open, then stood quite still for several seconds unable to move.

"Who the Hell are you?" she finally found her voice. Not only had Sean had the temerity to stay out until the early hours of the morning, but he'd apparently invited a young woman she'd never seen before into their home!

Mere seconds passed, but Imogen's thought process sped up as she took in every detail of the person before her. The first thing she noticed about the woman was her long luxuriant hair which was the kind of blonde that women everywhere attempted to achieve artificially with the use of expensive chemicals and never quite succeeded. A few strands had been plaited about her forehead to form a kind of headband but the rest fell past her shoulders to her waist to provide a thick shawl for her upper arms. Imogen ran her fingers through her own hair which she kept long because Sean had always said he liked it that way. She usually tied it back during the daytime, though, because it was forever getting in her way. Unlike this young woman's hair, it was fine and never grew more than about six centimetres beyond her shoulders. Imogen's heart sank. If this was her adversary, their marriage was certainly in trouble. Imogen noted the woman's slender frame and the clothes she wore. She had on a pink tie-dyed shirt beneath a slightly grubby, fringed denim jacket of pale blue. The shirt was belted loosely at the waist, and her long, red flowing skirt, the fabric printed with tiny flowers, spilled over her legs to the floor. She'd made herself comfortable, half lying on the sofa with cushions supporting her back and her feet up, flat sandals resting on Imogen's coffee table. She was holding the CD case to the Don McLean *American Pie* album in front of her face and appeared to be studying it.

Sensing Imogen's presence, the young woman looked up and smiled. Multi-coloured bangles jingled on her wrist as she laid the CD case on the cushion beside her.

"Cool, I wondered when you'd be down." The young woman's gentle voice had just a trace of an American accent which made it all the more attractive. The song started up again - she had it on repeat. "Sorry, can we just listen to this song one more time?" she said. "Aren't the lyrics just to die for? It's as if it was written about me." Imogen had been about to protest, but the young woman placed a finger to her lips, "Shhh. Listen," she said, then closed her eyes.

Trembling with indignation and, although she hated to admit it, fear, Imogen crossed the room to pick up the remote to the compact disc player, intending to stop the music immediately, but then she paused, looking at the young woman who had such a wistful expression on her face. Who am I kidding? she thought. My marriage isn't just in trouble. It's over. No amount of make-up, trips to the hair salon, or trendy new clothes could even begin to help me compete with this exotic butterfly. And she looks young - she can only be in her mid-twenties!

Imogen found herself listening in companionship with the young woman, to the soulful voice of Don McLean, and recognised the song as *Crossroads*. Imogen hadn't listened to the album for years, even though it had been downloaded onto her iPod. They rarely played CDs now. However, this particular album had been a birthday gift, several years ago, from her mother who had always insisted on sharing her own taste in music with her daughter. It must have been the music that had triggered the dream. The lyrics were indeed thought-provoking, advising the listener that no matter what decisions you made in life, you would always end up where you were supposed to be. At least that was how Imogen understood them, and she briefly wondered what the song could mean to the young woman. The last few piano chords were played and Imogen came out of her trance and pressed the off switch on the remote. The woman removed her feet from the coffee table and sat up, flicking a strand of her hair over her shoulder. She smiled at Imogen again – blue, blue eyes in a flawless complexion. Imogen decided to take control of the situation and accept her defeat with dignity.

"So, where's Sean?" Imogen asked.

"Sean?"

"Yes, Sean. The man I happen to be married to," she said.

"I don't know Sean, sorry." The young woman looked genuinely puzzled. "I'm here because I wanted to see the house. I used to live here, you see, and wondered whether it had changed much. I was keen to see inside."

Imogen experienced a confusion of relief and anger surge through her. She doesn't know Sean, she thought. Yet still he had stayed out all night and hadn't even thought to call her. She took her annoyance out on the young woman.

"Hmm. You thought you'd just break in, I suppose, and find out if **my** house would make a good squat. What are you, some sort of druggie? I should call the police."

The woman stood up, her palms raised towards Imogen. "Easy, sister, you've got me wrong. I don't do drugs, not even weed, and I didn't break in. The front door was open when I arrived. I thought it was strange since there were no lights, so I tried knocking and calling out before I came in."

Imogen raised her eyebrows and stared the young woman down, hands on hips. She believed her, but wasn't ready to admit it just yet.

Her thoughts raced. She knew the front door hadn't been open when she'd gone up to bed, so Sean must have been home and gone back out again. He was never particularly cautious about pulling the door to for the latch to catch and over the years the catch had become faulty. Why did I ever imagine he would care that I was sleeping in the spare room? she thought. Why had she believed for one moment that he would regret his recent neglect of her? All she'd managed to do was give him yet another opportunity to avoid talking about their problems.

"You expect me to believe that?" she said.

"Sure," the woman replied, "It's the way it was. Listen, I even went upstairs and saw you fast asleep through your open door. You looked completely out of it, so I wasn't sure what I should do. I didn't like to disturb you." She shrugged. "I obviously have, though, and taken liberties playing your music. I'm sorry, I just wasn't thinking straight. It's just that I always loved this house very much and it still feels like home. I really dig what you've done with the place," She glanced about her then looked back at Imogen. "Look, I'll just go. I've intruded enough." She stooped to pick up a cloth shoulder-bag from the floor.

"No, wait. I think perhaps it's me who should apologise."

An odd kind of acceptance had settled over Imogen and she no longer felt cross, just sad again.

"That door needs repairing. It doesn't always shut properly," she said. "If it hadn't been for you, I might well have been burgled or even murdered in my sleep." She tried to smile. "You're quite right, I was out for the count. I suppose it's because I haven't been sleeping properly lately. You have to admit though, not many people would just make themselves at home and wait for the householder to wake up if they found the front door of a house wide open."

"Yeah, I get what you're saying. I'm truly sorry."

"It's fine. Please sit back down and I'll make us some coffee. I'm Imogen, by the way, and you are?"

"Alicia. Great to meet you. Would you mind if I came with you? I'd love to see the kitchen."

Imogen shrugged. "Okay."

The young woman wandered about the kitchen, trailing her hand along the worktops and looking about her as Imogen filled the kettle and retrieved a couple of mugs from the cupboard. She was out of decent coffee. Instant coffee would have to do, she decided.

15

"Your sleepless nights, do they have anything to do with your man? Tell me to mind my own business if you like, but you sure seemed stressed about him."

Imogen turned for a moment to face Alicia. "Sean, yes, and life in general, I suppose. I'm fond of this house too, although I've recently been wondering if I should leave it and move on. You say you lived here before," she changed the subject. "You must have been very young. We've lived here eight years, unless … are you related to Mr. Stockman, the previous owner?"

"I'm probably older than you think," the young woman threw her head back and laughed. Imogen watched her until, regaining her composure, she said, "Yeah, I guess we are related, although I haven't been in the area for an age. I'm fairly certain he wouldn't want anything to do with me."

Imogen returned her attention to making the coffee, considering Alicia's comment. Maybe she was right, but then who would have guessed the stern-faced man in his seventies, who had first shown them around the house, would also be the type to take the brave decision to travel the world before the cancer, discovered in its early stages, robbed him of his faculties? He hadn't seemed the type to confide his reasons for wanting a quick sale, either, so they had respected his trust and hadn't quibbled over his asking price, which had been well within their budget anyway.

"If you really want to know what to do, the house can help you make a decision," Alicia said. "Just go back to sleep in that bedroom. Think about what you want to know and, well it helped me to decide what to do."

Imogen kept her face turned away to hide her expression. She continued to make the coffee in silence, trying to work out how to reply without offending the girl. "I wish it was as easy as that," she began, turning with two steaming mugs in her hands, but the young woman had gone.

"Alicia?" she called, taking the drinks into the lounge and setting them on the coffee table. She must be using the bathroom, Imogen thought. She waited a few minutes then went to call up the stairs. No answer. Bemused, she wandered around the house, searching, yet it was as if the woman had never been there.

Tiredly, Imogen went to the front door to discover her key was still in the lock on the inside, the keyring with the silver heart dangling from it attached. She'd forgotten she'd left it there. No wonder Sean isn't here – he couldn't get in! she thought. That young woman... I must have been sleepwalking and dreaming. I'm really beginning to lose it. She went and sat down on the third stair from the bottom and waited for her heart to stop crashing into her ribcage.

It was a while before her panic subsided and she was able to think calmly again. She went to fetch her mobile, resolving to text Sean and ask where he was. Even if he didn't reply right away, she'd cook a special meal for when he was due home that evening and she'd make him talk. She'd convince him they needed to sort out their problems, maybe see a marriage guidance counsellor. That decided, Imogen yawned and made a mental note to make an appointment with the doctor as soon as the surgery was open. She'd tell Dr. Macey the tablets she'd prescribed for her depression weren't helping. In fact, they seemed to be making matters worse.

Imogen went back to the lounge to get her coffee, deciding she might as well take it up to bed with her and read or something. She wasn't ready yet to begin the day. She took the spare drink and emptied it down the sink, rinsing and drying the mug and replacing it in the cupboard. Then, out of habit, she went back to the lounge to plump up the cushions and make sure everything was tidy. That's when she noticed the empty Don Mclean CD case still lying on the sofa cushion.

17

All the planning in the world would not have made the slightest difference to the outcome of that evening. Imogen had spent much of the day cleaning, vacuuming, dusting and generally ensuring the house was at its best – warm and inviting. She'd gone shopping for the ingredients for an exotic beef dish she'd found in one of her many cookery books, and had been persuaded, at an off-license in Rainham, to buy a rather expensive wine which she hoped would complement the food. She'd also treated herself to some wonderfully smelling bath oils and had then spotted a divine crimson midi-dress in a store window, which she went in to try on. It was a flattering fit and the colour set off her dark hair so she bought that too.

Her culinary skills were nothing compared to those of her in-laws who owned and ran a popular restaurant in Canterbury, but she felt she deserved top marks for effort after an hour and a half of peeling, chopping and mixing as she prepared the meal and set the timer on the oven before going up for her bath. When Sean arrived home, the dining table had already been set with a crisp white cloth and cutlery and glassware gleamed in the soft light of two tall flickering candles. Imogen was in the kitchen humming along to the latest Adele hit as she put the finishing touches to the meal. She turned and smiled, as Sean joined her in the kitchen, handing him a glass of wine. Sean was immediately on the defensive.

"Alright, I know I should have rung you myself, but I was running late and I had to hand my mobile over at the reception of the factory I was visiting. Sharon promised she'd let you know. Then I took the customer out for a meal and it was late when I got back to the hotel. I'm sorry."

Imogen took off her apron and hung it up before taking up her own glass of wine. "Okay, apology accepted," she said.

"Do you mean it?" He looked hopeful. "I gave Sharon a good telling off when I got your text this morning." He sipped the wine then held the glass up to look at it, swirling the ruby liquid around and around in the glass bowl. "Poor kid burst into tears and then I felt pretty mean because I know she's got problems at home. Still, I told her if she wants to continue working for me she'd better focus a bit more on her job."

Imogen nodded trying to look sympathetic, although she did wonder why he hadn't excused himself for a few minutes to make a quick call before dining with his client. She decided not to pursue it. Sean took himself through the archway into the dining room and sat down.

"Did you get the contract?" she asked as she carried plates laden with food through from the kitchen.

"Contract? Oh, yes, well nothing's certain yet. This looks delicious," he said, spreading his napkin over his lap and taking up his knife and fork.

That was when things had really started to go wrong. The meal was virtually inedible; the beef was tough and some pieces were charred from overcooking. After several minutes of chewing, Sean declared himself defeated. Crestfallen, Imogen had removed the plates.

"I should have stuck to something plain – a nice roast, perhaps. I've always been able to manage a reasonable roast," she said.

"I don't know why you worry so much," he said. "You know I've never really been into all that fancy food. Why'd you think I left the family business to work in a factory that makes cardboard boxes?"

"You wanted to make something of yourself, and be your own boss one day," Imogen said, trying not to sound snappish. She brought in the dessert - a sherry trifle.

19

"I managed it, didn't I? I'm the boss of my own company. I run the show!" Sean caught her about the waist as she placed the bowls on the table. "Let's go to bed for afters," he suggested. "You look wonderful tonight."

Imogen pulled herself free. "No, Sean. I really think we need to talk first."

"Oh, come on, why spoil things? This is the first time in months we haven't either been at each other's throats, or avoiding one another. Let's just go with the mood."

Imogen sat back down at her place and began to spoon trifle into the little glass dessert bowls. "I can't just pretend everything's alright. There are things we need to discuss."

"Discuss? Oh, that's right. I forgot. You're not interested in having sex unless it's the right time of the month. We can't just have fun anymore. We've always got to be trying to make babies. Well I've had enough!" He got up from his chair and threw his napkin onto the table. "It isn't my fault you can't conceive. God knows, I've tried to make it happen. We've spent a fortune on IVF. You need to get over it." He strode out of the room, pausing in the hall just long enough to grab his jacket. "I'm going to the pub," he said and left the house, slamming the door behind him.

Imogen had plenty of time to get over the shock of his outburst and was waiting in their bedroom, when he got back, relieved that he hadn't stayed out all night again. She was wearing a negligee and had arranged herself to lie provocatively on top of the bed, intent on making peace. However, Sean just ignored her, switching off the light so that he didn't have to avoid seeing the hurt in her eyes. He undressed, slipping into bed on the far side and turned his back to her. Feeling humiliated, yet refusing to be defeated, she slid beneath the bedclothes herself, and snuggled up closer to him. He smelt of stale beer and cigarettes. Wrinkling her nose, she put her arm around him, and kissed his shoulder.

When he didn't respond, she said. "You're right. We don't have fun anymore. We never laugh." Still nothing, although she knew from the way his breathing had slowed that he was listening. "I uh had this really weird dream last night. I walked into the lounge and there was this pretty hippy woman sitting on the sofa listening to Don Maclean and I thought … I thought …" She couldn't bring herself to ask: *Are you playing away from home?*

Sean rolled over to face her and Imogen thought she could just make out the glint of his eyes in the darkness. She took a deep breath to steady her nerves. "We don't communicate any more, Sean. I think we need help. I've been looking online for information about marriage guidance sessions. We might have to wait a couple of weeks but …"

"I'm not doing that with you," he growled. "Not now, not ever. Now if you want to sulk and go sleep in the spare room it's up to you. I need to rest."

He turned his back on her again, moving away from her once more and this time she left the space between them.

Chapter Four

Matilda Worthington, better known as Tilly to just about everyone who knew her, sat at the breakfast table at number 2 Whitewood Close, the picture of comfortable middle age, with laughter lines, rather than wrinkles, and hair that was never untidy. She was spreading a thin layer of marmalade on a piece of toast, and waiting for her husband, Neil, to lower his copy of *The Financial Times* so she could talk to him. Her patience was rewarded as he reached for his tea cup and, finding it empty, passed it to her for a refill.

Neil was still a handsome man, Tilly thought with pride. In his early fifties, his dark hair was flecked with grey, as was his closely cropped beard, yet it suited him. However, even though he was wearing his reading glasses, she could see this morning there were dark smudges under his grey eyes.

"You didn't sleep very well last night," Tilly commented. "Are you worried about work?" She poured his tea and handed the cup back to him.

"Not really. We're considering recruiting more graduates and that can only mean business is good. No, I was thinking about Adrian," he said, as if that explained everything, and really it did. He folded his newspaper and drained his teacup. "I suppose I'd better get going in a minute if I'm going to miss the traffic. How about you? What are your plans for the day?"

"Me? Oh, I think I'm going to have a nice lazy start to the morning, go back to bed and maybe read for an hour or so. Then I might go in and make a start on my classroom displays; school's open until midday. On the other hand, I could just stay home, sit out in the garden and enjoy the sunshine while I catch up on paperwork."

"Well whatever you decide, have a good day," he kissed her cheek and left the house.

They both knew she wouldn't be able to unwind properly for at least a couple of days into the summer break and he'd long ago realised it was pointless trying to persuade her to give up work. It was true they didn't need the extra income, but she still enjoyed the sense of achievement her work brought and until her passion faded, she wanted to continue teaching.

Tilly got up to clear the table and found her husband's mobile phone concealed beneath his newspaper. She hurried after him and was just in time to stop him, as he backed his Mercedes off the drive, and she handed him the phone. She waved as he drove out of Whitewood Close and onto Darrington Way, then, turning to go back inside, she spied Imogen Miles kneeling at the edge of her lawn digging at the border with a little trowel. She watched for several seconds before speaking to her.

"Hiya Imogen, you're up and about early. How are you?"

Startled, her neighbour looked up and got awkwardly to her feet, brushing soil from her hands. "Oh! Hi Tilly. I'm fine, thanks," She looked down at her apparel as if suddenly realising she was still in her bathrobe. "I'm waiting for the locksmith. My door isn't latching properly and he said he'd be here at seven, so I came to look out for him." She gestured towards the borders. "I just saw a few weeds and decided to deal with them before they took hold. I guess I'd better go and get dressed."

It was clear to Tilly that her neighbour, who was some twenty odd years her junior, was far from fine. In fact, she looked haggard. It was also obvious from the bloodshot eyes and puffy face Imogen had been crying. A brief image of bare display boards flittered across Tilly's mind, taunting her, but she dismissed it; her classroom could wait for another day.

"Before you hurry off, would it be okay if I popped around for a coffee while you're waiting for the locksmith? I need to put some clothes on myself, of course. I can be with you in

23

about ten minutes, though." Seeing the hesitation in Imogen's eyes, she added. "I could really use some advice."

There had always been something pleasing about Imogen's kitchen that Tilly had never been able to replicate in her own home, despite copying the sunny yellow paint on the walls. It wasn't the fitted cabinets, shiny work surfaces or appliances, or even the ceramic tiling on the floor. Tilly's kitchen was laid out in a similar fashion, as was the rest of the house, so it wasn't that either. No, it was something intangible like a familiar scent that stirred half-forgotten memories of happy times, yet when she sniffed all she could smell was a faint odour of orange blossom from the cleaner Imogen used, and of course freshly ground coffee.

"How's school been?" Imogen asked as she helped herself to a biscuit. She looked better than she had earlier, Tilly noted with some satisfaction, more like her usual self. It was, she suspected though, probably due to carefully applied make-up.

"Another year over," Tilly replied. "I'm on summer break now and looking forward to spending some time with Julie and my little grandson, Timothy. Did I tell you he's started walking already? And he's beginning to talk! He's just so cute." She took her mobile phone from her pocket and opened it to find the latest photos to show Imogen. She swiped past several Julie had taken of Tilly with the toddler, shuddering. The camera, or in this case, mobile phone, always made her look old and fat, she thought. She was beginning to put on a few extra pounds, and being only five feet tall it was bound to show, although it was only to be expected, a little middle-age spread. She looked after herself apart from that, had her auburn hair styled and coloured every six weeks to banish any trace of grey, and enjoyed the occasional facial and manicure. She shrugged off these thoughts and quickly found some pictures of Timothy by himself and with his mother for Imogen to see.

24

Once Imogen had finished admiring the pictures and had returned Tilly's phone to her, Tilly asked, "What have you been up to lately?"

"Not much. I've spent a bit of time in the garden now the weather's fine, and I'm toying with the idea of taking cookery lessons, although my computer work will still take precedence. It's just that I ruined a perfectly good piece of beef last night and I wouldn't mind but it took me over an hour of preparation to do it!"

"I always thought Adrian would make a good cook," Tilly mused. "He always liked to try out recipes and experiment with different herbs and spices when he had the chance. That's one of the things I miss about him now he doesn't live with us – he used to give me a break from the kitchen every once in a while."

"How are things with your step-son these days?"

"With Adrian?" Tilly sighed. "We haven't heard from him since his brother, Keith, left for Australia and that was eighteen months ago, now. Keith told us his brother had dropped out of university and got mixed up with some unsavoury characters. What Adrian's up to now is anybody's guess. Neil's worried and I don't know what to do to help."

"Do you think he's still in touch with his mother?"

"No idea. She's not replying to Neil's emails or phone calls and she was never very helpful when it came to the boys, especially Adrian. I think she's a bit too wrapped up in her own personal life to worry much about her sons."

"That's tough, having no way to get in touch with him. It's a pity you can't see him on social media websites. I don't suppose he ever answers his mobile when you call, or reply to your texts?"

Tilly shook her head.

"Don't fret, it's not all bad. Adrian's always known you and Neil are there for him. I think if he ever got into any real trouble he'd ask for your help." Imogen said.

"I hope so." Tilly was silent for some minutes as she worried about her step-son, trying to organise her fears into words. Then she said, "I'd like to think he hasn't got involved with drugs, but I'm not convinced, and neither is Neil. I guess when he did try to speak to Adrian, before he left home to live with his mother, he didn't deal with it very well. That's partly what bothers Neil."

She was quiet again for a while, remembering with dread an evening, about a week after Adrian was back in Kent. She'd arrived home late, having stopped off at Morisons to get eggs and bread, and walking into the kitchen she'd discovered Adrian, pale and obviously shaken, with blood from a cut lip smeared about his mouth, his face bruised, one eye so badly swollen he couldn't open it. Before she could cry out in alarm he'd lifted a trembling finger to his lips, and then slipped out the back door. Neil had been in the lounge, presumably watching the evening news. For some reason, she couldn't even now fathom, she'd dumped her handbag and groceries on the kitchen floor and hurried back outside in search of the boy, without even calling through to her husband.

It had been useless. Although she'd walked as far as the end of the lane towards Bushwell, Adrian was nowhere to be found, and by the time she'd returned to the house Neil had already left for a local Neighbourhood Watch meeting. That had been the very last time she'd seen her step-son. She had never mentioned it to Neil because Adrian had obviously not wanted her to, and whichever way she looked at it, she felt she would be betraying one or other of them by either speaking out or continuing to remain silent. She still wasn't sure whether she should broach the subject with her husband.

Tilly took another gingernut and bit into it. "Do you think I should pay a visit to his mother to see if she knows anything?" she asked. "I could try camping on her doorstep until she opens the door to me. That's the advice I was after: What would you do?"

"I'd quite forgotten you'd said you wanted some advice. Well, if I were you I'd think very carefully before you do anything like that. Neil might not like it, for one thing, and Adrian might resent it too if he found out. After all he isn't exactly a child anymore."

Tilly nodded. "You're right. I know you're right. I just feel so helpless."

The doorbell rang and Imogen pushed the coffee pot towards Tilly and hurried off to deal with the locksmith. By the time her neighbour returned to the kitchen, Tilly had made a fresh pot of coffee, rinsed and refilled the mugs and was halfway through her second drink.

"Thanks," Imogen said, sinking back into her seat with a weary sigh.

Tilly came straight to the point. "You've put up with me wittering on about my worries. Now it's your turn. You looked really upset this morning, and there's no use denying it," she wagged a finger at Imogen. "I wish I could say I don't want to pry, but I'd be lying. Talk to Aunty Matilda, I might be able to help."

She waited, looking expectantly at the woman sitting opposite her.

Imogen had the wary look Tilly imagined a deer might have when it caught the scent of a hunter in the forest.

"It's just that time of the month," she said at last. "I went into town yesterday and suddenly everywhere I look there are pregnant women, prams and pushchairs again, and I'm reminded once more that time is passing and the likelihood of my ever being a mother is diminishing with each passing day."

In the ensuing silence the women could hear the click and scrape of metal in the hallway as the locksmith removed the faulty mechanism from the door.

Tilly reached forward and patted her friend's hand. "I'm so sorry, Imogen, I hadn't realised. You and Sean have always seemed so content together, I'd just assumed the pair of you didn't want a family. How long have you been trying, if I might ask?"

"Seven long years." Imogen shrugged. "Please don't feel sorry for me, I don't think I could bear it just now."

"There's still time for you to have a family, surely. You're young yet – you can't be more than thirty-two?"

"I'm thirty-three, actually."

"Okay but that's no age. People wait longer these days because of careers. If you read the tabloids you'd know there are even women in their late fifties producing healthy babies with a little medical assistance. There's still hope."

"Not for me," Imogen assured her. "We've been through various investigative procedures, endured five failed cycles of IVF. I just can't seem to conceive and nobody can work out why," Imogen's voice broke on a sob. "The specialist even suggested that leaving work might help – I used to be Sean's PA until a couple of years ago – but it's made no difference whatsoever. I know some things just aren't meant to be. It doesn't mean I feel any better about it."

"I don't know what to say," Tilly said.

"I'd be grateful if you wouldn't mention it to anyone else," Imogen said. "It would affect the way people behave around me."

"Of course I won't say anything. How could I be so insensitive as to go on about my little grandson …" Tilly was distressed.

"See what I mean?" With a watery smile, Imogen dried her eyes and blew her nose on a tissue.

The locksmith tapped on the lounge door. "It's all finished, Love." He eyed his customer with curiosity, and Tilly wondered whether he'd been eavesdropping. "I've had to change the lock, I'm afraid, which will make it a little bit more expensive than we'd anticipated. Not by much, though," he said. "Oh, and you'll need these." He handed Imogen two identical keys. Then he retrieved his toolbox from the hall on the way out, promising to send his bill by the end of the week.

"I suppose I ought to let you get on," Tilly said, standing up. She paused, "Look, can I give you a piece of advice, Love?" Imogen nodded.

"Try not to let the baby thing colour the whole of your world. I know that's easy for me to say when I haven't had the sort of disappointment you have. I just think, well, you're young and healthy and who knows what the future will bring for any of us? In the meantime, make the most of what you do have. Take a few more chances, create opportunities, live life to the full. You don't want to get to my age, and be weighed down by regrets."

From the look on Imogen's face, Tilly wondered if perhaps she'd gone a little too far, stepped over some invisible line. Oh well, there was no point worrying about it now. She took the coffee cups to the sink and quickly rinsed them under the tap, leaving them on the draining board. "No point using the dishwasher just for them," she said in answer to Imogen's mild protest. She dried her hands. "Thanks for the coffee and chat," she said.

"Thanks for coming," Imogen replied, her brow creased. She surprised Tilly by saying, "I'll think about what you said. Perhaps next term I could come into school and listen to some readers for you."

It was a start, Tilly supposed. "Now there's an idea," she said, "or better still you could help out with my ICT lessons if you have time – that would be more your thing." Tilly glanced about the kitchen again. "I wish I could work out what it is about your house that's so different. It has a certain, I don't know, ambience. It always feels so welcoming."

Imogen hung the keys on the hook near the window, her mind seemingly elsewhere for the moment. She accompanied Tilly to the front door. "Do you remember much about Mr. Stockman, the previous owner?" she suddenly asked Tilly. "You were here a while before us, weren't you?"

Tilly stopped at the door, turning back to face Imogen.

"Vaguely. He was a bit of a recluse, worked from home, I believe," she said. "A delivery van visited the house regularly to pick up and take away various packages."

"Do you recall if he had any relatives who came to live or stay with him, a child perhaps?"

"How long ago are we talking?"

"I'm not sure. Fifteen, maybe twenty years?"

Tilly shook her head, looking thoughtful. "No, I don't think so. I remember our predecessor, Janet Nicholls, told us about his wife, a young American girl: Melony or Melody, I think her name was. Yes, that was it: Melody-Aria, I remember saying what a pretty musical name it was and Mrs. Nicholls telling me it suited Mrs Stockman because it perfectly described the young woman."

"What a lovely thing to say!" Imogen said.

"That was Janet all over, a generous soul, even if she did love a good gossip. She'd been widowed about five years before she decided to sell the house. I think she was lonely so we visited her a fair few times before we bought the place. Anyway, she told me they hadn't been living here long themselves when they realised Melody was gone. She said it was a shame because everyone liked her. General consensus was that she probably got homesick and returned to the States. Going back to what you were asking, though, Janet didn't say anything about any children, and I would have enquired because ours were young then. Why'd you ask?"

"I just wondered. I think Gillian McKenzie at number 5 said something about a little girl staying during the school holidays, although I probably misunderstood," Imogen replied, scratching her nose. "Or perhaps it was someone else. It doesn't matter."

The telephone rang in the hall behind them, making them both jump. Tilly stood silently for several seconds speculating about her friend's 'tell', the nose scratch, that revealed she was hiding something while Imogen hurried to answer it. "Probably another call concerning Payment Protection Insurance," she called over her shoulder. "Just about everyone else rings my mobile. Won't be a minute."

Tilly decided she might as well leave and opened the door, lifting a hand to wave at Imogen. However, her neighbour was looking the other way and Tilly then realised from the urgent tone of Imogen's voice that something was very wrong. Concerned, she waited on the doorstep. Imogen hung up the telephone receiver and turned to look at Tilly with frightened eyes.

"Tilly, would you be able to take me to the hospital?" she asked, "Only I don't think I should drive. Sean's been involved in a serious accident."

Bluebells, interspersed with whitebells, fought for space with the few remaining daffodils and tulips, and the magnolia bush near the end of the garden was in full bloom; the grass had been neatly cut and the hedges trimmed back, and happily it was a brilliant sunny day, despite the forecast. Standing on the patio with a prospective purchaser on a Saturday morning, Imogen was confident that her hard work had paid off and the garden looked well enough to be the deciding factor on a sale.

"It's very reasonably priced," her visitor said. "It's a lot of house for what you're asking. Why are you in such a hurry to sell?"

Imogen studied the woman before her. She was dressed casually in designer jeans, the kind that had deliberate fraying and holes on the thighs, and an expensive looking cream sweater that under different circumstances Imogen might rather covet. Imogen guessed she was of a similar age to herself, maybe a year or so younger, which meant she was probably in her early thirties. The woman was about 5ft 10, and slender. She used her small hands a lot during conversation, reminding Imogen of little birds fluttering about as she gesticulated. She was a brunette, her glossy hair cut to just below her chin and shaped in a flattering bob which framed the woman's heart-shaped face. Her hazel eyes, which never strayed from Imogen's, were inquisitive yet grave. Imogen decided to be honest.

"My husband was recently involved in an accident that left him disabled, well I say recently - it must be almost a year ago, now," she said. "He's paraplegic and we want to move into a bungalow in the village so that he can be more independent."

"Ahh, I'm so sorry. I feel I'm benefitting from your husband's misfortune." The woman was equally frank and looked uncomfortable which gave Imogen a sense of affinity and a desire to put her at ease.

"I can't pretend it hasn't been difficult. We've been very fortunate, though, in many respects. His parents have been extremely supportive and have been paying for him to have private residential health care up until now. There'll probably be some sort of financial compensation in time and, in the meantime we have this house to sell. I'm actually relieved he wants to make changes. I hate sponging off his mum and dad. Are you married, Ms. Everton?"

"Dawn. My name's Dawn." The young woman replied. "No, I'm not married. I've just accepted a position at your local primary school and want to move down from London. Believe it or not, the proceeds from the sale of the flat I've just put on the market will easily cover the price of this place, even if I'm offered a couple of thousand less than I'm asking, so I'm really tempted to make you an offer before anyone else snaps it up. I'm glad the estate agents gave me a call before advertising, and that I had the first opportunity to look around."

Imogen's thoughts flew back over the years, remembering the estate agent who had similarly called her and Sean before the house went onto the market. It was like a sign that Dawn should be the next owner. She returned the woman's smile.

"Well, Dawn, since we might occasionally be seeing each other in the village, it's only right we should be on less formal terms. I'm Imogen. Perhaps I can tempt you into making a positive decision over a cup of tea?" she said.

"That would be great, although before we go back inside, can you tell me which room the window at the side of the house belongs to, the upstairs window with the net curtain that you can just about see through the tree when you're looking from the road? Only I don't recall seeing the view from the side of the house or the branches of the Silver Birch through any of the bedroom windows, and I didn't notice a window on the landing."

Imogen felt the tension return to her body; she should have known better than to relax and let her guard down. "Ah, I wondered whether you would notice that," she kept her voice light. "It doesn't belong to any room. I'll explain what I mean while the kettle boils." She turned and went back into the house, expecting Dawn to follow and hoping she would not be put off buying a house with a mystery.

To Imogen's surprise Dawn lingered longer in the garden than she'd anticipated and the tea was already brewing in the pot before the woman joined her at the kitchen table.

"I love gardening and I can tell you have green fingers too – this one's well laid out. You have plenty of room for planting out there. I have to admit I'm impressed with everything about this property. If I do move in I hope you're serious about buying a bungalow in the village and not moving right away from the area. It would be nice to have someone who could introduce me to the locals and show me around – that's if you have the time. I'm usually very good at first impressions and I have a feeling you and I would get along really well together."

"Yes, we're definitely staying nearby," Imogen assured her as she handed Dawn a cup and saucer. "I'd introduce you to Tilly next door who already works at the school, but I'm afraid she and her husband are both out at the moment."

"So, tell me, was your mother a fan of Shakespeare?" Dawn asked, spooning sugar into her cup and stirring. "I'm talking about your name," she said, in answer to Imogen's questioning look. "It's believed Imogen came from a printer's misspelling of the name Innogen in Shakespeare's play, Cy*mbeline*. I like the name, Imogen, I mean, not Innogen, although the play isn't a particular favourite of mine." She sipped her tea, studying her new friend over her cup.

"No. My parents enjoyed trips to the theatre occasionally, but they preferred more contemporary plays. I was named after my maternal grandmother. My parents married and had children quite late in life and my grandparents went back to live in Ireland shortly before I was born. My gran was suffering from the onset of dementia, so granddad wanted to go home."

"That must have been hard for your mother. Are you and your mum very close?"

"We were." Imogen's face felt stiff as she attempted to smile, then to her horror she could feel tears start to well. She reached for a tissue and screwed it into a tight ball in her fist. "I lost her a couple of months before Sean's accident. Cancer. She was never one to want to trouble the doctor with aches and pains, even when she was quite ill, so she didn't even know she'd got it until it was too late."

Dawn shook her head slowly, her eyes full of sympathy. "I'm sorry," she said. To Imogen's relief, however, she made no further comment on the subject. Instead she took another sip of tea and said, "Tell me about the mysterious window."

Imogen took a deep breath and gathered her thoughts. "Well, unlike you, when we first looked at the house we didn't notice there was a window missing on the inside. It wasn't until a few weeks after moving in that we realised. We were sitting in the car one evening after work, planning a trip to buy paint and wallpaper and, as we studied the exterior of the house, we noticed the extra window. We couldn't believe it at first. We tried to locate the possible position inside the house and came to the conclusion it should be an extra side window in the middle bedroom which, as you will have seen, has a fitted wardrobe."

"How intriguing! I wonder why the glass wasn't removed so it could be bricked up. Do you mind if I have a look, at the inside of the wardrobe I mean? I quite understand if you'd rather I didn't go poking around in your possessions, although I'd love to see for myself."

"No problem. There's nothing in the wardrobe now, anyway."

The two women finished their tea and climbed the stairs, Imogen leading the way. She went into the bedroom they'd been discussing and opened the wardrobe doors wide for her visitor to see inside. Dawn stepped forward and ran her hand across the back of the cupboard then rapped with her knuckles. She looked back at Imogen, frowning slightly then knocked louder.

"That's weird. I expected it to sound hollow." She continued knocking the wall along the whole width of the wardrobe stepping right inside to do so. "It's a nice closet space, although I'd probably consider having the wardrobe removed to re-use the window," she said. "It's odd there being brickwork beneath the plaster. I guess I assumed it would be plasterboard or wood." She stepped back out into the bedroom and closed the doors. "'Curiouser and Curiouser', said Alice.'"

"Yes, it does seem a bit *Alice in Wonderland*, doesn't it?" Imogen tried to sound flippant.

"Ahh but I think Lewis Carroll might have enjoyed the puzzle. Did you ever read *Through the Looking Glass*? I know he's had a bit of bad PR over the years, but I still think he was rather a clever man. Did you know he was quite a mathematician? He invented Carroll diagrams."

"No, I guess I thought he was just a writer. I saw the Disney version of *Alice in Wonderland* as a kid, but I never read the Alice books," Imogen said. "I take it as a teacher you've read a lot of children's literature, classics and modern, and need to keep up with the latest books for the classroom. I know my friend, Tilly, is into Julia Donaldson at the moment."

Dawn raised an eyebrow and seemed about to say something, although several seconds passed and she turned away, making no comment. Imogen said, "Listen, before you go imagining anything sinister about the window, let me tell you Sean's theory."

Dawn shrugged. "Go ahead. You don't need to worry, though. I'd still like to buy the place."

"Good, I was hoping you'd say that. Anyway, my husband thought it was probably to do with building and planning regulations. The owner didn't want to be bothered with all the hassle, or he might even have been refused permission to remove the window. Either way, he simply built a wall a few inches away from it so that nobody could tell from the outside that he'd done away with it."

"Sounds plausible to me," Dawn said, following her back down the stairs, "much more likely than a murder victim incarcerated behind a false wall."

Imogen shuddered. "What a horrible idea!" she said. "Have you been watching too much *CSI*, by any chance, or *Crimewatch*?"

"I read newspapers online, even the tabloids. Think about Fred and Rose West. They weren't the first to hide bodies in their home, and don't tell me you've never considered the possibility."

"What of hiding my murder victims?" Imogen turned her head and shot back a wry grin. She liked Dawn. If anyone was to have her lovely house she hoped it would be her. "I admit it, I did wonder whether it was something foul and I wanted Sean to remove the wardrobe and investigate," she continued, reaching the last stair and turning back towards the kitchen, "but he persuaded me it would be a waste of time and cause a lot of unnecessary mess and expense for no good reason, especially as the fitted wardrobe was a selling point when we viewed the place."

"I'm just teasing," Dawn responded, laughing. "Whitewood Close is much too nice a place to have anything nasty like murder go unnoticed."

She followed Imogen back into the kitchen, pulling a sheet of paper from her jeans pocket before sitting back down at the kitchen table, waving a dismissive hand at the offer of more tea.

"I notice on the particulars, the estate agent gave me, that the freehold includes a garage. It's obviously not attached to the house. Where is it?"

"Oh, that's partly hidden by the Leylandii trees. It's to the side of the house near the bottom of the garden. You have to drive up past the house to gain access. We've never actually used it."

"I take it the garage isn't in very good condition then?"

"It's fine. Or rather, it looks alright from the outside. We were told it's identical to the garages of the neighbouring houses. There aren't any windows to see inside, although from what I've seen of Tilly's garage it's more than adequate for a modern family saloon, if that's what you're worried about. Your car will fit with space to spare."

"Yet you've never used it before or been inside?" Dawn was clearly sceptical.

"No. Somehow the key to the garage got overlooked when our purchase was completed and by the time we'd contacted the agents they were unable to get hold of the previous owner. He did tell us he hoped to travel, so we guessed he must have already gone away. It's probably full up with rubbish anyway, or that's what one of the neighbours told Sean; he said the old man only ever went in there to stack boxes. He apparently never used it for his car either."

Dawn shook her head. "You've got to be kidding me! Did you never think to get a crowbar and force the door just to see what's inside?"

"Why would we do that? It would just mean having to clear it out and we didn't need it for anything. Sean would never have considered parking his company car anywhere but outside the front of the house where he could keep an eye on it."

"How long have you lived here?" Dawn asked her face still incredulous.

"Almost nine years."

"And you've never been curious about what might be inside the garage?"

"Not enough to break in and damage the door and we didn't see the point of going to the trouble of hiring a locksmith when we had no intention of using the garage," Imogen said. "Besides, I suppose we thought the agents would get in touch with the previous owner to ask about the key when he eventually returned to this country. Then we just forgot about it."

Dawn stood up, the sudden sound of her chair scraping the floor making Imogen turn from the task of rinsing the cups in the kitchen sink.

"Come on. I've got an iron bar tyre jack in the boot of my car we could use as a crowbar. Let's go and have a look now. After all, I'm going to buy this house anyway, so it will be me footing the bill for any damage and there might be something valuable inside. Have you got a small hammer?"

Imogen dried her hands on a tea towel and shook her head. "Sean would be furious if you damaged any part of the property before it legally belongs to you and besides, surely anything of value in the garage would still belong to the previous owner if he put it there. And if the door was broken we'd then have to think how to keep the contents from being stolen until they were returned to him."

"Okay," Dawn lifted her hands in resignation. "I'll wait until I move in, but I insist you come and help me when I do force the door. I'm not sure of the legality concerning ownership of the contents. I guess I could look into that." She smiled and stuck out a hand. "It's been lovely getting to know you a little, Imogen Miles. I'm going back to see the estate agents now to put in a formal offer. In the meantime, are there any other little mysteries concerning this house that I ought to know about?"

"Not that I'm aware," Imogen lied, although her smile was sincere as she shook the hand Dawn proffered. She accompanied her to the end of the front garden path and watched as the woman got into her Audi and drove away. Then she turned and looked up through the branches of the Silver birch tree beside the house, seeking out the window on the side of her house. She looked at her neighbour's house; it was identical in appearance from the outside, as was, she knew, the detached neighbouring house on the other side, except for one difference. Neither of the houses or any of the other houses in Whitewood Close for that matter, had upstairs windows at the side.

Chapter Six

Imogen mounted the steps that had once been so familiar and paused before the door, reading the plaque: Messrs. Cartwright, Harper and Green, Solicitors, Established 1891. She'd been given the tour when she'd first applied for a job here as a teenager and she'd been told that the three original partners, Thomas Cartwright, James Harper and Edgar Green, had started their firm in a modest Victorian terraced house at the end of a street, close to the main road through town. In the years that followed, the other houses in the terrace had gradually been acquired and the necessary building works completed to allow the five previously separate residences to be used as one impressive establishment.

Imogen pushed the door open and went inside. She didn't recognise the young woman manning the switchboard and didn't expect an immediate response to her presence. As she waited she glanced about the newly redecorated office space. The heavy oak counter that served as a reception desk, creating an effective barrier between the staff and the general public, hadn't changed, but the colour scheme of the walls and carpet were different and she could see more modern office furniture beyond the new switchboard. The receptionist finished her conversation, scribbled on a notepad and then turned her attention to Imogen.

"Hi, I'm Imogen Miles, here to see Mr. Morgan."

The woman nodded and politely directed her to a chair, promising not to keep her a minute. Indeed, Imogen had barely settled herself into her seat when Ernest Morgan himself pushed open the door from the corridor to personally escort her to his office. She realised she hadn't seen him in a very long time, yet still she was shocked to see how much he'd aged.

"Imogen, how good to see you!" He shook her hand and took her arm to guide her out of the door. "Sheryl, hold my calls for the next half hour," he said to the young receptionist.

"First of all, let me say how sorry I was to hear of your husband's accident. I understand his injuries were quite serious."

Imogen sat in a huge green chesterfield chair to the side of the matching sofa on which he sat. She was grateful he hadn't taken his seat behind the imposing writing desk near the window, as she would have felt intimidated sitting opposite her former boss. Behind the sofa, shelves of heavy legal tomes lined the wall. Ernest Morgan's office hadn't changed at all in the intervening years, she noted, with the exception of the updated framed photographs on the wall near his desk portraying his two sons, both young men resplendent in graduation robes, holding degree scrolls. She supposed to him they'd be old photographs by now.

"Yes, Sean was very badly injured and almost died. His spine was damaged quite severely and we've been told he'll never walk again, but with advances in technology," she shrugged, "who knows?"

"Did they ever trace the driver of the other vehicle?" Ernest Morgan leaned back in his chair.

"Yes. Fortunately, Sean remembered the markings on the delivery van and the police were able to locate the driver because it belonged to a supermarket chain. It's taken a while, though, because Sean was in a coma for several weeks and couldn't remember anything at first when he did regain consciousness."

"I heard that the impact to your husband's car was such that it left the road and was found on its roof in a field. Could he tell the police exactly what happened? Obviously, the other driver committed a criminal offence in failing to stop or report such a collision, regardless of who was at fault."

Imogen had the distinct impression that he was talking to her as if she was a prospective client.

"All that Sean remembers is that the other vehicle was on the wrong side of the road, travelling quite fast and, although he tried to take evasive action, the van struck him. The police have since produced evidence that the driver had been using his mobile phone at the time of the accident, so they've charged him. We're still waiting for the date of the court case and of course we intend to pursue a civil suit for damages, but that's not the reason I came to see you. The insurance company have their own legal department and they're looking into that."

Imogen gripped the handles of the handbag on her lap tightly, determined to hide her nerves. "I'm in the process of selling our present home and I would, of course, like the firm to deal with the conveyancing. However, while Sean is still in private care, I find I have rather a lot of free time on my hands. I was wondering whether you might have any vacancies for secretarial work. You know I'm computer literate and I've kept my office skills up to date. I did a lot of the administrative work for Sean's company until relatively recently, it's only been about two years since I stopped."

Her old boss eyed her with a gaze that was non-committal. "What have you been doing with yourself since?" he asked.

Imogen didn't want to go into the whole infertility problem, and after a moment's thought she said, "Now I design web pages on the internet as a hobby. I can show you, if you're interested. I started out trying to help one of my neighbours who wanted to advertise her florist shop. I did quite a bit of research, bought an idiot guide book and did an online course in order to achieve what she wanted. Then the PCC for our local church heard about it and the vicar approached me after the Sunday service and asked if I'd be willing to have a go at putting together something for them. They already had a website, but it seriously needed updating. I've been experimenting with different ideas ever since. My latest project is Sean's company. Like the church, he had a web designer put together a website for him some time ago. It definitely needs changing now, so I'm working on that."

"That's very impressive."

"Thank you. I still have an awful lot to learn and it's time-consuming, but I enjoy it. However, with Sean still convalescing I need to supplement our income without worrying him. Do you have any vacancies...?"

She waited, trying not to look too desperate. If he couldn't offer her a job she was sure he would give her a decent reference, even though it had been more than a decade since she'd worked for him. She didn't really want to have to apply to the DHSS for income support.

Ernest Morgan stared at her for a while longer and she fixed her eyes on his face, waiting. He must be well into his seventies now yet remained corpulent. He'd always reminded her of the protagonist in Charles Dickens' *Pickwick Papers*.

"I do wish you'd called me or come into the office a week ago," he said at last. "We've just employed an undergraduate for the summer while Mr. Watkins' PA is on maternity leave." He took his pen from his inside breast pocket, and studied the writing implement, twiddling it between his finger and thumb. "Let me think. Many of the staff you worked with have long-since gone. Times have changed and the firm has had to evolve to keep up. I don't have clients myself, these days. Or at least, very few. Still, we're going to be taking on a new man, chap from Australia, to ease the burden on our litigation team soon. He doesn't get here for another two months, so I suppose that doesn't help you much at the moment. He's going into Tumber's old office and we haven't even got around to employing someone to clear it out yet."

"I could do that." The words were out of her mouth before she had chance to rethink them.

"There now Imogen, apart from the removal of clients' files, the room's barely been touched since he died. It will be a dusty, boring job going through all the old paperwork, archiving and throwing out rubbish. I don't think you really want to be troubling yourself with that."

"Mr. Morgan, I hope you don't think I'm speaking out of turn but I know the partners, yourself included, had great respect and affection for Mr. Tumber and I believe that's why his room has been left for so long. Don't you think you would all be happier knowing the person who does clear it remembers him too?"

She immediately realised her mistake when she saw the man opposite change posture in his seat. He seemed to swell as he sat forward. He frowned. He never had liked anything that even hinted at criticism. Imogen could see a deep red hue creep up from his neck to his face. She bit her lip.

"It wasn't due to some sort of sentimentality, you know," Ernest Morgan blustered. "He had no immediate family, none that we could trace at any rate, nobody to whom his personal effects could be given. His Will provided for his estate to be divided up between several charities and none of them would have wanted anything that was left in his office, yet it hardly seemed right to throw his things out."

"That's understandable, Sir. However, now you have need of the space, and it makes sense that the PA for the new solicitor should be involved in organising his work environment." She gave him time to challenge her assumption that she would be that assistant. When he didn't she added, "Besides, I'm sure some of his books are very old and might be quite valuable, perhaps could even be auctioned off for charity. I know if I put aside those I thought might be interesting, you could make an informed decision."

She saw the compliment had the desired effect and he nodded, becoming at once business-like. "Very well, Mrs. Miles, if you're certain you are equal to the task, I will put your suggestion to the other partners and let you have our decision by tomorrow evening." He re-pocketed the fountain pen and she realised this was her dismissal. She paused before rising to her feet. She had rather liked being addressed by her Christian name as if she was an old friend, before he'd decided she would be an employee again. It was obvious he was now set on offering her the job; the other partners might be more youthful with new ideas, but he was the Senior Partner and they would really have very little say in this particular matter, except in coming to some agreement concerning remuneration. She stood up and walked over to the wall displaying the photographs of his sons.

"Robert and Frazer look very distinguished in their academic robes," she said. "Did either of them choose law as a profession?"

"As a matter of fact, both did. Frazer's a junior barrister at present. Robert decided to become a solicitor and works for another partnership. They are both doing exceedingly well, thank you for enquiring." He had risen to his feet slowly and carefully, as she'd crossed the room, and she was aware of the slight stoop as he walked over to join her. However, he seemed to grow in stature as his eyes followed the direction of her own, yet she also sensed a great sadness in him.

"Like arrows in the hands of a warrior, so are the children of one's youth. I am very lucky, Imogen, and very proud. You, my dear, ought rather to be thinking of having offspring of your own, not concerning yourself with a career." Then he coughed suddenly, embarrassed again. "Forgive me, Imogen, that was unkind. I forgot for the moment your husband's situation. Welcome back to the firm, my dear."

Chapter Seven

An hour and forty minutes later, Imogen drove into the car
park to the side of the private medical facility where Sean was,
for the time being at least, residing. She sat looking up at the
building, wondering what sort of mood her husband would
greet her with today. The sky was a little cloudy, but the
weather forecast had promised a bright, warm afternoon. She
didn't believe it would rain. She thought back to the day of the
accident, when she'd been thinking about leaving Sean and
how fate had stepped in to make a mockery of her plans. It
had been overcast that day too. Then, as day turned into night,
she'd sat in the 'families' waiting room with Sean's parents as
he underwent a nine-hour operation.

Afterwards, she'd been by his bedside while he was in a
coma, talking because the doctors and nurses had said it might
help. She said all the things she thought he would want to
hear, the things she felt she ought to say. She told him that she
loved him and needed him, and as she talked she realised her
marriage really would be 'until death us do part'. Perhaps that
had always been the case. She had just fooled herself that she
could live without him, she thought, pushing down a hard
lump of uncertainty seasoned with doubt, which was lodged in
her chest.

The day he'd regained consciousness she'd been absent,
had left him still lying silent and inert as if in a deep sleep;
she'd slipped home for a much-needed bath and change of
clothing and arrived at the house to a ringing telephone and
the news that sent her scurrying back to the hospital.

When Sean had discovered that it was unlikely he would
ever walk again he had become deeply depressed. For a while
he tried to refuse to see her, but she conspired with the nurses
and, after listening quietly to his protests, firmly insisted on
spending as much time as possible with him. She was the loyal

wife she'd always pictured herself to be. After a while he ceased protesting, although he remained subdued. The hospital put a nurse on full-time suicide watch, ensuring he wasn't left alone during the brief spells when Imogen left his side.

However, Sean was nothing if not practical and after some time he became willing to work towards improvement. Once he had finished the course of rehabilitation, had undergone training to use a wheelchair, worked with the medical staff to organise appropriate exercise and physiotherapy regimes, and participated in group therapy where he was able to discuss his fears, he quickly regained his former love of life and, also it seemed, of Imogen.

During her visits, they began to talk again in a way they hadn't in such a very long time, discussing their marriage and the future. He seemed oddly certain that they would still one day have a family and this troubled Imogen, although she didn't argue about it. She was just relieved they were communicating again.

Sean talked about his plans for the business; his Manager, Tony Shoreham, had stepped in and taken on Sean's role since he had become incapacitated, but the man was struggling (this had been evident when Imogen confiscated Shoreham's laptop when she caught him on the way in to visit) and Sean was keen to get back in control. Imogen's in-laws had been generous, cashing in an insurance policy to pay for his medical care. However, Sean and Imogen both knew his parents would be glad when he was able to go home so they could be relieved of the growing financial burden of his health care. That's when Imogen and Sean had discussed the house and decided to sell and buy something more suitable to their needs. She had found and shown him the details of a small bungalow in Bushwell that might suit their purposes. She had yet to tell him of the offer Dawn had made on their own house.

Imogen now glanced at her watch and got out of her car, making her way along the path to the side of the building. It had become Sean's habit to be out in the open air in his chair, enjoying the well-kept grounds at this time of day, perhaps with one of the other residents. She was surprised, therefore, when she heard shared laughter, not from the gardens, but from the patio area beside the doors to the orangery, particularly when she found him seated alone at a wooden garden table with his laptop in front of him.

"Oh, I thought you had company!" she said. He looked up.

"Come and look at this – I think it might be just the place for us!" he said, ignoring her comment.

She pulled up a garden chair to sit beside him and peered at the computer. Reflections of the sky and nearby tree branches dazzled her until he tilted the screen slightly.

"But I thought we were going to make an offer on the bungalow in Mill Road," she said.

"Imogen, we're only young once and that's a pensioner's bungalow. We need space to entertain if we want to, room for our hobbies." He leaned over, giving her a hug. "We don't have to give up living just because I can't walk. You said that yourself. Just take a look."

She clicked her way through the photo slides. It was certainly more suitable than the bungalow they'd originally considered. This place had already been remodelled with a disabled person in mind. The final picture was of the outside of the house.

"Oh, it's Mr. Gantry's house! I didn't even realise it was up for sale."

"That's because he didn't want it advertised in the village after all the commotion over the possible closure of the Post Office."

"Can we afford it?"

49

"That's just it. He wants a quick sale and thinks the fact it's been converted for a disabled person will impact on interest, particularly as it's sandwiched between the Post Office and the school. He says he hasn't time to wait around. I've no idea why. I think he has a new lady friend.

Imogen giggled. "That *would* cause a bit of a stir – everyone sees him as a confirmed bachelor. Hang on, though, who will run the Post Office if he moves?"

"Not our problem. There again, maybe you could take it on. You wanted another job." Imogen said nothing about that idea. She clicked onto the email from the old postmaster and read it, then smiled at Sean.

"Okay, let's go for it. We've just been offered the asking price for our place and I've accepted it, so I think we can afford this place with a little money to spare."

She told him about Dawn's visit earlier in the week and her enthusiasm for the house (omitting the part where she wanted to break into the garage) and then said she'd been to see her old boss at the solicitors about a job and was waiting to hear from him. He seemed pleased, although he didn't ask for details and she felt no compulsion to tell him that her first duty would involve clearing out an old office. When she left, he was tapping away on his laptop, communicating with the former postmaster, Bill Gantry.

It was good to see Sean so enthusiastic and she found herself humming cheerfully as she crossed the car park and clicked her key fob to unlock the doors of her Kia. She decided on impulse that she would find somewhere to eat before tackling the long drive home.

She wasn't in the mood for a microwaveable meal for one in front of the television set this evening. Besides, she felt she had something to celebrate at last.

Chapter Eight

The following couple of weeks passed swiftly. Sean was making excellent progress at the private care facility and there was talk of preparations for him to come home. Mr. Morgan had telephoned Imogen as promised with an offer of a temporary part-time job to clear the office space for the new litigation operative, and she was pleasantly surprised by the figure mentioned as a one-off payment which she was told would be advanced to her bank account. She immediately accepted, and although Mr. Morgan had made it clear there was no promise of future employment at present, she was confident this situation would change in due course. If it didn't, she thought wryly, she could always apply to take on the village Post Office. She'd work on her web pages during her free time.

The office space Imogen was required to clear at Messrs. Cartwright, Harper and Green was located in what would once have been attic space. There were two offices and the main one, which the old solicitor had used, was a large room which overlooked the street. The smaller office leading off from the main one was where the solicitor's secretary had worked and this was bare, except for an empty desk (the computer having long since been removed and utilised elsewhere) and an uncomfortable looking chair. Imogen wandered over to look out the window and found herself peering down onto the back gardens of a row of houses in the next street over, behind the solicitors' building.

"I expect you remember old flash 'arry used to live in one of those houses." Imogen turned to see a robust, ruddy-complexioned woman in her late sixties, wearing a floral print overall over her clothes. She was carrying a loaded tray of tea and coffee in her hands, which she placed momentarily on the desk.

"Sally! I can't believe you're still here!" Imogen cried, stepping forward to embrace the woman. She didn't reciprocate the hug, but didn't seem to mind it either.

"They can't get me to retire. I 'spect they'll carry me out in a box one day. Well, what else am I gonna do now my Jim's gone? Do you want tea or coffee?"

Once Sally had used the fire door which provided an escape route through to the next building, Imogen wandered from the old secretary's room through to the main office which remained almost as a time capsule, as if the occupant had just that moment walked away. It wasn't quite as gloomy as Mr. Morgan had depicted it, for it was still cleaned each evening, the carpet vacuumed, surfaces dusted and windows polished in the same way all the other offices, were, so there was no dirt or cobwebs, just a little dust among the papers and books which the cleaners would not have touched.

Imogen enjoyed a certain amount of privacy once she began work, for nobody but Sally ever used the fire-door through to the other offices. Imogen was able to take her iPod in with her so she could listen to music through her earphones to relieve the boredom while she worked, without fear of being disturbed.

There were few personal items in the room: a couple of faded framed photographs, one of Mr. Tumber's long-dead parents hanging on the wall, and another of a curly-headed toddler holding a ball, which she found hidden in the bottom of a filing cabinet. Both pictures had fancy, intricately carved wooden frames. She put the photographs on the secretary's desk in the adjoining office just as Sally appeared with her morning coffee.

"I'll find something for you to wrap those in before you pack them in a box," the char lady said, handing Imogen a mug of steaming coffee. "There you go, no sugar, plenty of cream, just as you like it."

"I think they're only going to a charity shop – someone might want the frames," Imogen said.

Sally picked up the picture of the toddler with the ball and looked at it. "Wonder what happened to his little'un," she said.

"What? Do you mean Mr Tumber had a child?"

"Ha! Depends who you ask. There was talk of an illegitimate kid, a girl. I reckon this was the nipper." She put the photograph back onto the desk. "There were rumours about the partners trying to find her when he died, 'course, that was just after you'd left, but I don't think they had any luck. Then Mr. Morgan got wind of the gossip and gave the staff a right talking to and put a stop to it. I 'spose she must be dead." She sniffed. "Right, I can't stand here all day. I've a lot to do. If you leave the black rubbish sacks near the fire door, I'll make sure they're carried down this evening. Save you a job like." She waddled off towards the fire door and pulled it open. "See you later, Love." Then she was gone.

Imogen finished her coffee sitting on the rickety old chair near the window and looked down into the back gardens of the houses in the next street. It was a grey morning, yet someone had hung a line full of bath and hand towels out and these hung limply in the still, damp air. Nobody was about. Imogen left her mug on the desk next to the photographs and went back to the office that Mr. Tumber had once worked in. She sighed and looked about her again.

There was an outdated computer monitor on Tumber's desk and next to this was a stack of papers pinned down by a chunky paperweight with a seahorse and sea shells embedded deep within the amber-coloured glass. In the desk drawers, she found a few bills from a local tailor (his store long since gone), a wine merchant, a bookshop, and some old receipts. There was an ancient blotter that was so worn it was falling apart, an ink pen that had long ago leaked out into the desk drawer, along with a bottle of Indian ink, some writing paper and a rather beautiful, blank-paged notebook with a soft leather jacket, the edges of the cover decorated with trailing foliage. There was also some half a dozen or so paperback novels on top of the filing cabinet. Mr. Tumber had apparently enjoyed reading spy thrillers and tales of espionage. Imogen felt sad that she'd never known that about him when he was alive, and she doubted many other people working there had either.

There were plenty of other books to look through, including books of essays, an anthology of nineteenth century poetry, books on art appreciation and several volumes of Gibbons' *Decline and Fall of the Roman Empire*. There were, of course, a wide range of hardback, expensive looking books about law, neatly lining the bookshelves behind Mr. Tumber's old desk. Apart from these books and personal items, there was a whole collection of papers to sort out, although Imogen was certain that most documentation would already be saved in computer files. She would have to check each and every document and that would be time-consuming.

Mr. Tumber had been a little like Ernest Morgan, old-fashioned as if born out of time, and his workspace evidenced this. Certainly, by the time Imogen had joined the firm as a junior office clerk, fresh out of school at sixteen, the old boy had been well beyond retiring age. Like Mr. Morgan now, he'd no longer had any clients, but simply couldn't get out of the habit of coming to the office. He'd never been a partner, of course, although he had given years of loyal service to the firm, so the partners had indulged him, eventually re-assigning his secretary to another department and calling him a consultant, allowing him to while away his hours reading or napping in his chair. The new solicitor coming to work for them would be a completely different species of lawyer.

On the third Monday morning after she'd started clearing the office, she was ready to call into Mr. Morgan's office at about eleven, having stayed late the Friday before in order to finish up the task she'd been given. She quickly explained that she'd boxed up the books she thought he might like to look through. He seemed pleased and asked if she could come in to see him the following morning to discuss her future with the firm. She quickly agreed. Then she asked if she might keep the leather-bound notebook with yellowing pages that had, along with various other personal items, been destined for the rubbish bin.

"You can see, the book hadn't been used," she said, holding it out for him to inspect. "It seems a shame to throw it away. I've always had a bit of a penchant for notebooks of different shapes and sizes."

Ernest Morgan took the book from her and examined it, turning it over in his hands as he looked at the tooled leather cover. "Of course, you must have it if you wish. I have to say, it hardly looks like the sort of thing old Tumber would have liked. I wonder why he kept it." Her boss handed the notebook back to her and waved a dismissive hand. "Off you go. Enjoy the rest of the day." She thanked him and left, tucking the book into her bag as she walked down the road towards the High Street.

She had a few hours to kill before visiting Sean and the notebook had given her a taste to have a look at the new stationery shop that had recently opened in the town centre.

After that she'd gone to the public library to look for books that might enhance her knowledge further, with regard to her computer work, then she'd bought a stack of clip together cardboard boxes for packing, since few shops seemed to keep those in which goods were delivered anymore. "They're a fire hazard," one shop assistant had told her, "we have to flatten them as soon as they're empty and store them outside." Funny she should be buying cardboard boxes when her husband's company made them. She felt a bit like the cousin who lived on a farm and was criticised by her family for purchasing oven chips instead of using their home-grown potatoes. She hadn't experienced an ounce of guilt, however, as she put the flat packs into her car; time was of the essence, as solicitors often stated in correspondence when a need for prompt action was required. Besides, Sean's company made boxes and cartons to order so there were rarely spare samples available, unless of course they were defective and destined to be sent for re-pulping.

Daylight was fading to dusk before Imogen's car finally turned into Whitewood Close and, although she was tired, she felt more positive about the future than she had for a long time. A small glass of red wine, a long soak in the bath and an early night with the latest Kate Mosse novel would make a perfect end to the day, she decided.

She always dressed as a professional when she went to work, even though she'd merely been clearing out an old office. Appearance counted. Now, she took off her jacket, hanging it by the door and slipped off her patent high heeled shoes, relishing the cool wood beneath her aching feet. She'd put the lights on a timer switch shortly after Sean's accident so that she would never have to come home to a dark house and, although the hall and lounge light had come on, the kitchen remained unlit. She didn't bother to throw the switch as she made her way to the cupboard where the glasses were kept because grey twilight still filtered through the kitchen window. She never drew the blinds at the back of the house, since the back garden wasn't overlooked by any of the other houses, and she paused now to look out as she reached into the cupboard for a glass.

A flicker of movement near the trees at the end of the garden caught her eye. She put the glass down and leaned forward slowly to make sure she hadn't been mistaken. The child was there again, standing looking up at the house. Imogen watched, unmoving, as the little girl slowly walked across the lawn, her eyes fixed on the top of the house as she did so. She could only be four or five years old, skinny with untidy fair hair hanging loose about her shoulders and the same grubby pink dress she always wore.

As soon as she moved out of sight to the side of the house, Imogen sprang towards the back door, throwing it wide and calling out, trying to sound friendly. As usual the little girl was nowhere to be seen. Imogen checked the tall side gate which was fastened and bolted at the top from the inside. She didn't believe in ghosts and besides the child seemed perfectly human – flesh and blood – not some wraith melting into the early evening air. There must be a way through the hedge, a small gap the little girl could have squeezed through. The past couple of times she'd seen the child, she hadn't got around to investigating further, deciding she must be a visitor to one of her neighbours, although it irked her that such a little one should be allowed to roam freely. This time, however, she unbolted the gate and pulled it open to look out onto the green and there the small girl stood, beneath the silver birch, looking up at the window on the side of the house. The hopeful expression on her face gave Imogen pause and kept her from calling out again.

Imogen stepped through the gate and was about to walk slowly forwards, careful not to startle the child, when without warning the little girl turned and ran towards the access road. Imogen was gripped by panic that the child might run straight out onto the lane into the path of a car, so with a yelp she gave chase.

However, by the time Imogen reached the bend leading out of the Close, running painfully, her bare feet feeling every tiny sharp piece of loose gravel, the little girl was nowhere to be seen.

Imogen turned and walked, limping slightly, back towards the house. Neil's car was not on the Worthingtons' drive. She glanced at her wrist watch and decided it was not too late to call on her neighbour. Perhaps Tilly would know something of the child – as a teacher she seemed to know just about everyone between the ages of four and eleven in Bushwell, and the children's parents too. It was also time to tell Tilly that she and Sean would be moving.

Since the immediate aftermath of Sean's accident, Imogen hadn't seen much of her friend, except for the occasional wave on the way in or out of their houses, and the odd quick exchange of news. Tilly probably had no idea she and Sean were in the process of selling the house and it was time to put that right.

Chapter Nine

Imogen was standing on the Worthingtons' doorstep, about to press the bell, when the door opened and a young man stepped out, pushing angrily past her. She recognised him immediately as her friend's step-son, Adrian. As Imogen moved aside, Tilly appeared in the doorway and called after him, her face anxious. However, he continued striding away from the house as if he hadn't heard her. Tilly watched him for several seconds before becoming aware of Imogen, then she apologised and invited her inside.

"I thought when he telephoned to ask if he could see me it was too good to be true! He wants to borrow money, a couple of thousand, for some new business venture, but he doesn't want me to tell Neil! I mean, Imogen, how can I not tell his father?"

It was obvious the question was rhetorical so Imogen sat quietly, hands in her lap and watched Tilly as she pointed the remote at the television set to switch it off.

"Sorry, I'm always wrapped up in my own worries," Tilly said. "How are you?"

Imogen had almost forgotten the reason for her visit. "I'm okay, thanks," she responded. "I just thought I'd come and ask if you'd seen a little girl wandering about the Close. I'd say she was around five or six years old, and she has long fair hair."

Tilly pulled a face and shrugged, "No, I can't say I have," she said.

"I've caught her playing in my back garden three times now in as many weeks," Imogen said. "I'm not bothered, except she seems rather young to be left to her own devices. She actually ran out of the Close tonight on her own and I was scared she'd get knocked over or something. I ran after her, but I wasn't quick enough to see where she went."

Tilly sat down heavily on an armchair, frowning. "I don't think there are any kids that age staying in the Close, and you're right – that is young to be on her own if she's come all the way from the village. Blonde hair, you say? No, I can't say off the top of my head which family she might belong to. I'll ask around."

"Thanks." Imogen relaxed then, feeling relieved to have told someone about the incident. She said, more cheerfully than she actually felt, "Nearly the end of term again – hasn't that year flown?"

"It has and it's been a tough one for you. I'm glad Sean's getting on okay. School's been interesting. We have a new Head teacher starting in September, and she came in last week. She's young and ambitious, so I expect there will be a few changes, but she seems alright – ready to listen, you know?"

"It'll be a bit strange without your old Headmaster though, won't it?" Imogen had heard countless stories, gossip really, about the retiring head teacher who'd been a bit of a womaniser. "Actually, a couple of weeks ago, I met one of the new teachers who'll also be starting at your school in September. I should have told you before. We're selling the house, you see. Have to really, it won't be practical to stay here unless we make some fairly drastic changes, and most of our money is tied up in the business so we wouldn't be able to afford to sort the house out any time soon. It just makes sense to move."

"Oh Imogen, I am sorry to hear that. I'm going to miss you dreadfully. We all are." Tilly got up to hug her friend, looking upset.

"Thanks, but don't think you're getting rid of us that easily! Hopefully we aren't going too far. We could be buying Mr. Gantry's bungalow next to the Post Office, so you and I could visit each other for the occasional coffee and chat." She didn't want Tilly to see just how miserable the prospect of leaving the Close and her beautiful home made her. "Anyway," she rushed on, "this new teacher is moving from London and buying our house. Her name's Dawn Everton."

Tilly stared at her. "Heavens, that's our new Head!" she gasped. "She's going to be next door? I can't believe it …"

"No, she's a teacher. She can't be your Head teacher, she's too young," Imogen blurted out, then blushed when she realised what she'd said.

Tilly raised her eyebrows, shaking her head slightly. "Really, Imogen, you wouldn't have thought that if she'd been a man. Shame on you."

"I know, I know. It's just that she didn't seem anything like a Head teacher. I'm not sure if I can explain why exactly, I mean she certainly comes across as assertive, intelligent, well-read and interested in everything. When she told me she'd got a job at the school, I guess I assumed she was a teacher." She sighed. "The woman's got a lot of spunk, I will say that. I was rather hoping we'd become good friends."

"No reason why you shouldn't, if you're only moving to Bushwell."

The two women were silent for some minutes, busy with their own thoughts. Imogen was remembering other friends she and Sean had made since moving to the Close. Michael and Penny used to jog with them, and pair up for badminton at the leisure centre in town. Imogen smiled at the memory; they'd all worn electronic wristband trackers to record the exercise they did and had competed against each other in the fitness stakes. Imogen missed that. They lived in Scotland now and had two kids.

There'd been a whole group of friends who used to go with Imogen and Sean to the theatre, the cinema and even to an occasional nightclub in the Medway towns, including Amber and Nick, although that couple had gone their separate ways long ago, Amber back to her parents in Gravesend and Nick – who knew where Nick had gone?

Heather had been the hardest to lose. Imogen had believed her to be her closest friend. Heather had been obliged to move to London to further her career as a television presenter. To Imogen's great disappointment she hadn't even attempted to keep in contact. In fact, though most of her friends had tried to stay in touch, communication had gradually become evermore sporadic with all of them. They were busy with their new lives, she'd realised, and different friends. Imogen felt lonely and left behind.

Her neighbours, especially Tilly, were lovely, of course, but she missed the social interaction with people her own age, especially since Sean's business had expanded and he'd had less time for leisure. She knew Dawn's friendship could make all the difference to the way she felt.

"I have to admit," Tilly broke into her reverie, "I'm a little nervous about having my boss for a neighbour." She pursed her lips in dismay.

"She seemed very nice," Imogen assured her, "quite good fun actually. I don't think it will be a problem for you. I wonder why she didn't tell me she was going to be Head teacher."

"Perhaps she didn't think it was that important. Are you going to tell the rest of the neighbours you're moving, at the barbeque next month?" Tilly changed the subject.

"Um, I'd forgotten all about that! You're right, it is the beginning of next month, isn't it? I haven't organised anything …"

"Don't worry. We discussed it after the Neighbourhood Watch meeting last week. As you know, I don't usually attend – that's Neil's responsibility in our house – but he insisted I go along this time. Everyone's sympathetic to your situation with Sean's medical care and everything and they've all taken on different tasks to help out. I don't think anyone realised before now just how much effort you've gone to every year in the past to organise it all and they want to show their appreciation. All you need to do this year is be here to enjoy it with us."

"That's so kind of everyone."

"Not at all. It seems as good a time as any to tell them you'll be moving into the village."

"That's not a bad idea. Perhaps I could invite Dawn and introduce her to everyone. With any luck, Sean should be able to be here too."

***

By the time Imogen was back inside her own home, the little girl no longer occupied her mind. That was until she saw the still open door to the glassware cabinet and the empty wine glass sitting on the kitchen worktop waiting to be filled. Then she also remembered her original intention to have an early night with a glass of wine and a book. Instead she closed the kitchen cabinet door, switched the garden lights on and went out back to check the fence and hedges to see if she could find a small gap where a child might scramble through.

After a fruitless search, she re-bolted the side gate. She glanced up at the mysterious window at the side of the house that was just about visible from where she stood, and wondered why the little girl had been so interested in it. Had she seen something? Ridiculous notion – was she thinking of ghosts again? Someone looking out? Such nonsense and not like her at all. Imogen shivered in the cool evening air. She went back inside the house through the front door, which she locked, before checking and relocking the back door too. Then she filled the waiting empty glass with Shiraz and took it with her upstairs, although she decided she was no longer ready for an early night. There was far too much to think about and do. She felt restless, as if she should be pacing up and down like a caged animal.

Imogen went into the smallest bedroom which they had originally planned to use as a nursery and sipped her wine as she looked around. It had been used as some sort of office or workroom by the previous owner, and she and Sean had taken down the old-fashioned, homemade shelving and stripped off the outdated woodchip wallpaper. The room must once have been a child's bedroom before that because they'd discovered a frieze depicting Noah's Ark, complete with animals lined up in twos, half-way up the wall, across the length of the room on one side. Imogen had wanted to keep it. Sean, however, insisted he wanted something more modern for his child. As a compromise, they'd papered over it using a wallpaper designed to look like a summer sky full of birds, butterflies and rainbows, and the Noah's Ark remained intact beneath this. Though empty, the room still appeared fresh and ready for some child other than her own.

She left the nursery, closing the door behind her with a soft click. The attic – that needed to be cleared and the contents sorted. It had gradually been filled with odd scraps of furniture, bags of clothes, books and old vinyl records. She would have to do something with all of it. She took her half empty wine glass into her bedroom and, after another sip, put it down on her dressing table. Imogen changed into an old sweatshirt and jogging bottoms before locating the rod with the hook which was kept in the airing cupboard. She used this to unlatch the cover to the hatchway in the ceiling on the landing and hooked the attic ladder to bring it down. She straightened her shoulders, determined to banish any further hint of sadness from her mind. She walked back to her wine and drained the glass, leaving it in her room, before returning to climb the steps. Junk, all rubbish, she thought, once her head was through the hatchway.

Imogen worked hard, sorting the items with any value that could be given to charity shops from those that could be discarded. The pleasant light-headed sensation from the wine sustained her. Eventually, with a feeling of achievement, she climbed down the ladder and closed up the attic space for the last time. She glanced at her wristwatch; it was two o'clock in the morning! Imogen looked about her. She had a pile of black plastic sacks for dumping at the bottom of the stairs and labelled boxes of items to deliver to charity shops on the landing.

Imogen realised she was tired and it was time to go to bed, although her brain was still very much awake. Suddenly she remembered the young hippy woman, Alicia, and her advice to allow the house to help her to make important decisions. She shrugged the thought away – what decisions were there to make anyway?

She took a quick shower and pulled on an old pair of Sean's pyjamas, hoping it would help her to feel closer to him. As she drew back the duvet she kicked something that she'd left on the floor near the bed earlier. It was a plastic carrier bag containing her library books. She pulled the books out of the bag, opened one and began to read, perched on the edge of her bed. Then she decided she needed some post-it notes or something to mark different pages she might wish to refer to at a later date, or to make notes. She remembered the leather notebook in her handbag and went to fetch it, along with a biro.

Imogen plumped up her pillows, switched off the main light and lit the bedside lamp, then got into bed. One of the library books, together with the notebook slid off the duvet. Irritated, she reached down to the floor to retrieve them. As she picked up the notebook something slipped from between its pages. It was an old colour Polaroid photograph of a young woman. She picked up the photo and stared at it for a long, long time. It was a picture of the beautiful young hippy woman she'd been remembering earlier. It was a Polaroid snapshot of Alicia.

Chapter Ten

In three days' time Imogen and Sean were due to sign the contract for the sale of their house. She sat in the Costa shop just around the corner from the firm of solicitors she now worked for, sipping a cinnamon latte and mentally making a 'to do' list. She was waiting for her mother-in-law who had sent a text that morning asking if she would meet her for half an hour at about three. She was rather late, it being well after four now, but Imogen was unconcerned. She'd had a good morning.

She'd been offered the job as Personal Assistant to the Australian solicitor and been ordered to prepare for his arrival. She had finished organising the office space for her new boss and indeed for herself too, and had even been given the go-ahead to order new furniture and equipment. Mr. Morgan had then called her in to see him again, before she left at lunchtime, and asked if she'd be prepared to step in if they were short of staff for holiday cover. The firm would, of course, begin to pay her full salary, although she may or may not be needed before the new solicitor arrived. She'd been pleased; it was all money in the bank.

Imogen stared out the large plate glass window of the coffee shop at people hurrying past. A fresh wind had got up and a light drizzle wet the pavements. She looked towards the door as it opened, hoping to see Sean's mother, but a couple of skinny teenage girls, deep in conversation about fashion, walked in and headed for the counter. Imogen watched as they continued chatting, pausing only to choose and pay for their coffees, before deciding to take them upstairs.

She wondered why her mother-in-law had suddenly requested this meeting. Imogen supposed it would be something to do with Sean's homecoming. He'd been really moody whenever Imogen had visited of late. He'd hardly spoken and had spent a lot of time either tapping away on his laptop or looking at his mobile phone and texting. Imogen felt relieved he'd become so engrossed in business matters again as it meant he was getting back to his old self, and when he suggested she cut short her visits, she willingly complied, content to let him get on with his work. Jo would probably say he needed cheering up, maybe even suggest a welcome home party, although if that was the case, it would have to be at the in-laws' place. Imogen had enough to do with packing up their house ready to move. It was taking longer than she'd at first anticipated because she kept procrastinating. The house held her heart; it still seemed to harbour all her hopes and dreams from the past and it would be hard to let it go.

The shop door opened again and this time Imogen stood up, an expectant smile on her face. She got on well with Jo, although she was different in every respect from her own mother. Johanne Miles was determined to stay young-looking for as long as possible. Her hair was short and spikey with blonde highlights, and she had both studs and small gold loops in her ears. She wore smart black denims with kitten-heeled boots, a white cotton top with a lacy neckline and a rust-coloured suede jacket. Everything about her appearance looked expensive and in perfect keeping with her position as part-owner of a trendy restaurant.

Imogen went to the counter for fresh coffee while her mother-in-law took off her jacket to hang it on the back of her chair before settling herself at Imogen's table.

"Imogen, you know we're very fond of you, don't you?" she began the moment Imogen regained her own seat, having placed the drinks before them. "Gary and I think of you as the daughter we never had," she said. Imogen nodded. She wasn't sure where this was leading to and guessed it was the precursor to some sort of criticism. "Only we wanted you to understand the position we've been put in. It hasn't been easy.

I told Sean he needed to talk to you properly before he came home, but he's refused. I don't know what he's thinking, it's the least he could have done. Anyway, we've decided it will be best if he comes home to our house when he leaves the nursing home."

Imogen shrugged, unable to comprehend why the woman seemed so uncomfortable. "Well I guess it would be helpful if we could stay with you until we get the bungalow organised. We're supposed to be exchanging contracts on Thursday, by the way," she said.

"No, Imogen. Not you. Just Sean. And as for the bungalow, he really is going to have to discuss that with you. I can't do everything."

Imogen began to feel uneasy. "I don't understand. What do you mean?"

In answer, Johanne Miles opened her handbag, took out her purse and pulled a photo from the back of it. She laid the picture on the table in front of Imogen.

"This is my grandson, Ethan. He's eighteen months old and he's Sean's son. I would have told you before, but we've only just found out about him ourselves. I'm furious with Sean, I really am, and so, so sorry to hurt you like this. His girlfriend, well I suppose she's his mistress really, is expecting another one, you see, and we told him he needs to do the right thing, by them and by you."

Imogen stared at the photograph of the gorgeous baby boy. It couldn't be Sean's son, it just couldn't and yet, and yet he had eyes just like Sean's and the same shaped nose.

"Honey, say something. Please." Johanne was blinking back tears when Imogen looked up at her, and she wondered why she, herself, felt so numb, not hurt, not angry, nothing.

"I see," she said.

"I know I probably shouldn't say it, but I did wonder whether the girl would still want him, you know with him being an invalid and all, yet she seems determined he should get a divorce and be a father to his children. Charlotte, her name is, although he calls her Charlie. He met her on one of his business trips."

A million questions hurtled through Imogen's mind, although she couldn't for the life of her put them into coherent words. She stood up. "I'm sorry, Jo. I'm going to have to go," she said. "I need some time to process all of this."

"Yes, of course you do, Sweetheart. It must be an awful shock. Give me a call when you're ready." Openly weeping now, she hugged her daughter-in-law, sooty tears wetting her face where her mascara was running. Imogen pulled a tissue from her pocket and handed it to her before walking away.

Dazed, Imogen made her way to the carpark where she'd left her little red Kia. Once she'd started the engine she realised there was only one place she could go – to see her husband. She'd been due to visit him later that afternoon anyway. As she drove, she thought carefully about what she would say. She'd stay calm, she told herself. She wouldn't let him see her cry.

When she arrived at the nursing home, the sun was out, evaporating all signs of the earlier light rain, and the wind had died away. She entered the building and asked the woman on the desk if there was somewhere private she could speak with her husband. The receptionist telephoned the Manager and after a brief conversation he agreed to allow Imogen the use of his office. The man then personally went to find Sean to tell him Imogen was waiting to see him. Sean arrived about five minutes later, a sheepish expression on his face.

"She told you then, my interfering mother?"

"Yes, she told me. So, you have a little boy. Ethan, isn't it? Congratulations."

"Listen, Imogen. I'm really sorry, okay? It's not what you think," he said.

She leaned back in her chair, watching him. After a moment, she said, "I knew. I mean, I've suspected you were having an affair for a while now, but I couldn't get you to talk. Now I understand why. You were getting ready to leave me. There was nothing I could have done."

"No, you've got it wrong."

"Really? Tell me then."

"I was feeling kind of low just after your last IVF cycle failed and then, when I went to London to see about the order from the shoe factory I met this woman. I'd been drinking, drowning my sorrows in a bar because they didn't renew the contract for shoe boxes. I thought, what the hell I'd stay over at the nearby hotel. It felt like my whole world was falling apart and I couldn't face you that night with yet another failure. So, I ordered one more drink." He stared down at his knees, unable to meet her eye for the moment. "Then this young woman came up to the bar. She sat alone for some time alongside me, watching the door. She'd been stood up and after a while we started chatting. I guess I felt flattered by the attention and what with the booze, well I never thought for one moment she'd get pregnant after just one night. I had no intention of seeing her again, ever, I swear."

"And you think that would have been alright? You cheating on me? Did you ever consider telling me?"

"No. I don't know. Not at first, I don't think. I felt awful the next day and I left before she was even awake. She managed to trace me, though, because I'd told her about the business, but not until the boy was born. I insisted on paternity tests and he was mine alright. So, I got advice from my solicitor." He looked up at her again, pleading. "I was thinking of us, I swear. I asked him if I could fight for joint custody or even full custody. I know it wouldn't be the same as having one of our own, but I thought maybe she'd agree to let us adopt him. We'd have a son."

Imogen just stared at him. She couldn't believe what she was hearing.

"Anyway, she wasn't interested in giving the baby up and my solicitor advised me I would have a stronger case for joint custody if I was an integral part of his life. So, I arranged to meet up with her again and spent as much time with my son as possible."

"And his mother, Charlotte, of course, since she's pregnant again. You didn't think to share any of these 'plans' with me to see how I'd feel about it all?"

"I was going to. That's why I suggested we buy the bigger bungalow! I'm sorry I didn't tell you sooner. I needed to charm the woman, gain her trust. I'd have an even stronger claim if I could prove her to be an unfit mother ... then she got pregnant again. But it doesn't change things. We could go for custody of both the children!"

Imogen sighed, her heart heavy. She'd promised herself she wouldn't cry so she inhaled deeply, holding her breath for a few seconds, then said, her voice dangerously quiet brooking no interruption, "You'd do that, would you? Steal another woman's children? Oh, silly me. You already thought it was okay to treat me as a fool by sleeping with someone else. Why would I think you wouldn't lie to, cheat and betray another woman that you aren't even married to?' She gave a short, bitter laugh. "What makes it even worse is that you believed I'd go along with it." She stood up. "It's over, Sean. I want a divorce. My solicitor will be in touch."

She walked out then. She didn't even slam the door.

Imogen was sure that she'd give vent to her feelings once she'd got into her car, clipped on her seatbelt and started the engine for the long drive home, yet no tears came. Her heart had been beating painfully hard in her chest, making it difficult to breathe, when she'd walked out of the Manager's office. She'd been trembling and her legs felt as though they were hollow, but she'd held her head high and kept her back straight, ignoring the curious look of the receptionist as she left the building.

Imogen was already driving back through the Medway towns before the numbness began to thaw and a mixture of anger, frustration, hurt and despair overwhelmed her. She drove into the carpark of a large industrial estate with a B&Q and a Homebase. At last she knew exactly what she intended to do. She made a number of purchases then continued on her journey home.

As she got out of her car, back at the Close, she waved to Stephen Miller, who'd just finished mowing his lawn at number 2. He watched her as she carried her shopping in from the car, his arms resting on the handle of his grass rake, then as she opened the door and stepped inside, turning to give a small wave, he continued about his own business.

Imogen closed the door and slipped off her shoes, took off her coat and hung it in the hall then climbed the stairs. She went into the spare bedroom, the one with the fitted wardrobe, and dropped her packages onto the bed. First, she found a screwdriver and went to work unscrewing the wardrobe doors from their hinges, and laying them neatly on the floor near the window on the other side of the room. Then, having stepped back to admire her handiwork, she pulled on a pair of workman's gloves and took up the sledgehammer she'd bought. She fixed her eyes on the wall at the back of the wardrobe and swung the hammer back. It felt heavy as she brought it forward and she almost lost her balance as she hit the brick wall. There was a satisfying crunch as plaster cracked, accompanied by a little puff of dust. Imogen thought about Sean's betrayal, her inability to have children, having to sell her house. She wasn't just angry and disappointed with her husband, she realised as she studied the small dent in the wall, she was mad at God.

She stepped back, parting her feet for better balance and braced herself, swinging the hammer again. This time she gave a scream of fury, putting the full force of her rage behind the blow, following it with another blow and another. The wall began to crumble. Pieces of brick fell inwards to the space behind the wall and clouds of dust filled the air, causing her to cough and splutter as she worked, but she didn't care. Imogen swung the hammer again and again.

Chapter Eleven

Daylight was almost gone by the time she stopped attempting to demolish the wall, although there was still so much dust in the air it made little difference to visibility. She had no idea how long she had been smashing away at the brickwork and was only mildly surprised that nobody had come to investigate the noise. She didn't think she would have heard the doorbell or telephone anyway, if her neighbours had decided to check she was alright. Exhausted, she dropped the hammer at last. It landed on the carpet with a heavy thud. Imogen stared at the gaping, jagged hole in front of her. She could just make out the rectangular window beyond, draped with a net curtain. She turned away, crossing the room to the door, pausing at the light switch, but deciding instead to make straight for the bathroom.

Imogen's arms no longer seemed to belong to her and her whole body ached from the exertion. She was covered from head to foot in dirt and sweat and her clothes were ruined, beyond repair. She stripped and turned on the shower, stepping beneath the warm spray to wash her hair and rinse the dirt from her body, soaping herself from head to toe with jasmine-fragranced body wash. Then she wrapped a towel about her head and ran a hot bath, adding plenty of bubbles. There would be time enough to examine the gap between the hole and the window tomorrow. For now, she had to think what she was going to do about her future.

She supposed she would have to go ahead with the sale of the house and split the proceeds with Sean. He could then take out a small mortgage, if he still wished to buy the bungalow. Imogen would have to find somewhere else to live. She needed to talk to Ernest Morgan and ask if one of the partners could represent her in the divorce. Messrs. Cartwright, Harper and Green were already dealing with her conveyancing business and they would need to know that she would no longer be buying the bungalow with Sean. She turned the bath taps off, lit several scented candles, fetched extra towels from the airing cupboard and switched off the electric light. The candles filled the bathroom with a warm glow. She lowered herself into the warm soapy water, laid back and tried to relax.

Imogen woke with a start. She must have drifted off as the candles had burnt themselves out and the water was cold. Something else was different. She felt, rather than heard, a faint humming. Imogen clambered out of the bath in the semi-darkness, groping for the bath sheet she intended to wrap about herself, before making her way out onto the landing. The noise or vibration or whatever it was appeared to be emanating from the spare bedroom. She entered the room to find it surprisingly well-lit, the light coming from the newly uncovered window.

Imogen glanced back at the window on the other side of the bedroom which seemed to show it was dark out. It must be a street lamp, although she didn't remember one being so close to the house. She crossed the room towards the hole in the wall. Cautiously picking her way across the rubble, she stepped into the gap and taking just two small steps found herself at the window.

She pulled the net curtain aside and looked out through the branches of the tree, and saw a full moon, low in the sky reflecting silvery light on the scene below. A slim, dark-haired woman stood on the front part of the side lawn with her back to the window. She bent down to retrieve something large from the ground and when she stood back up, Imogen saw that it was an estate agent's sign. The woman lifted it and brought the post of the sign hard down into the ground, then proceeded to hammer it in place with a mallet. As far as Imogen was concerned Dawn was still buying the house – the agents had not received instructions from her to put it back on the market. Perhaps Sean had decided to stir up some trouble. Imogen tried to open the window but it was jammed shut. She turned and raced out of the room and down the stairs, flinging open the front door, shouting, "Hey!"

The front lawn was deserted. There was no woman and no 'For Sale' sign. Imogen stepped out just as the moon disappeared behind a cloud. She looked all about the Close, straining her eyes to see in the darkness. Nobody was about. Bewildered, still damp and naked, but for a towel, she went back inside, closing the door behind her.

She hurried straight back up the stairs. Surely, she couldn't have imagined it... She grabbed her bathrobe on the way past the bathroom, struggling into it as she entered the spare bedroom again. With some trepidation, she made her way back to the window.

Sure enough, the woman was still there and she'd fixed the sign firmly in place. Imogen rapped hard on the glass, trying to attract the woman's attention, then watched as she walked away from the house towards a smart BMW, parked at the kerb. Imogen heard the bleep of her key fob perfectly clearly as she unlocked and opened the driver door, even though the woman had appeared not to hear her own attempts to attract her attention. Then something made the woman hesitate before she got into the driver's seat. She turned and looked up at the window, the expression on her face one of abject misery.

Imogen's heart skipped a beat, then the world seemed to lurch and send her into a spin and she felt her legs buckle as she struggled to remain conscious. She stumbled backwards, her legs coming hard against the jagged opening to the hole, before falling back into the bedroom. She scrambled for the bed, pulling herself onto it, panting hard. She had recognised the affluent but unhappy woman. She had been looking at herself.

Imogen told herself to breathe deeply and slowly as she waited until the adrenaline rush had eased and her body stopped trembling. If only Sean were still here and the whole miserable business of his adultery and the accident had never happened. She missed him terribly, even though they'd been drifting apart for some time. A vague thought, unpleasant, insidious crept into her mind. Supposing she'd made a mistake? Perhaps she should have given him another chance … then she began to feel heavy with sleep and she struggled to fight it. She must have been dreaming all along, she thought drowsily, and if that was the case it wouldn't hurt to look out the window again, just to check.

She slid off the bed and made herself walk back to the broken wall, and once again she stepped into the space and towards the window. This time the scene was different. The moon could no longer be seen through the tree branches at the side of the house, as pale sunlight brightened the sky. It was either dusk or dawn, although she was unable immediately to determine which. The other Imogen was there again with her back to the house and she was watching two workmen loading furniture and belongings from the house onto a removal lorry. They finished and one of the men brought papers attached to a clipboard to her for signing. Then the other Imogen stood and watched as he got up into the cab of the removal vehicle. As the lorry pulled away, a familiar man hobbled out from the house to stand beside her. He was leaning heavily on a crutch, but managed to put an arm about her shoulders and she leaned her head against him. The man was Sean, no longer in the wheelchair, and he could walk!

Imogen watched from the window, fascinated, as another car drove into the close and pulled up at the kerb. A slim, mousey-haired woman emerged from the driver seat and strode round the car to open the rear passenger door. A little boy of about four climbed out. The woman leant into the car out of sight, while the little boy stood patiently on the pavement waiting. When the woman reappeared, she was holding a toddler – a little girl with tiny bunches in her hair. She was sucking on a pacifier. The woman took the children towards the couple, spoke for a few moments then kissed both the little boy and the little girl and fetched an overnight bag from the boot of her car before leaving them with a wave as she drove off. The children began to howl piteously and, although the woman had put on a brave face, Imogen – the one looking out the window – could see it was an act, a brave front, to reassure the children.

Imogen backed away from the window and, turning, scrambled back through the hole. No. No. She wouldn't, couldn't do that to those children, to their mother. Sean really did need to stand up to his responsibilities, she thought grimly. She would never enable him to deliberately hurt others, regardless of her love for him and her own desperate longing for children.

She accidentally stood on a piece of broken brick and gave a yelp, hopping to the bed to sit on the edge and inspect the underside of her foot. There was a long cut in the skin, not too deep but it was bleeding and would need washing and a plaster to be applied. She hopped to the bathroom, found what she needed in the cabinet and perched on the edge of the bath to dress the wound. As she stood to close the mirrored door of the medicine cabinet, she looked at her reflection. Surely if she was dreaming she wouldn't have felt any pain? She decided to take one more glance through the window. Steeling herself, she went back to the spare bedroom. Daylight still graced the mysterious window. However, this time her other self was standing talking and laughing with Dawn at the kerb. Dawn had just got out of her car and was lifting a cardboard box from her passenger seat as they conversed. The car appeared loaded with a number of boxes, so it seemed likely she was moving in. Then the slow growl of a motorcycle could be heard heading into the Close and a motorcyclist drew up on a fancy machine behind Dawn's car. The leather-clad figure switched off his engine, dismounted, kicked out the stand and took off gloves and helmet before turning towards the house. He was a complete stranger, as far as Imogen could tell. He was probably in his late thirties, slightly taller than either of the woman, and he had ginger hair. He said something as he approached the two women which Imogen, watching from the window, could not quite hear, and he grinned. The women laughed and the three of them stood talking to one another.

Suddenly the motorcyclist turned and looked up at the window, and for one heart-stopping moment Imogen thought that he could see her, but then he turned back to continue talking with the women. She was certain she didn't know him, yet something about him was oddly familiar. The scene was so vivid, the sound of chatter so real, she couldn't believe it wasn't actually happening. She decided to go once more to her front door and check outside. However, as soon as she moved away from the window, the babble of conversation abruptly ceased as if someone had switched off a radio.

Imogen went back to the window and looked out to find nobody there, and, from her limited view through the branches of the tree, Whitewood Close appeared to be quiet. It was morning and judging from the cool grey light, people were probably only just getting up and ready for work, preparing for the day. She took hold of the old net curtain that still hung bunched at one side of the window and tore it down. Scrunching it into a ball, she cast it aside. Imogen stepped back over the lower part of the jagged hole in the wall and turned to look at the mess she'd made the previous evening. It was fortunate she wasn't expected at the solicitors to cover holiday leave yet. She would need time to clear up and find a builder to take down the rest of the wall safely and remove the remaining parts of the wardrobe. Imogen was fairly confident it would not affect Dawn's decision to buy the house because she'd already announced her intention to knock down the wall herself.

Imogen sighed. She'd have to phone the solicitors later to postpone the exchange of contracts, to allow time for her to file for divorce. For the moment, she was going to go back to bed because the only explanation she could come up with, concerning what she'd seen from the window, was that she was dreaming and, unless she was sleepwalking, she was probably already in bed anyway. She returned to the double room she had previously shared with Sean. The bed looked neat, un-slept in, the duvet smooth with no indentation in the pillows. She climbed in and wriggled about until she was comfortable. It had to be a dream, she decided tiredly, because if it wasn't she needed to face up to the harsh reality that she was having some kind of a nervous breakdown and was well on the way to losing her mind.

Chapter Twelve

The workman had been as good as his word. His task had taken two and a half days but the jagged hole in the wall was gone, the room was freshly redecorated and appeared as if the extra wall hiding the second window had never been there. Imogen had even had him replace the carpet so that all the floor was now covered. It had cost most of the money Imogen had earned in her first fortnight at the solicitors, and yet she had to admit, as she paid the man cash in hand, it was worth it.

"My friend thought there'd be a dead body behind that wall," she quipped as the workman collected together his tools.

"Did she, now? That reminds me," he said, and pulled a package from his tool bag. It was about thirty centimetres long and five wide, wrapped in brown parcel paper and tied with string. "I found this hidden in the corner behind that false wall. It's a bit grubby." He handed it to her and she turned it over in her hands, feeling the shape of it, pressing her fingers lightly into the paper.

"I wonder what it is."

"Well, it's not big enough to be a body, that's for sure," the man grinned.

Imogen shuddered. She thought, not unless it's a very small body, such as a premature baby. Feeling slightly ridiculous, she raised the parcel to her nose, tentatively sniffing. The workman was clearly attempting not to smirk as he watched her. She quickly put the package down on the dressing table.

She saw the workman to the door and as he left, Tilly arrived. Imogen wasn't at all surprised; she'd heard the raised voices coming from her neighbour's house earlier, and the slamming of the front door. She led her tearful friend to the kitchen to sit down.

"Can I get you anything? Water? Tea?"

"Have you anything stronger?"

Imogen laid a hand on her neighbour's shoulder, then went to fetch a bottle of Chardonnay from the fridge and a couple of glasses. "This do?" She asked, showing Tilly the bottle. She pulled the cork and poured two generous drinks. They chinked glasses together before tasting the cool refreshing liquid. The wine barely seemed to be alcoholic, such was their shared appreciation.

"Why is it that no matter how hard I try to do the right thing, I always seem to be on the receiving end of recriminations?" Tilly began. She took another large gulp of wine. "I tried to tell Neil that he needed to talk to his son and before I could even explain why, he started accusing me of going behind his back and interfering. That boy's in some sort of trouble, Imogen, I just know it, but Neil's so far up on his high horse he won't listen to reason."

Imogen reached across the table and squeezed Tilly's hand, forgetting her own problems for the moment. "Give him a couple of hours and he'll calm down and see sense," she soothed.

"I very much doubt it. He slammed out of the house and has gone off to play golf. He knew Adrian was coming home to talk to him, and Imogen, it's taken me an age to convince the kid it would be for the best, yet his father's deliberately gone out to avoid him."

"That's awkward. What are you going to do?"

"I've already done it. I've written a note to Adrian telling him I've had to go out and won't be back until late and I've left dinner in the oven. He's still got his own key, so when Neil gets home he will jolly well have to face him and sort things out. I'm not going to be there. I'm going to drive into town and book a room at The Golden Hope for the night."

"Don't do that."

"Why ever not?"

"Three reasons. One, you need to be close by in case it all goes terribly wrong and ends in a fight, not that I think it will but you can't be sure. Two, you shouldn't drive after you've been drinking," Imogen paused and refilled her friend's glass, then as an afterthought topped up her own. "Three, why pay good money for a room in town when you can stay here in my newly decorated spare room."

"You're very kind. I don't want to impose ..." Tilly began. Imogen cut her short. "It's not an imposition. I could do with the company. Now what shall we do about your car? If they realise it's still in the garage they'll probably guess you're somewhere nearby."

"I don't think they'll even look. In fact, I don't think they'll even talk to each other, so this whole idea is probably a waste of time."

"You'll never know if you don't try. Anyway, it could be quite fun having you stay over for the night. We could sit up late and watch a rom-com. Besides, I've got some more news. I'm divorcing Sean."

Tilly's mouth dropped open, but before she had chance to respond the doorbell rang. The women looked at each other. Imogen hurried into the lounge and peered out the window. She couldn't see who stood on her doorstep, but a familiar Audi was parked at the kerb.

"Panic over, it's neither of your two," she called through to the kitchen on her way to the door.

Dawn didn't wait to be invited in. She was obviously upset and as soon as Imogen opened the door she pushed past her, stopping and turning to confront her in the hall.

"I've just been informed by the solicitors that you've postponed exchanging contracts." She didn't raise her voice. However, her eyes were sparking with anger. "I can understand if you've had a problem with the place you're buying. What I don't get is why you wouldn't tell me yourself and why the solicitors refuse to give me a reason for you stalling. I thought we were friends."

Imogen sighed. "We are. Listen, Dawn, a lot's happened since we last spoke. I obviously owe you an explanation, so please just come through to the kitchen. We were having a glass of wine. Imogen led the way. "I believe you know Tilly," she said, nodding to her neighbour. Perhaps I can get you a drink, Dawn?"

"A glass of water, thank you." Dawn sat down at the table with a stiff little smile in Tilly's direction, then spoke as if she wasn't there.

"I'm sorry, Imogen, I shouldn't have burst into your home like that. I guess I'm panicking a bit as I was counting on moving in before the end of the summer break. I don't much fancy driving to school from London every day, and the people buying my flat are ready and waiting."

Imogen gave Dawn a glass of water and sat back down, taking up her wine glass again. "It's me who should apologise. I meant to warn you, but I lost my mobile and with it your number." In fact, she had smashed her mobile and thrown it in the bin to prevent further persistent calls from Sean, which she had no intention of answering. She'd done it in a moment of spite, furious that he was ignoring her request not to contact her again. Silly really. She should have simply blocked his number. "I was just telling Tilly, I'm getting divorced."

Her two friends looked at her. Neither made any comment. They waited for Imogen to continue.

"It turns out my husband has another woman, a young son and another child on the way." She smiled cheerfully as if she found it all a huge joke. "You've heard Stevie Wonder's song about a part-time lover? Well, Sean planned to make me a part-time mother. Or perhaps a full-time replacement mother? I'm not entirely sure which. I, of course, declined." She drank, emptying her glass, then picked up the now finished wine bottle and got up to fetch a replacement.

"More wine?" she addressed her neighbour who still sat motionless, a look of disbelief on her face. Tilly abruptly roused herself. "Please. That would be lovely."

Dawn rested her elbows on the table and put her head in her hands. "To hell with it," she said, looking up. "I'll have some too. That's if you wouldn't mind putting me up for the night?"

"You can have my room. Tilly's got the spare. I'll sleep on the couch," Imogen said, "and I don't want any arguments. I can't seem to sleep at the moment without the television on for background noise."

Dawn said she'd drive into Bushwell to get more wine, then they got into a discussion about food and Imogen rang an Indian restaurant in the next town and ordered supper. While Dawn was gone, Tilly and Imogen flicked through the film titles on the satellite channel.

"Dawn isn't as intimidating as you thought, is she?" Imogen said.

"Stop, I want to see what it says about that one," Tilly said, staring at the screen. "Oh, okay. Bit morbid. No, you were right as usual. She seems fine. Perhaps she's learnt to compartmentalise work and home life."

Imogen pointed the remote control at the TV and pressed the button again.

"How about this film? *Love and Time,*" Tilly put a hand on her arm to stop her scrolling through the films. "It says it's a cross between *The Time Traveller's Wife* and *About Time*. There's no happy ever after. Apparently, the couple split up, but it's very moving and uplifting. Oh, and it's a comedy, what do you make of that? Look, it's got five stars."

"Sounds like fun, I don't think. What about *The Lake House?* I could do with having my faith in mankind restored," Imogen said.

At that moment, Dawn came through the back door, carrying a couple of bottles. She stood in the doorway for a moment watching them.

"It's a lovely story but I watched *The Lake House* a few days ago. I need to be able to forget the story a bit before I watch it again," Tilly said. "Sorry."

"Here's a suggestion," Dawn said. "How about we watch the latest Star Trek movie? It's got everything": excitement, adventure, romance..."

"Brilliant idea! I watched a programme the other night whereby Christies were auctioning off all the old film props. It was amazing what people were prepared to pay for some of those things," Tilly told them.

"I never took you to be a Trekie fan, Tilly," Dawn smiled.

"And I never realised you were the new Head teacher at the school," Imogen said, "Let alone a Sci fi geek!"

"I wasn't really into science fiction until a guy I've recently started seeing got me interested." Dawn ignored the comment about her job.

"Ah, so you have a boyfriend too," Imogen teased.

"Not sure," Dawn said, her voice serious. "He isn't the type I generally date."

"Let's hurry up and open that wine before the food arrives," Tilly suggested.

Chapter Thirteen

It was late. The film credits were rolling and Tilly was snoring in her armchair, her breast gently rising and falling.

"That passed a couple of hours and helped me forget my worries for a while," Imogen said.

"What do you intend doing about moving, then?" Dawn had something on her mind and came straight to the point. "You obviously don't want to move to the bungalow now. Will Sean still buy it, do you think? He'll have to share the proceeds of the sale of this place and you'll even be entitled to a share of his business, you know. You could move right away from here. Have a whole fresh start."

Imogen looked mortified. "I don't want to move away," she said.

"Sorry, I didn't mean to upset you."

"It's okay. I've thought about little else since I found out about Sean's secret life. I've even dreamt about how my decisions could affect my future."

"That's probably your mind trying to rationalise what's happened and help you come to terms with it. The brain is a remarkable organ. Tell me about the dream."

"I was looking out the bedroom window and I could see myself in different situations according to what I had decided. It was really vivid. That reminds me. I took out the wardrobe in the spare bedroom and knocked down the wall so that the window you asked about can be seen from the inside as well as outside. Don't worry, the wall was taken down properly and the room's been redecorated."

"Sorry, I'm confused. It must be the wine. Was that part of your dream or have you really had the wall removed?"

Imogen laughed. "I knocked a hole in it then thought I'd better pay to get rid of it properly."

"I presume there was no corpse then," Dawn said. She sat up straight, having noticed Imogen's expression. "Whatever's the matter, you look quite peculiar."

"You've just reminded me, the builder found a small package hidden behind the wall. It's up on the dressing table. I'd forgotten all about it."

"Come on," Dawn said, getting up and pulling Imogen up by her hand. "Let's go find out what it is. Then we'd better get Tilly to bed. She's going to have a real thumper of a headache in the morning."

Somehow in Dawn's company, the package no longer seemed in the least bit worrying and yet Imogen passed it over for her friend to cut the strings with nail scissors and un-wrap the brown paper. She didn't tell Dawn of her horror that the package might contain something sinister, and when the last fold of paper tore slightly to reveal a small, delicate baby's face, Imogen uttered a cry of dismay. Dawn glanced up at her then pulled the last of the paper away.

It took several seconds for Imogen to grasp that the object Dawn held carefully in her hands was not the body of a dead infant. It was a baby doll with a face made of what appeared to be flesh-coloured porcelain painted in an attitude of repose. It had a soft cloth body with delicate little hands and feet made of the same porcelain-like material that the head was made of, and it was clothed in a long cream linen dress hemmed with lace.

"This looks like it could be antique," Dawn said, showing the doll to Imogen. "It's quite exquisite, isn't it? I don't think I've ever seen such a life-like doll." She passed it to Imogen. "You need to keep it somewhere safe – it could be valuable. I wonder why it was put behind the wall. Who do you think it could have belonged to?"

It had taken a while for Imogen to regain her composure. She looked down at the remarkable little doll in her hands.

"One of the previous inhabitants of the house, I suppose," she said. "As to why it was hidden, we'd have to find out who built the wall to solve that mystery. I've an empty shoe box in my room that I was going to use to pack ornaments. It would be ideal to keep the doll in for the time being."

Once the doll was wrapped in tissue paper and safely stowed in the box which was placed on the top shelf of her walk-in closet, Imogen collected her nightclothes and left Dawn in her bedroom, wishing her a good night. She fetched a spare duvet and pillow from the airing cupboard and went back downstairs to rouse Tilly. When she gently shook her friend by the shoulder, the woman jerked awake, eyes wide in panic.

"Is Adrian home? Has there been any trouble?"

"Calm down," Imogen said. "I haven't heard a thing from next door and if you look out the window you'll see your house is in darkness. They must have gone to bed. It's quite late." She began to arrange the pillow and duvet on the sofa. "Dawn's already gone up and I just wanted to ask if you needed anything else. There are fresh towels in the airing cupboard if you want to help yourself."

"Is the film finished then?" Tilly asked. Imogen had already changed channels and lowered the sound on the television set. "How did it end?"

Imogen had finished organising her bedding on the sofa and sat down. "The spaceship flew off through the stars to continue exploring space," she said.

"Right. Well I'd better get along to bed then. I can't believe I fell asleep while watching it." Tilly heaved herself from the armchair and slowly plodded up the stairs.

Imogen settled on the sofa beneath the duvet, reached over to pick up the remote from the coffee table and flicked through the channels, the sound still low. She left it on an American sitcom, put the remote down and lay on her back, staring at the ceiling, thinking about the doll they'd found. That made her think of the little girl in the garden and the photograph of Alicia that had fallen from the notebook. That in turn led her on to wonder about the things she'd believed she'd seen from the window. She moved onto her side and stared unseeing at the television screen, believing she would never manage to get to sleep. A floorboard creaked overhead; it was strange not to be alone in the house for once, although she had enjoyed having some female company this evening.

She must have fallen asleep because the next thing she knew the kitchen light was on. She got up and went to investigate. Tilly was filling a glass with water. "Sorry," she said, "I didn't mean to disturb you. I had a weird dream." Imogen yawned and looked at the kitchen clock. It was quarter past four in the morning. Tilly looked pretty shaken as she drained the glass of water. Imogen noticed her hand trembled as she placed the glass on the table and pulled out a chair to sit down. Imogen joined her at the table.

"Would you like me to make some cocoa or something?"

"No, no. I'll be okay. It's just the dream seemed so real."

Imogen felt goose bumps. "Tell me about it," she said.

"I dreamt I woke up, got out of bed and looked out the window. I'm not really sure why. I saw Adrian with two men arguing. They started to push him about a bit so I knocked on the window and yelled and tried to open it, but couldn't. I ran down the stairs to the front door, yet when I opened it the Close was deserted. You were fast asleep on the sofa so I relocked the door and crept back up to the bedroom.

"I was so baffled I went over to the window as soon as I got to the room I'd been sleeping in and peered out again. This time I saw myself standing next to a hearse and a coffin was being carried out from my house. It really frightened me and I knew then I must be dreaming, or rather having a nightmare. I screwed up my eyes tight to try to wake myself up. When I

90

opened them again there was sunshine pouring in through the window, so I assumed I'd been sleepwalking and it was now morning.

"As I looked out, a car pulled up at the kerb and Neil's ex-wife was driving. Adrian stumbled out of the back of the car and limped towards the house. He was in a bad way and his face was battered and bleeding. Then one of those fancy four-wheel drives sped into the Close and a man I've never seen before jumped out. There was a huge to do as Neil's ex tried to grab the man's arm. He was shouting at Adrian. Then Neil came out of our house to investigate. Adrian said something to him and Neil must have told him to go inside the house, which he did. Neil turned, pulled his ex-wife aside and with one punch flattened the man. I've never seen him raise a hand to anyone before, he's the most gentle and quiet man I know, yet he seemed really angry." She shook her head and rubbed a hand over her face.

"Well, I thought it was really happening this time, so I raced back downstairs – I'm amazed you didn't hear me – and flung the front door open and again nobody was there and it was still dark. That's when I decided to get some water. I think the wine we drank must have had a bad effect on me."

Dawn padded into the kitchen and joined them at the table. She placed a hand with neatly manicured nails over her mouth as she yawned.

"Has there been trouble next door? I heard someone running up and down stairs, so I thought I'd better come down and check you were alright, Tilly."

Tilly shook her head again. "I was just having a nightmare. I'm sorry I disturbed you."

"Ahh, I caught some of what you just said and was quite concerned until I heard the bit about alcohol and I realise now you must have been talking about a dream. I expect you were worrying about your husband and son when you fell asleep and that's why you dreamt about them." She leaned forward, elbow on the table, chin in hand, interested.

"Adrian's my step-son actually, but yes I was thinking about him and Neil."

Imogen was busying herself making three cups of cocoa. "Bit of a strange coincidence, though, Tilly dreaming exactly the same type of dream as I did," she remarked. "I mean, I had a dream about that window, Tilly, and Dawn suggested my dream was about my personal anxieties too," she said over her shoulder.

"It's just how the mind works," Dawn reasoned. "I really do believe the brain uses dreams to sort through the day's concerns and try to make sense of them." She looked from one woman to the other. "The window part is probably simply because you were sleeping in a room with an extra window which faces the bed."

"What did you dream then, Imogen?" Tilly asked at last.

"Yes, tell us and I'll show you what I mean," Dawn said.

Imogen gave out the cocoa and sat down, took a sip from her mug then began to relate her experience the night she'd begun to knock down the wall in the spare bedroom. Her two friends listened in silence. When she finished, she said to Dawn, "Well, go on and tell us what it all means then."

"Uh huh." Dawn stared off into space, thinking for a moment. "I think you believe if you sold the house and moved on you might be better off financially, but you don't necessarily think you will be happy. The expensive car and designer clothes you were wearing denote wealth. That means you're confident that rather than merely surviving, when striking out on your own, you could actually prosper. Your sadness illustrates it's not enough, not what you really want."

"Okay, I can accept that," Imogen said.

"The part where you were with Sean and he was able to walk probably means you feel he'd do better if you remained with him, yet you can't accept his idea about custody of the children."

"I get that too, but don't forget I've never seen this other woman and yet I could see her quite clearly in the dream and she was obviously as upset as the little ones."

"It wasn't the actual mistress you saw. The woman in your dream probably represents a facet of your own personality that's grieving over the loss of your marriage."

"Imogen pressed her lips together. She wasn't convinced by Dawn's theory. She looked at Tilly whose eyes seemed to dart from Dawn to herself and back again, her expression unreadable.

Dawn drank from her mug, her eyes on the table, obviously thinking about the last part of the dream and what it might mean.

"In the final part of your dream I was getting boxes from my car, obviously moving in and we were all chatting in a friendly manner, so you must unconsciously feel you are doing the right thing selling the house and moving on, but you want to stay close by as was your original plan."

"What about the motorcyclist, though, the guy with the red hair?"

"That's the guy I've just started seeing, or rather it sounds like him."

"Yet I only learned you've got a boyfriend tonight! How could I possibly know what he looks like or that he has a motorcycle?"

Dawn shook her head and put her cocoa mug down. "That is a bit weird, I have to admit," she said.

Tilly said, "I think there's something strange about that window. I'm not even sure now that I *was* dreaming when I saw everything I told you about, Imogen. Like Dawn, I guess I just tried to rationalise it by believing I was dreaming. What if I wasn't? What if you weren't dreaming either? Supposing we've seen some sort of premonitions about what could happen according to the decisions we make?"

Dawn laughed. "That's ridiculous! Look, before we allow our imaginations to run away with themselves, let's go look at this 'extraordinary' window."

"Fine. I rather think we should," Tilly was on her feet, leading the way back up the stairs to the spare bedroom, before Dawn had chance to change her mind. She got to the window seconds before the others and looked out.

"There!" she cried. "Now there's a police car outside my house. An officer is getting out and he's taking his cap off and running his hand through his hair. Oh my, – bad news!"

Chapter Fourteen

Dawn was at Tilly's side in seconds. She peered out of the window. Then she turned to Tilly, took her by the shoulders and insisted she look at her, rather than through the window. "There's no police car, Tilly. There is no officer going to your house," she said, her voice firm. Once the older woman had calmed down, Dawn allowed her to join her in looking out the window again. Tilly just said, "Oh!" and with a bewildered expression turned towards Imogen, who was waiting by the bed. She left the window and went to sit down next to her. Imogen gave her a reassuring hug. Dawn continued to gaze out of the window, her back towards them, saying nothing. Imogen wondered what she was thinking.

After a moment, Tilly stood up and began gathering her clothes together.

"I think I'm going to go home, if you don't mind, Imogen. Perhaps a couple of hours in my own bed will help."

"Of course," Imogen said. "Dawn and I will leave you to get yourself organised," Dawn turned and nodded her agreement. "I don't think I'll be able to go back to sleep though," she said. "I think I'll get dressed too, if you don't mind."

As she followed her onto the landing, Dawn caught Imogen's arm before she started down the stairs. "Imogen?" Imogen turned, surprised at the look in Dawn's eyes. She stopped. "What is it?" she asked in alarm.

"I, er," she shook her head. "Nothing. I was just going to say I ought to think about getting back to London as soon as it's light."

"We haven't spooked you, have we? It wouldn't surprise me if we had. It's been a weird night," Imogen replied.

"You haven't spooked me; that would be absurd. I think we are all just over-tired and stressed by recent events and we exacerbated the situation by drinking too much."

95

Imogen's glance was inquisitive. "Well, okay then. You go ahead and get ready. I'll make a pot of tea and some toast for when you come down."

She went back to the lounge and folded the duvet, placing the pillow on it ready to put away. Then she went into the kitchen, filled the kettle and switched it on. She put bread into the toaster then sat at the table waiting for Tilly to leave. Ten minutes later Dawn joined her. Neither of them spoke. Dawn made tea, although it remained on the table before them untouched. They each ate a piece of buttered toast. When Tilly finally left, closing the door behind her Imogen said, "Do you think she'll be alright?"

Dawn shrugged, rather unsympathetically Imogen thought.

After a moment, Imogen said, "Tell me, why all the secrecy about you being the new Headmistress at Bushwell Primary School?" She shook her head. "You knew I thought you were a teacher, why didn't you put me right? I felt rather foolish when Tilly told me."

"I wanted you to judge me for myself and not my job."

"I'm not in the habit of judging people, either by their career or otherwise," Imogen shot back. "Why should it make any difference what you do for a living?"

"It will to some people. You obviously care very much about the village and people who live hereabouts. I didn't want my position to affect your decision to sell me this house."

"I don't get it."

Dawn's reply was matter of fact. "Are you aware that the school is failing? The pupils aren't achieving or making the progress they should be. I've been sent in to get Bushwell Primary out of Special Measures, otherwise the school could well close. There will be major upheavals. Some of the staff might have to go. That doesn't always make the person responsible for instigating change popular with the locals."

"Is Tilly's job safe?" Imogen was almost too afraid to ask.

"I haven't had time to completely evaluate staff performance yet, or decide whether I agree with the powers that be as to where the principle weaknesses in the school lie. I wouldn't tell you even if I did know."

Imogen nodded. "I appreciate your honesty."

"Good, then I can be candid. The people that I generally keep as friends are those that are most useful and beneficial to me. I know that sounds mercenary but it's the way I am and it's probably the reason I'm excelling in my career."

"And how will I be useful to you?" Imogen was quickly realising that, as well as being fun and sociable, Dawn could also be both sharp and ruthless. She was a bit of an enigma, one moment seeming incredibly young, witty almost to the point of being outrageous, the next serious and mature beyond her years. She was certainly, as Tilly had said, ambitious.

Dawn blushed. "Don't forget I said beneficial too," she laughed. "As I told you before, it will be good to have a friend who is nothing to do with education, someone who can introduce me to people in Bushwell. Also, you have a great sense of humour and that's crucial, as you will discover, if you intend to be friends with me."

"The fact that I own the house you wish to buy was just a bonus then?" Imogen decided she should be equally blunt.

"Ouch, you really know how to put a person in their place, don't you? Actually, I have an idea about the house."

"You do?"

"Yes. You clearly don't really want to leave this house. Why don't you re-mortgage and buy Sean out? You could take me as a lodger until I find something else. I'd pay the going rate in rent and that would help with your mortgage re-payments. It would help me, too, as I haven't time now to organise alternative accommodation. I don't know how long I shall be able to keep driving from London each day. I believe it would benefit both of us."

"You've really thought this through, haven't you?"

"I began to consider it as an option after you mentioned seeing me from that window getting boxes from my car, and us standing chatting with Eli. So, what do you think of my idea? Would it work?"

Imogen suddenly felt as though the world had become a lighter, brighter place. Dawn was right. She didn't really want to move from this house, despite its oddities. At the very least Dawn's suggestion provided a reprieve while she decided what to do next. She smiled. "Sounds like a plan to me. The boyfriend's name is Eli, is it?"

"Not a boyfriend yet. We've been out a couple of times, that's all and he's had a meal at my flat. I met him, believe it or not, in the British Science Museum during a school trip. He's the Managing Director of the Jaxen Foundation. You might have heard of him?"

"You don't mean Elijah Croft, the guy responsible for all that scientific research into mental health issues?"

"That's the one. He's also very keen to encourage young people's interest in science and was at the museum to look for ideas for a number of workshops he's considering setting up. He approached me because he wanted to gauge my views as a teacher. Of course, I was deputy head of my old school and still taught part-time. We had a brief chat and then he asked me out to dinner to discuss the matter further. After that he invited me to a discussion group at the university where he apparently lectures from time to time. Not what you'd call romantic dates."

"What about when you dined at your flat?"

"I thought it only polite to reciprocate in some way, and I don't have an awful lot of free time. He was an absolute gentleman."

"I thought he looked vaguely familiar when I saw him from the window. He's been on the covers of magazines and on T.V. Wow, Dawn, he's loaded!"

"He is probably reasonably affluent, although I'm not particularly bothered about that. He's a nice guy, genuine – you know what I mean? The trouble is I'm not sure he's my type. I tend to go for the more dangerous type, and that's why my relationships invariably end in tears." She paused for a moment, holding a hand up to inspect her nails, before adding, "Anyway, thanks for agreeing to let me move in for a while."

In a moment of spontaneity, Dawn hugged Imogen. They laughed together, faces flushed with pleasure. They were going to be housemates. Imogen suddenly stopped laughing. "Wait a minute, don't you mean when I *dreamed* I saw you?" she said. "I thought you didn't believe the window really showed us what we saw? You said you didn't see anything when Tilly saw the police car."

The smile faded on Dawn's lips. "No, what I said was there wasn't a police car outside."

Imogen was perplexed.

"When I looked out of the window it was daylight," Dawn said. "I saw myself carrying a tray of cup-cakes towards the green. You were with me, struggling with a crate of beer. There were loads of people on the green and music and food."

"The barbeque on the green! I intended inviting you to join us." Imogen's eyes widened. "No wonder you went all silent on us."

"I knew I couldn't be dreaming and just didn't know what to say, I mean, how is it possible that a window can show something entirely different to what's actually going on outside of it? How long has it been like that? Do you think that's why a wall was built in front of it? Why didn't whoever built the wall report it to someone, so that it could be investigated properly?"

"Yeah, I have just as many questions as you," Imogen said. "There's always been something special about this house, and I don't think it's just because of that window. I was heartbroken at the prospect of having to leave this place."

Imogen chewed her lip and looked about her as if expecting to find the answer somewhere in the kitchen. She thought about how Tilly had only recently commented on how much she liked Imogen's kitchen but couldn't say why, and she hadn't been the first of her friends over the past nine years who'd complimented her on the atmosphere of her home. She'd always put it down to the peaceful rural setting, yet recently she'd begun to wonder if there was more to it than that. She mused how even the strange young hippy woman had talked about how much she had missed the house.

"I've just had a thought," Dawn said. "Don't you think, Imogen, it's time we jimmied your garage door to see what's in there?"

"My garage? Hmm, you're right we ought to have a look. It might have something inside that could throw some light on things. Didn't you say you had to get back to your flat, though?"

"London can wait," Dawn assured her. "Now I'm beginning to understand just how unique this house is, I'm burning with curiosity."

"Okay, then. Why not!"

They agreed to wait until the majority of the residents had left the Close for the day before taking some tools, including Dawn's iron wheel jack, to force open the garage door. They made quite a bit of noise, working together jamming the jack through the slim gap near the lock, knocking it deeper in with a hammer and pulling with all their might. Just as they were ready to give up, the edge of the door buckled and the lock bust apart. The door slid up and over with a clang. The two women stood for a moment, waiting for their eyes to adjust to the darkness of the interior.

"It's just a lot of cardboard boxes, piled one on top of another," Imogen said. "I bet they're either empty or full of paper and rubbish."

"Let's find out," Dawn said, stepping into the garage. She reached up to take down the top box of the first pile she came to and set it on the ground. Imogen had also taken down a box from the other side of the garage and placed it next to the one before Dawn. They glanced at each other before squatting down to rip the tape from the tops of the boxes and pull open the cardboard flaps. Dawn took out an object and held it up for her friend to see.

"There must be dozens of these in here. What have you got?"

Imogen plunged her hand into the box before her and pulled out several of what appeared to be oddly shaped beads. Turning them over in the palm of her hand, she exclaimed, "They're eyes for toys!"

Dawn threw the miniature leg she'd been holding back into the carton she'd opened. She stood up and took down another box and opened it. "Just as I suspected," she said. "Arms!"

"Roger Stockman restored and sold antique dolls." The woman's voice came from outside the garage. It had a light American accent that was somehow familiar to Imogen.

Still crouching beside the boxes, they looked towards the opening to the garage, both holding their hands just above their eyes as if saluting, to shield their faces from the glare of the sunlight outside. Imogen gasped.

There stood the beautiful young hippy woman, Alicia, and she was holding the hand of the child Imogen had seen in her garden, the little girl with the blonde hair and pink dress who she'd recently chased out of the Close.

Chapter Fifteen

Imogen stood up and walked towards Alicia, reaching out a hand to touch the woman's arm as soon as she was close enough. Watching, Dawn also straightened up, her hands brushing the front of her jeans as she came out of the garage.

"You're real," Imogen said, letting her hand drop to her side once more. "I thought I'd imagined you! And this little one," she said looking down at the upturned face, "I've seen her before too!"

"My daughter, Echo. Yes, once I showed her the secret gate, she couldn't resist using it. Sorry. She's not quite as bad as her brother, Lee. He's more of a wanderer, though he prefers the woods and fields to other people's gardens. It's a full-time job trying to keep track of the pair of them."

"You have *two* children?"

Alicia laughed. It was a warm, musical sound. "Yes, twins. Lee's older by seven minutes. I don't mean to be rude, only do you think I could take Echo in to use your bathroom? She's getting a bit desperate." Imogen looked at the little girl who nodded her head vigorously, hopping from one foot to the other.

"Er, Yes, of course, as long as you don't vanish again." Imogen gestured towards the house before turning back to close the garage door. She moved as if dazed, in a dream. Alicia, on the other hand, scurried towards the side of the house, the child running beside her.

"Say, is the back door unlocked?" Alicia paused and called back.

"Yes, yes, it is," Imogen replied, then murmured to Dawn, "Come on." They too began to hurry back towards the house. As they watched, the young woman pulled on part of the iron fencing behind the dense foliage of the conifers. To Imogen's amazement there was indeed a secret gate which, with very little coaxing, opened out to allow access to the garden. Imogen broke into a jog, Dawn close on her heels. They entered the open gate and rushed into the garden towards the backdoor.

"Why are we running?" Dawn asked, panting.

"I don't want to give that woman chance to disappear again," Imogen replied.

"Imogen, you aren't making sense. Who is she?"

"You stay there by the back door. I'm going to lock the front."

Seconds later she returned to the kitchen, closely followed by Alicia and her little daughter. Alicia sat down at the kitchen table. "Echo, you go on into the garden to play, Darling, while I talk to these ladies. Is that Okay?" she added, looking at Imogen who nodded. "Don't wander off," Alicia instructed the child who needed no further prompting and was out of the door in a flash. Alicia turned her attention back to Imogen and Dawn. "Imogen, I sure need to apologise to you profusely. I never should have slipped away that night; it was ill-mannered," she said. "I guess I felt kinda guilty visiting your house under false pretences."

"Who is she?" Dawn asked again, before turning to Alicia. "Who are you?"

"Me? I'm the granddaughter of the man who built this house. My name's Alicia Chloe Fisherton-Downing. My husband's Gerald Downing. You may have heard of him? He's a fashion designer, famous for his retro label..." She gave the women time to absorb this information. Imogen and Dawn pulled out chairs from the table and sat down, never taking their eyes off their visitor.

"I love Downing clothes, even if they are a bit pricey. They're so stylish," Dawn said.

"Wait a minute. What do you mean by false pretences? Do you know anything about the doll I found hidden behind a wall in the middle bedroom? And the window? Do you know about the window?" Imogen asked.

"Yeah, I do, kinda. Let me explain."

"I think you ought to." Imogen met the young woman's eyes with a penetrating gaze.

"I don't blame you for being suspicious of me. I came back to see if you'd found the doll. I waited at the edge of the woods until the house was dark and silent and then I came in through your back door." She pushed her hand into the hip pocket of her jeans and pulled out a door key which she placed on the table. "This was concealed by the post of the hidden gate years ago, by my aunt."

"How could you possibly know the back door wouldn't have been changed, or the lock?" Dawn wanted to know.

"I couldn't be sure. When grandpa built the house, it was quite isolated. He wanted to make sure the place was aesthetically pleasing and the design of the external doors reflected that, but I think he also had security in mind. They're good strong doors that have stood the test of time so it seemed unlikely anyone would want to change them unless it was really necessary."

"You're right about that," Imogen conceded. "We always liked the design of the doors, although I have had to have the lock on the front door replaced recently because it was no longer working properly."

"Seems I was lucky with the back doorkey, then. Anyway, I searched for and found it during one of my walks with the children. The night I met you I just let myself into the house and crept upstairs. At first I thought there was nobody in the house, then I saw you sleeping alone in the very room I needed to look at, so I decided on the tale about wanting to see the house again and was about to leave and return in the morning, ringing the bell like any other visitor, when I saw the CD player and hit on the idea of waking you with music. After all, you might not still be alone come the morning."

"You must be mad! Why didn't you just ring the bell during daylight hours in the first place? Why all the sneaking around?" Imogen's voice was hard.

"I know. I'm a coward, I admit it. I thought Roger Stockman might still be living here and I was always a bit wary of him. More than wary, actually. I'm rather scared of him, even after all these years. I didn't even dare ask after him in the village in case he found out. Anyhow, I took the opportunity to have a look at the closets after I used your bathroom that night, and saw the wall was still intact in the middle bedroom, so I left. I went out through the front, closing the door as quietly as I could behind me. I'd already re-locked the back door. Sorry, I didn't mean to alarm you," she said, her expression contrite.

"Tell us about the doll." Dawn was becoming impatient.

"The doll was given to me a long time ago: it's always been called Baby. I slept in that room and had some real strange dreams and consequently felt I should leave Baby behind. I told my aunt to hide it. I can tell you, it's a very long, weird and complicated story."

Imogen sat back and folded her arms. "That's okay, we have plenty of time. Then you can explain why you came back. Surely anything left in the house now belongs to me, the current householder, including the doll."

"I'm not denying that." Alicia got up and went to check on her daughter from the kitchen window. Then she returned to her seat. "It's taken my family a long time to piece everything together. I'll try to tell you everything I know as best I can. I'm here because I, we rather, need your help."

"Do you live near here?" Dawn asked, her voice quiet in an attempt to calm Imogen.

"Gracious, no, though I've distant relatives nearby. They used to be farmers in my grandpa's time. Then eventually the place became an animal sanctuary."

"I know the place," Imogen said.

"I came over as a teenager and helped out there and that's where I met my dear friend, Tamsin. I guess it must be eight or nine years ago, now. She was looking for a dog and we introduced her to a lovely old collie called Ben. We've kept in touch ever since," Alicia went on. "I almost named my daughter after Tamsin, until I saw how much like her brother she looked. My twins were so alike, virtually identical apart from the obvious, although my little girl was slightly smaller and quieter except that every time her brother cried, she copied him like a little echo, so that's what I named her! Sorry, I know I'm babbling. Nerves."

"It's a cool name, very original, but you *are* rather straying from the point," Imogen said, her tone rather kinder now than before. "You were telling us about your friend, Tamsin, although I'm not sure why?"

Alicia grinned. "We've been staying at her house – that's what I was going to tell you. She lives at a place in Rainham called Silverspot. She invited us to stay while the rest of her family are away on holiday visiting her in-laws for a month. The invite couldn't have come at a better time, I can tell you. Do you know Silverspot?"

"That's the little estate off Mierscourt Road, isn't it?" Imogen asked.

"Sure is. Gerald and I generally split our time living in London, England, and New York with the kids – we've homes in both places."

"I've just sold a flat in London, St. John's Wood," Dawn put in. "I loved living there. I used to teach in one of the inner-city schools." She was obviously warming to Alicia, Imogen thought, while she, herself, still had reservations.

"I don't mean to be rude, but can I just ask you something?" she said. "Something personal?" Alicia nodded and Imogen continued, "You're hardly short of cash, so why do you let your little girl run around in that same awful pink dress all the time?"

Alicia gave a little laugh. "Gee, you sure believe in speaking your mind!" She raised a hand to halt Imogen's protest. "It's cool. I'm not offended. That's Echo's play dress. She insists on wearing it because it's pink. I'd rather she wore denim pants and a T-shirt," she lifted her hands in a resigned shrug, "but that's what she chooses to wear when her pa's not around to object. Kids need a bit of freedom, occasionally, don't you think?"

Dawn nodded. "I couldn't agree more. It doesn't pay to be over-protective. Children need to be able to choose occasionally, and to explore outside and discover things for themselves," she said.

"Well there you go then," Alicia looked back at Imogen. "It doesn't matter if that old dress gets soiled or torn when she's scampering about with Lee, playing at camping or trying to climb trees in the woods."

"The woods?" Imogen queried. "Do you mean the woods behind the Close?"

"Yes, you might not know it, but the woods and fields and all the land surrounding this little estate ..."

"Darrington Way," Imogen supplied.

"Yeah, Darrington Way, excluding the area on which these houses stand, still belongs to my grandpa's family. Whenever I'm down I make a point of telling the kids about dear old Henry, and we go for long treks to explore the land."

"Henry?" Dawn queried.

"My grandpa, Henry Fisherton." Alicia flicked a long strand of hair back over her shoulder. "If you're sure you have time I could begin by telling you everything I know about him."

Chapter Sixteen
1960 - London

Henry stood beside the hospital bed and looked down at his father's face, which was white and lined with pain. Even in his sleep, he was struggling for breath. Henry wondered whether he should be stroking his father's forehead and whispering words of comfort, but the faint sheen of sweat on his brow seemed uninviting and his father had never been particularly tactile anyway, offering kind words of wisdom to illustrate his love for his son as he grew up, rather than hugs and kisses, therefore Henry doubted he would appreciate it. The matron, who had shown Henry to his father's bed, had advised a short visit. Then she had placed a screen around the bed space to allow for some privacy. Henry shuffled uncomfortably from one foot to the other and had just decided to sit on the chair next to the bed when his father opened his eyes.

"Henry, my boy." His voice was husky, every word an effort.

"Hi Pop. Yes, it's me. You don't need to talk." It seemed the appropriate thing to say. However, in response his father became agitated.

"Henry," the man croaked, "you have to look after the meadow between the woods and fields at Darrington Way."

"Okay, Pop. I'll do my best." Henry had absolutely no idea what his father was talking about, he just wanted to soothe him and offer reassurance.

"No. No. Listen to me, Henry." His father, frustrated and anxious, tried to pull himself up into a sitting position, groaning and gasping for air.

"Hey, hey, lie back down. I'm listening, Pop. I'm all ears, just take it easy."

His father lay back on his pillows, a hopeless expression on his face, his tired eyes unhappy. A tear rolled down his cheek.

Shocked, Henry no longer worried about his earlier reservations. He placed a tentative hand on his father's forehead, and stroked his hair now mostly grey, damp with sweat.

"It's a lonely place," his father whispered urgently, the sound reminding Henry of the rustle of pages being turned in an ancient book, "and there's something unnatural about it. The locals stay away, rumours of restless spirits." He paused, fighting for breath before continuing in a fretful whine, "I should have blessed it or done something. It needs protecting, Henry, or the world needs protecting from it." He made a grab for Henry's hand, his grasp surprisingly strong, compelling his son to look at him, to pay attention. Then a fit of coughing took hold of him, so violent it brought the night sister running. She scolded Henry for exciting her patient and insisted he leave. Henry squeezed his father's hand before he left. "Don't worry, Pop. I'll remember," he said.

He made a quick exit because he didn't trust himself to keep his own emotions in check. His father was all he had left in the world since his mother passed early last summer. He'd only just finished college. It wasn't fair, but then as Pop would once have said, whoever it was that claimed life was fair was delusional.

Henry's father died the very same night that he'd first mentioned anything at all to his son about Darrington Way. Henry had been staying at the vicarage in Woolwich London, the only family home he could remember, since his father had been taken into hospital. He spent the next couple of days going through his father's roll-top desk to find the names and addresses of people he might need to inform.

He rang one of his father's friends from another church nearby and appealed for help to arrange the funeral. Fortunately, the man was very generous with his time. Henry found the address, also in London, of his father's solicitor, a

Mr. Nigel Barnworthy who had a string of initials after his name. Henry telephoned him and was informed, after Barnworthy offered his condolences, that his father had left a Will and instructions regarding his internment. This made life easier for Henry.

The funeral took place at the church for which his father had been responsible, and most of those who attended were people Henry knew to have been part of his father's congregation. One or two clergy and a bishop also attended and there were about half a dozen relatives – aunts, uncles, cousins whom he barely recognised or remembered, having not seen them in years. They had turned up to show their respects. Henry had organised a small tea at the vicarage for after the service, with sandwiches and cake. He felt strange standing in the lounge making polite conversation.

Fortunately, nobody stayed too long and he was able to tidy up and ensure the vicarage was presentable again and still be in bed by nine. He slept, exhausted by grief. All the time he'd had the funeral to organise he'd felt he still had something he could do for his Pop. Once it was over, the pain of loss was unbearable and sleep was the only remedy.

The next morning, Henry attended the prearranged appointment with the solicitor and handed over the vicarage keys.

There had been little to wind up by way of an estate, Nigel Barnworthy explained. The vicarage, of course, belonged to the Church and his father had directed that all other possessions, including his books, be sold and the proceeds given to charity. His father had known Henry wasn't intending on a life in the church, then. The thought gave him some small comfort, although he wished he could have shared the news that his first novel had been accepted by an American publishing company; his writing career was on its way. His father would have appreciated knowing he had made a good start on the path he had chosen.

The solicitor handed Henry a box containing photograph albums and a few personal papers. After that, the man had read his father's Will in which Henry was bequeathed (without the impediment of death duty which would come directly from Nathaniel Fisherton's estate) the land known as Darrington Way.

In this manner, Henry found himself not only an orphan (he felt the term still applied, even though he was no longer a child) at the age of 21, but also homeless. The lease on his college digs had expired, of course, and the vicarage was to be cleared with the help of some of his father's parishioners.

Thinking he must remain in London to live, Henry found himself a room at a small bed and breakfast establishment in Plumstead, and after some discussion with the Landlord, which involved handing over part of the money from his book advance, he was able to stow his few possessions, clothing and books in his new living space. The room would be his for the foreseeable future, providing rent was paid promptly. Henry was entitled to breakfast along with the guests, but his lunch and dinner he would be obliged to find for himself (which he invariably did over the next few weeks at a little corner café down the street). He was given a key to the house and one to his room and was free to come and go as he pleased.

For a few days, he tried to write, sitting at the old Imperial typewriter he'd bought second-hand whilst still at college, blank page staring back at him. The publishers had given him a year to come up with his next novel, but they wanted to see an outline of the first three chapters sometime within the next six weeks. Henry, however, found himself unable to think of anything other than his father's last conversation with him. He took to walking the streets, late at night to try to clear his mind and help him sleep better.

After several weeks of contemplation, he came to the conclusion he would have to travel to Kent to take a look at his newly acquired land and see what could be done about his father's peculiar request. That decided, he sat at his typewriter and within three hours he had typed out the outline required by his publishers ready to send.

By two o'clock the next day, which was Friday, Henry found himself on a bus, travelling towards the village of Bushwell. He'd caught the train from Victoria, early in the morning, had eaten lunch further down the line at Gillingham then, having requested directions from the station master, had walked to the bus station, rather than wait two hours for another train. Although he'd had to change buses at Rainham, the journey had been straightforward enough.

The bus now lurched to one side, the engine roaring in protest as the driver changed gear and turned a corner to drive up a hilly country lane. Henry looked around at the other passengers and caught the eye of a pretty girl who'd previously had her nose buried in a book. She peeped at him now from beneath a fringe of shining blonde hair cut just above her eyes. Meeting his gaze, she quickly looked away, turning her head with a small smile to stare out the bus window, and for a second he found he couldn't take his eyes off the gentle curve of her slender neck. Then he noticed the rest of that glorious fair hair, tied back with a yellow ribbon in a high pony tail which curled up at the end. There were small pearl studs in her earlobes and her yellow cardigan, worn over a simple summer frock, was left unbuttoned to show off the little necklet of pearls which matched her ear studs. She took a peek back at him again and he smiled – he couldn't help it – and he was rewarded by her returning smile, soft pink lips parting slightly to reveal even white teeth. He faced forward again, yet couldn't resist sneaking one last look over his shoulder at the girl several seats behind on the other side of the bus. She was still watching him, a look of merriment causing her blue eyes to sparkle. Henry didn't believe he'd ever seen anyone as stunningly beautiful as this girl before.

The bell rang and the conductor called out, "Darrington Way. Last stop before Bushwell." Henry returned his attention to the window. They were at a sign-posted crossroads. He might save himself a walk if he got out now. He stood up, shrugging his shoulders regretfully at the girl behind him as he made his way to the bus door. To his surprise, she stood up and followed him. He stepped down from the bus into dazzling sunlight, heard the door close and the bus engine protest again as it continued on its way.

Henry looked up at the signpost which showed Bushwell to be two miles further along the road which the bus had taken. Rainham was, of course, in the opposite direction, while the third sign pointed towards Halstow. The fourth part of the sign indicated Darrington Way to be along an adjoining narrow lane from where he now stood. He was very aware of the girl standing nearby. He gave her a long sideways look. She had an open basket over one arm with various grocery items and a couple of library books inside.

"Do you live near here?" Henry asked, his heart hammering in his chest. He hadn't had much experience talking to members of the opposite sex since he'd left school, well not people of his own age. He didn't believe the middle-aged housekeeper at the college accommodation halls counted, or for that matter his new landlord's plump forty-something wife.

"I'm Henry Fisherton," he added as an afterthought and felt himself flush with embarrassment. The girl moved slightly closer and held out a hand.

"Pleased to meet you, Henry," she said. "My name's Eleanor Harrison, although most people call me Ellie. I'm staying with an aunt who lives just across that field there. I've a bit of a walk, although it's a lovely day, isn't it?"

"It is indeed. Would you, that is, could I walk you home?"

Ellie smiled. "Aren't you catching the next bus to Halstow? I thought that's why you got off, and it'll be here in ten minutes. Besides, my aunt would have fifty fits if I turned up with a young man in tow without first warning her."

"Oh, right. Well I'd better let you get along then," Henry kicked at the grass verge at the foot of the lamp post. He didn't correct her assumption as to where he was headed. Ellie began to walk away, then turned back.

"Hey, do you like country dancing?"

"I'm not sure, I've never tried it," Henry said.

"There's a barn dance on at the village hall in Bushwell tonight at half past seven. It's not exactly my kind of scene either, but it's what passes for entertainment here. I could introduce you to my aunt and little cousins if you came," she suggested.

"I'd like that," Henry said, his voice sincere. "I'd like to get to know you too." Ellie nodded, smiling, then started off on her way again, ponytail bouncing as she walked. Henry watched her until she was out of sight.

Chapter Seventeen

Henry began to walk, turning up the narrow lane in search of the meadow his father had spoken about. He walked for about a quarter of a mile, in that time, berating himself for his stupidity. He couldn't go to a barn dance, he'd never get the bus back to Rainham in time to catch the last train back to London! He had only the clothes he stood up in and not a great deal of cash on him. Yet he couldn't forget the girl's face, and the way she'd smiled at him. His mother would have said she was forward, but then times were changing. Young people were becoming restless, motivating them to drive that change.

He remembered with a grin the way his mother had reacted when he'd played his first Elvis Presley record, and her despair at the music that followed. His father had been more tolerant of rock and roll because a lot of the young people in his parish loved it and he'd gradually talked her round for the sake of his son, and for family peace. Henry missed his father terribly and it wasn't just that he'd only recently been bereaved. He missed his mother too, of course, but the loss of his father he felt left a gaping hole deep inside him that hurt so much he could hardly breathe when he thought of him. Why hadn't he spent more time with him while he was still alive? Okay, so he'd expected his father to live well into his eighties, although he knew he'd lost some of his zest for living since Henry's mother had died, even though she'd been an invalid for some years. His father must have been lonely, Henry blamed himself. Why hadn't he gone home more often at weekends while he was at college? Why hadn't he told his Pop how much he meant to him, instead of wasting the last few precious minutes of his time with him listening to him fretting about this piece of land, this meadow on Darrington Way?

Henry thought about the girl again. He would go to the dance. Life was too short not to take chances. He'd walk into

Bushwell and see if there was somewhere he could stay the night. Perhaps the village pub would have a room. If push came to shove he was prepared to sleep rough in a field, since the weather was fine. He also decided to call at the vicarage to see if the vicar had heard of, or knew anything about, the history of the land on Darrington Way. Having come to this decision, he focussed more readily on his surroundings.

The lane he walked along was lined with tall hedgerows that maintained the boundaries of the fields beyond. Eventually he came to an opening in the hedge to his left, barely discernible through the nettles and weeds that grew out to the verge of the roadside. He pushed his way through, scratching and stinging himself in the process, and found himself at the edge of the very meadow he had been seeking.

Henry stood and gazed. This was exactly how he imagined Heaven to be. There was a wide expanse of grass of varying shades of green, sprinkled with wild flowers. Parts of the ground swayed and rippled like sea waves as the soft summery breeze caressed the grass, and there were butterflies and birds flitting about among the flowers. One solitary tree stood in the midst of all this glory, although beyond the meadow Henry could see woodland. He didn't know much about trees. However, he thought this particular tree was a variety of Silver birch because there had been such trees in the college grounds where he'd studied, although he'd never seen one so tall. It stood proud and graceful against the blue of the sky, its branches trailing down like a weeping willow. Its leaves hissed in the breeze, offering the sound of the sea that the grass appeared to emulate.

Henry walked towards the tree, his feet leaving a trail in the previously un-trodden grass. It had to be close to a hundred feet high, he approximated. On closer inspection, he could see it was dying, this beautiful old tree. Perhaps it was coming to the end of its natural lifespan. He could see dieback: dead branches hiding like so many sinners amongst the living. He touched the rough white bark of what seemed to be two trunks melded together. He looked up and noticed for the first time there were no birds resting in its branches, almost as if they avoided the tree out of respect because they realised its life was gradually draining away. There was a sturdy-looking branch at about the height of his chest. Henry grasped hold of it and hoisted himself up. He would climb up, he thought, as far as he could manage, taking care not to rely on any of the dead wood. From on high he would study the meadow below to see if he could spot anything that might hint at the reason for his father's unease.

He was some fifteen to twenty feet from the ground, resting on a sturdy branch close to the middle of the tree, when he first heard the noise – a sort of humming combined with an odd, disquieting sound. It was a little like the sound of a wireless being tuned, not quite music, not quite voices, but a blend of unnatural noise, whining and fading in and out. Rather more curious than afraid, Henry reached out to part the leaves which he believed were concealing its source.

There was nothing to be seen and yet there *was* something, something virtually indescribable. The air appeared to move as if in a heat haze, except the space in which this occurred seemed confined to an area with a diameter of approximately eight feet, although the space was by no means completely circular. As the air shifted and moved Henry saw it darken and then lighten again. When it darkened, it was as though he was looking at a night sky full of tiny moving stars, and when it lightened it was like a television screen that needed repair – the images on the screen too blurred to be able to make out what they were. Henry stared for a long time and concentrated, trying to make sense of what he was seeing. Shadowy forms swirled before him, until quite suddenly, and only for a moment, the image sharpened just enough for

Henry to make out the face of a man with dark hair, dark close-cropped beard and solemn eyes. The man seemed to be trying to say something, but his voice was extremely faint, accompanied by a whining and babbling sound and all that Henry could make out were the words: *Beneath the tree.* Then the image faded away altogether and the heat haze effect was back again, together with the unpleasant, unnatural noise of before.

Henry waited several seconds, before he carefully climbed back down from the tree, dropping the last few feet to the ground with a soft thump. He bent down and examined the base of the trunk, crawling all the way around it on his hands and knees. There was nothing to be found, just dry compacted soil, naked of grass where the tree had drawn the moisture out of the ground. Puzzled and weary, Henry got to his feet, straightening himself and brushing off his trousers. He looked back up through the branches, but could not now see anything untoward. He sighed. He was hungry. From the position of the sun in the sky he knew, without looking at his wristwatch, that it would soon be dusk. It was time to make his way to the village to secure a bed for the night and a meal.

He scanned the meadow once more and looked to the woods beyond, before moving away from the tree. At least he thought he had some idea now why his father had been so adamant Henry should do something about the meadow. What was it he had said? *It needs protecting, or the world needs protecting from it.*

Chapter Eighteen

Although Henry reached the village hall fifteen minutes before the barn dance was due to begin, he could tell he was one of the last to arrive from the buzz of conversation emanating through the open entrance door. The hall itself was well lit and warm inside. Bunting had been hung from the rafters and several hay bales were stacked at the far end of the hall to lend an authentic 'barn' look. There was a space for the musicians and caller to perform near the hay. Tables and chairs were pushed to the sides of the hall to allow room for dancing in the middle.

People stood around in groups chatting, the majority of the men wearing checked shirts, denim jeans or work trousers, and boots; the women wore summer frocks or flared skirts with blouses. Henry felt a little overdressed in his good suit. Children chased one another, winding in and out among the adults. There was a festive mood in the air. Henry went to the table at the corner of the hall nearest the door where most of the youth had gathered and cider was being served.

He'd just handed over his money when he felt a tug at his sleeve. He turned to face Ellie. She was even prettier than he remembered, if that was possible. She wore a blue dress that brought out the colour of her eyes and her hair hung loose about her shoulders.

"Hello. Come and meet my aunt," she said. Henry allowed himself to be dragged, not reluctantly, across the room, his glass of cider in his hand. He had imagined Ellie's aunt would be a stern-looking spinster, sniffing disapproval, and he was preparing himself accordingly. In reality she was younger than he'd expected, a brunette with a modern haircut in her mid-thirties looking a little harassed, as a mother of several lively youngsters might well do. She sat at one of the tables at the side of the room with her youngest, a boy of about three, on her lap. She was talking to another woman as Henry and Ellie approached her, but he could see she also kept a sharp eye out for her other offspring.

"So, you're the young man from Rainham," she said looking up at Henry when Ellie introduced him to her.

"No, Ma'am. I'm from London, Woolwich to be precise. I'm staying at the vicarage at present," he replied, conscious of Ellie's quizzical glare.

Ellie's aunt raised her eyebrows. "You're a guest of Reverend Jacobson?"

"Yes, Ma'am. He knew my late father, Reverend Fisherton."

"Fisherton?" her neighbour chimed in, barely able to suppress her excitement. "As in the Fishertons who own Darrington Way?"

Henry nodded, his expression polite.

"And what do you do for a living, Henry?" Ellie's aunt enquired.

Henry hesitated, thinking for a moment and then said, "I've just finished studying for my theological degree, Ma'am."

The little boy on the woman's lap began to pick his nose. Ellie's aunt brushed his hand aside and he squirmed to get off her lap. "Don't go too far, Billy. We're leaving at eight," she told the child as he scooted away. At that moment, a man at the end of the hall wearing a Stetson shouted to gain everybody's attention. He introduced himself as the caller for the evening and gestured towards a group of four musicians, asking everyone to put their hands together to welcome each of them as they were named.

Then the music began and there was no more time for conversation. People were told to take their partners for the first dance and Ellie relieved Henry of his drink, placing it on the table, and pulled him towards the dance floor.

"Nice to meet you, Henry," her aunt called after them, giving a little wave. "Please see that Ellie's home by half past ten."

The music stopped briefly while the caller walked the dancers through their steps. They were directed to stand in one large circle to begin, ladies on the left. Henry felt his hands grow clammy with nerves. He wasn't sure how he'd cope with this.

"You didn't tell me you're going to be a vicar," Ellie hissed in his ear. She was obviously annoyed.

"Didn't have time," Henry muttered back. "Besides, I'm not."

The music started up again. Henry made a few mistakes, stood on Ellie's foot once, and bumped into the couple behind them as they swung their partners, but he soon realised he was doing as well as many others. There was much laughter and apologies shared around the hall. He began to enjoy himself.

After two more dances, he left Ellie sitting at the table her aunt had vacated, while he fetched drinks. Looking about he realised most of the young children had now been taken home by their parents, leaving more space for the dancing and less noise between dances. Even so, it was difficult to have a proper conversation above the general hubbub. Henry sensed, with some amusement, that Ellie was bursting with impatience for an opportunity to question him further about himself. He didn't mind. He wanted to know all about her too, but was more than happy to wait until it was time to walk her home.

The cider was having some effect, as he hadn't had time to eat that afternoon, after all. He'd introduced himself to the vicar as soon as he'd arrived at Bushwell, and after a short conversation, had quickly been offered a place to stay for as long as he needed it. He hadn't wanted to push his luck by asking for a meal. Fortunately, halfway through the evening there was an interval. Baskets of food were produced and several women put together ploughman's lunches for the dancers to enjoy. Henry devoured the huge chunks of bread with cheese, pickles and ham with great relish, nodding from time to time in reply to Ellie's chatter. In truth, he could barely hear a word she said, although he understood she was saying something about dancing and the sort of music she usually preferred to listen to.

By the time the barn dance was over and the villagers spilled out of the hall, bidding each other goodnight as they parted company, the evening had turned chilly. The sky was clear, stars bright, as Henry and Ellie walked along the road leading out of the village. Ellie shivered and Henry gave her his jacket. They walked on in silence until they were in sight of the signpost at the crossroads.

"If you aren't going to be a vicar, why did you study for a degree in religion?" Ellie suddenly blurted out, unable to contain her curiosity any longer.

"I wanted to understand more about my father's convictions, I suppose. I also knew it would please my parents. However, I believe it's necessary to be called by God to become a priest and I'm pretty sure I haven't been yet."

Ellie persisted. "So why did you come to visit Reverend Jacobson, then? And why would you get off the bus before it got to Bushwell?"

"My original intention wasn't to visit with the good Reverend. I came to look at a piece of land I inherited from my father," Henry said. He didn't think it was necessary to explain that it was only through pure luck, or possibly divine intervention, that the local vicar had happened to know his father and therefore been willing to offer Henry lodgings.

They came to the stile that led to the path across the field to the farmhouse at which Ellie was presently staying. Henry took her hand to help her climb over.

"Are you rich then?" she asked, waiting for him as he climbed over the stile after her.

"Not yet. I hope to be pretty well off one day. I'm a writer." He felt a surge of unexpected pride as he said it. "My first novel has just been published in America. I write Science fiction."

Henry was disappointed when his pronouncement didn't have the desired effect. Ellie just trudged on ahead of him. He followed, occasionally straying from the path in the moonlight, his decent shoes sinking in the damp mud of the recently harvested field. "What about you, where do you live when you aren't staying with your aunt?" he asked.

"I don't get on with my parents," Ellie declared. "My dad's an engineer and he was offered a job in the States. They'll be gone for two years, maybe longer. They wouldn't take me, and said I should stay in England to help my aunt with her children," she sniffed. "I'd love to see America."

"Then I'm sure one day you will," he said. "If my book does well you might even come with me!" He laughed to show her his words were meant as a joke. She made no comment.

Henry could see the lights of the farmhouse ahead. He stopped walking and said, "Ellie, I'll probably only be here for a couple of days, but I'd like to see you again, that's if you want to, and your aunt doesn't mind."

Ellie stopped and waited. He trudged over to her.

"It isn't up to my aunt," she said, as soon as he was by her side. "I'm seventeen, old enough to make my own decisions. Plenty of girls are married by the time they're my age. Now, hurry up and kiss me, Henry Fisherton, before I change my mind."

Henry complied, feeling awkward at first, worried that they'd bump noses before their lips even touched, but he soon forgot himself as she pressed her body closer to his. He could feel the warm, soft contours of her breasts against his chest.

Time seemed to stand still. Henry lost himself as his emotions overwhelmed him. Finally, he released her. She took off the jacket he'd lent her and handed it to him, shivering slightly as she did so. He put it on then attempted to take her in his arms again, but she darted out of reach.

"Meet me at the signpost tomorrow at lunchtime," she said, skipping away from him. "I'll bring some sandwiches and we'll have a picnic somewhere."

"I'll be waiting," he called after her. "Mid-day. I know just the place we can go."

The village was quiet when he let himself into the vicarage with the key his host had provided. He was careful to make as little noise as possible as he closed the front door behind him. However, Reverend Jacobson was still up, working in his study and he must have heard the soft click of the door latch for he immediately called out for Henry to join him.

He was a thin man in his late sixties, clean shaven and mostly bald, although he had a little white hair growing on the sides of his head. He was seated at his desk, bent over a book reading with the aid of a magnifying glass. "Hello. There you are. Sit down, I won't keep you long."

Henry moved a pile of books from the seat of a rickety wooden dining chair, it being the only other place to sit in the room, apart from the floor. Reverend Jacobson took a notebook from the drawer of his desk.

"I haven't got much for you, I'm afraid. Your relative is, as I said, in the parish records, or rather the date of his baptism. No marriage and no entry for death either." He looked up from the notebook. "However, I telephoned the priest who was here before me and he did have some information. Apparently, Albert Darrington vanished in the year 1895. He was some sort of scientist, so the story goes, and was camping on a piece of the land you've inherited at the time he disappeared. Reverend Leybon, my predecessor, was privy to some village gossip when some of the teenagers in the village camped out on the land as a dare one Halloween. I'm talking thirty odd years ago, now."

Henry nodded to show he was listening.

"Something frightened them and they returned to the village in the early hours making a terrible din. They insisted the place was haunted. Well, Leybon wasn't having any of that. He decided to prove it was all nonsense and did some research at the county library where he discovered a newspaper article, about Darrington's disappearance, on microfilm. There were even photos of the abandoned campsite."

Henry found himself imagining a grainy picture of a large, white canvas tent, pegged down with ropes in a field, the entrance flap open and the interior dark, a Victorian policeman standing alongside staring at the camera.

"According to the newspaper report a local farmer who had been providing Darrington with supplies ..." the Reverend shrugged and lifted his hands, "milk, eggs, that sort of thing, probably even needed water, although I understand there's a stream that runs alongside part of the woodland. Anyway, I digress, this farmer found the camp abandoned and after returning on several consecutive days to find there was still no sign of the scientist, reported him missing to the police. The farmer said that Darrington had told him he needed some privacy, peace and quiet for his work and that was the reason he was camping there. Bit odd, don't you think?"

Henry nodded, frowning slightly.

"That's all I can tell you, I'm afraid. As I said before, the few people who've ever mentioned it to me have just said there's a field that everybody avoids. Some have laughed when they said it, but there does seem to be some sort of superstitious uneasiness concerning the place. I suspect it's become a sort of nature reserve by now. Wildlife thrives in undisturbed environments." He put his notebook back into the desk drawer. "May I ask if you have decided what you intend to do with it yet?"

"I'm not sure."

Henry considered telling the vicar of his own experience in the meadow. He studied the kindly man's gentle face and decided against it for the time being. He wanted to do some research of his own.

"It could be worth quite a bit of money if you were to sell it to developers, although I do hope you don't," Reverend Jacobson said into the growing silence. Henry shook his head.

"Thank you for looking into the history of the place for me and thank you once again for allowing me to stay in your home. You must let me reimburse you for my meals and lodging."

"No need, Henry. It's good to have some company, if only for a few days. I am so sorry about your father. I'm not ashamed to say I learnt a thing or two about faith during the time he worked with me as a deacon and I have always felt privileged that he considered me a friend ever since. He was a good man and a fine priest."

"Yes, I know he was," Henry said, "but it's nice to hear someone else say it. Goodnight Sir."

As he left the study, he heard the vicar slide his desk drawer shut. Henry's mind was full of the story he'd just been told as he made his way up the stairs to his room. In his head, he could see a picture of the campsite again but this time instead of a policeman, there was a wide wooden trestle table near the entrance to the tent with a man standing behind. The man was wearing a long dark jacket as was popular in the Victorian era, and he had dark hair, a dark, close cropped beard and solemn eyes.

Chapter Nineteen

At breakfast Henry learned that Reverend Jacobson intended, that morning, to spend a couple of hours weeding and generally tidying up in the vicarage garden. Henry offered to help. His host was pleased and as soon as they'd finished eating he found Henry some old clothes he could borrow to work in. Henry was surprised to find they fitted well and the vicar explained this by remarking that he'd lost weight over the last couple of years. Henry was then taken to the garden shed, shown an ancient-looking lawnmower and was left to cut the grass. The garden was large and the mowing took a couple of hours, but he enjoyed the work as it left his mind free to think about the meadow on Darrington Way and what he would do next concerning the strange phenomenon.

After he'd finished his task, had cleaned the blades of the mower and returned it to the shed, his host called him over to share tea and biscuits at a little wrought iron table with matching garden chairs. The two men chatted about the garden, the weather and a little about Henry's father. Reverend Jacobson confided that, like Henry's father, he'd lost his wife the year before after a protracted illness, so Henry felt able to talk about the intensity of his own grief which helped ease his pain. He was even able to relate a couple of anecdotes about his parents and laugh about them. Then the vicar thanked Henry for his help in the garden, said that he had some calls to make and that he had no further chores for the young man to do.

Henry had a couple of hours to spare before he was due to meet Ellie. He went to his room and carefully rolled up his own clothes to put them into the satchel he carried everywhere. He was grateful for the shirt and trousers the vicar had lent him as he'd had to work hard to remove the dust and dirt from his suit after his climb the day before in order to look halfway presentable for the dance. This morning he had borrowed a clothes brush to remove the mud splatters from the bottom of his trousers, and shoe polish to clean his shoes. The comfortable old trousers and shirt lent by the vicar meant he could explore the meadow and tree further and still have time to change and arrive promptly at midday to meet Ellie.

He set off at a brisk pace and within fifty minutes or so he was back in the meadow, looking up at the Silver birch. He took a few minutes to re-examine the ground around the base of the tree, then finding nothing began his climb again, listening the whole time for the unusual noise. After a while the first shadow of doubt crept into his mind. He continued his climb thinking perhaps he wasn't high enough. He searched frantically, parting swathes of leaves to peer about him before continuing to climb, until he realised he was much further up than he had been previously and could not safely go any further. Disappointed he began his descent.

Ellie was already waiting by the time he had changed and walked back to the signpost. She had her basket with her again, but this time it was covered with a bright cloth and he guessed it contained their lunch.

"Where shall we go for our picnic?" she asked brightly, kissing his cheek.

Henry could hear the bus approaching and as it appeared around the bend in the lane he took Ellie's arm, his other hand feeling in his pocket for change.

"I thought we could eat on the bus," he said, putting his arm out to halt it.

"How unromantic!" Ellie protested. "I thought you were going to take me to see your newly acquired land."

"No, we're going somewhere much more interesting than that," Henry said, helping her up into the bus. "I thought we'd go to the pictures. I saw a cinema in Rainham while I was on the bus coming here." He paid for their tickets and followed her to the back row of seats to sit down.

"You mean The Royal," she said. "Alright, that should be fun."

"There's a film I'm really dying to see being advertised in the London cinemas, an adaptation of H.G Wells' *The Time Machine*." Henry grinned, glad that she approved of his choice of venue for their first real date. "I doubt it will be showing here yet though, so we'll have to take pot luck."

They got to the cinema in plenty of time for the afternoon matinee and watched cartoons, film previews, and a western. Then Henry took Ellie to a little tea shop for a cup of tea and slice of cake before they caught the bus back. Ellie was safely home before ten, which pleased her aunt. Everyone was happy, including Henry who practically danced back across the field. As he climbed over the stile to the lane he suddenly decided he'd go back to the meadow. The evening was clear, the moon bright and he knew that even if he did immediately return to the vicarage, he'd be unable to sleep.

The lane with the opening to the meadow was rather dark and lonely. The meadow looked very different in the moonlight, no longer the heavenly mirage of his first impression, but rather a brooding, morose place. He made straight for the tree, his eyes quickly becoming accustomed to the pale light. The long meadow grass seemed to drag at his feet, trying to dissuade him from venturing further. Even as he approached it, the tree creaked, and moved and rustled in the night air as if impatiently waiting for him and beckoning him on. He felt for the branch at shoulder height and pulled himself up then began his climb, perilous in the half-light, yet he was drunk with the success of the afternoon and evening, determined to prove to himself that he had not imagined his odd experience when he'd first climbed the tree.

Very little time had elapsed before he was rewarded as his ears picked up the low humming. He paused, waiting. He carefully parted the foliage and as before, there was the hazy, almost liquid movement of air. He began to feel about him for a twig he could break off the tree, without taking his eyes off the mirage. Again, without warning, the haze cleared.

It was as though he was looking into a large mirror, for he could see himself in the moonlight, reaching for a stick of some sort. He stopped moving and watched, fascinated, as his mirror image continued in his search, apparently oblivious to being spied upon – if you can really spy upon yourself. His other self tugged at a piece of twig trailing from a nearby branch that was all but bare, almost losing balance as he did so. At last it came free in his hand, a spindly, crooked piece of dead wood about a foot long. For a moment, it was as though his reflection was staring straight at him, then he shuffled further along the branch and lifted the twig to throw it through the air in the direction of Henry. There was a blinding flash and Henry clung to the trunk of the tree, closing his eyes tight, fearful of falling. Strange how the brain works for, even as he wrapped his arms and hands tight about the tree, he found time to wonder at how the wood further up was smoother to the touch than that of the trunk below.

When he opened his eyes again everything had changed. It was as though he was looking at a cinema screen, rather than the reflection in a mirror.

The scene shown was in daylight. His other self was lying on the ground beneath the tree and there were people around him – paramedics. Henry looked on in horror as, after examining him, they placed him on a stretcher and covered him over with a blanket, including his face. He was dead.

Henry tore his eyes away from the scene and looked all about himself for reassurance that actually he was still very much alive. It was still night time, the moon still shone in a sky full of stars. He looked down below him, dreading what he might perceive, but there was nothing, just darkness.

He looked back at what he now thought of as the screen. To his amazement, he saw himself very much alive, in broad daylight again, this time standing with Ellie beneath the tree. He was pointing all around the meadow and talking. Ellie was nodding. She seemed happy, excited even. Henry strained to hear what was being said. The other Henry seemed to be talking about building, but his words were not quite audible. Then he produced something from his jacket pocket and Henry realised it was a tiny, velvet box. He opened it and showed it to Ellie who nodded vigorously and threw her arms about his neck. It made sense, Henry thought as he watched from his perch in the tree. He'd known from the first time he'd set eyes on Ellie that she was the girl he wanted to marry. He smiled as he saw himself slip an engagement ring on her finger then walk away across the meadow arm in arm with her. After the couple were out of sight he continued to gaze at the landscape - flowers and grass, the small white butterflies flitting about in the sunshine. It was then that his conscience began to trouble him. Could he really be prepared to sacrifice this wonderful haven of nature just so he would have the money to marry and have a home of his own? It seemed incredibly selfish. And what of the strange phenomenon he was at this very moment witnessing? His father's dying wish had been that Henry should find a way of keeping it from the rest of the world...

As he hadn't taken his eyes off the scene he thought it was his own imagination when the picture began to blur. He wanted to rub his eyes, only resisting the urge because he wanted to see what happened next. With some flickering a new scene emerged. The humming, which had been coming and going, became very loud then gradually died away and the sound quality improved. He could see himself standing in a laboratory with the man who had sombre eyes and he could hear the conversation quite clearly. The man was shaking his head, adamant. "No," he said. "I'm not Albert Darrington."

Henry watched and listened. He learned a great deal, and by the time the image finally faded out of existence and the humming had ceased, it was past midnight. Henry climbed back down to the ground and stood for a moment beneath the tree in the cool night air, thinking. Then he crossed the meadow towards the gap to the lane in order to walk back to the vicarage.

Henry believed in visions – he was a man of faith, after all, regardless of his decision about his future career. He'd studied the prophets in the Bible. He did not, therefore, consider what he'd seen as his tired brain's response to intolerable grief, although he didn't believe the visions had been some kind of message from The Almighty either. He was pretty certain he wasn't mad because he was able to speak and interact with others quite normally, and he'd read somewhere that insane people were unable to reason about the state of their minds anyway. Further, not only had his father warned him there was something inexplicable about the meadow, there was also the story of the village teenagers insisting the place was haunted, which meant if his mind was unsound because of what he'd seen, then they must also have suffered some sort of delusion too and this seemed highly unlikely, unless of course something here was causing it. Henry had always been an aficionado where science fiction was concerned, be it in films or literature, so the most likely explanation to him was that some sort of alien technology was involved. Why it was there he had no idea.

As he came out of the lane near to the signpost, Henry thought of the very different scenarios he'd witnessed. It was like arriving at a crossroads and having a choice which route to take with the foreknowledge of where each would lead you. He smiled to himself as he confidently strode towards

Bushwell. He would take none of the three choices, although what he'd learnt from the third vision that evening would certainly inform his decision about the future of the meadow. He would talk to Reverend Jacobson about blessing the meadow – it had been his father's intention and could do no harm. He also had another favour to ask the benevolent vicar when he saw him at breakfast. After that, all being well, he would write and post a short letter to Ellie, for tomorrow afternoon he intended to travel back to London.

Chapter Twenty

Forewarned – A Prophecy by Aliens Henry typed, then ripped the page out from the roller of the typewriter and screwed it up. He inserted a fresh piece of paper and sat staring at the blank whiteness of it. He had the story, or at least the beginning of it, but could not think how to start or even invent a decent title without giving the whole plot away. It was getting late. He would sleep on it. He sat back in his chair and ran a finger inside the front collar of his shirt. It was humid and he didn't cope well with heat at night. Who was he trying to kid – he wouldn't be able to sleep. He hoped there would be a storm to clear the air.

There was a soft tap on the door and he called out for his landlady to enter. She did so carrying a glass jug of water and a tumbler on a tray. She placed it on the little bedside cabinet and turned back to face Henry.

"You've settled in then," she said. "I thought, it being so hot, you might appreciate a drink and milk in this heat doesn't really quench the thirst," she gestured towards the water.

"Thank you, that's most kind," Henry replied.

"Am I disturbing you? You only have to say and I'll be out of your way," she hesitated and he could see she was reluctant to leave.

"Not at all," he smiled. "I was thinking about starting on my next novel, but I just can't seem to begin. It will be good to have a break." He watched as she perched herself on the edge of his bed. She was a spinster, a former librarian, probably in her late seventies, judging from the lines on her face and the careful way she moved, although she was active and alert. Henry liked her. She invited confidences without appearing nosy. She peered over her spectacles at him.

"So," she said, neatly folding her hands in her lap, "tell me all about yourself, Henry, if I may use your Christian name.

Reverend Jacobson gave you an excellent reference. He must like you. He said he knew your late father."

"I'm afraid I haven't anything very interesting to add to what you probably already know, Miss Noaks," Henry said. "As Reverend Jacobson probably told you, my father was a vicar in London where I was born and grew up." She nodded in acknowledgment and he continued. "I studied theology at college and began writing stories about space travel during my leisure time. I was lucky enough to gain a publishing contract for my first novel with enough money paid in advance to keep me while I write my next book and, since my father left me some land here, I decided I could live and work as well in Bushwell as I might in London."

"Ah yes, I'd heard about your inheritance. Tell me, did your decision to move here have anything to do with a certain young lady currently residing at Milltop Farm?" Her eyes twinkled with mischief.

There was a flash of light and a low rumble of thunder. Both Henry and Miss Noaks glanced at the window. They waited several seconds for the sound of rain. It didn't come. Henry looked back at his companion.

"I am seeing Ellie Harrison, yes. I expect you know her aunt."

The conversation was interrupted by another white flash of light, this time so brilliant it dazzled them. This was closely followed by an extremely loud crash which shook the whole cottage and made the windows rattle.

"My goodness," cried Miss Noaks starting to her feet, "That sounded very close. I believe it might have actually hit something" She rushed to the door.

"I'll come with you," Henry said. "I hope nobody's been hurt."

Despite the rain which soaked the pair of them, they met with a surprising number of other concerned and very wet villagers hurrying about the neighbourhood looking for the hapless victim of the lightning strike. However, a quick round of the village reassured everyone that none of the houses or buildings in Bushwell had been struck. With assertions that the mystery would surely be solved next day, people parted company to return to the comfort of their own homes. Back in the cottage kitchen, Miss Noaks found towels for Henry and herself with which to dry themselves. She raked the embers in the grate of the kitchen range and made Henry, whose teeth were chattering as he shivered, sit in one of the easy chairs close by with a blanket wrapped about his shoulders. She made some tea and toast, using a long fork to brown the bread in front of the fire.

"I know I should use my shiny new-fangled electric cooker over in the corner," Miss Noaks said, as she handed Henry a plate of buttered toast, "But on evenings like this I'm glad I kept my mother's old range."

Henry was glad too. The night air had cooled considerably since the onset of the storm, but they were cosy in the little kitchen as they sat in companionable silence, eating toast and drinking tea, listening to the wood crackle in the grate and the splatter of rain against the window pane.

That night Henry slept fitfully and woke early, worry nagging at him; perhaps the lightening had struck the farmhouse. Ellie's family could have been hurt. He dressed himself by the grey light of dawn and crept down the stairs, taking care to avoid the third step from the top which he'd already discovered creaked as if groaning in protest every time anyone stepped on it. He took his still damp jacket from the peg and let himself out of the cottage via the back door. Once outside he looked about. The heavy rain had certainly caused havoc in the garden. The hinges of the gate whined as he stepped out into the alley, shared with the neighbouring cottage, which led to the road. The village was deserted and nobody saw him walking away from Bushwell towards Milltop farm.

He could smell the acrid aroma of smouldering wet vegetation long before he could see any sign of a fire. It drifted on the air mocking him. As soon as he reached the stile that led to the field he would need to cross to reach Ellie and her family, it became apparent that the odour was not coming from the direction of the farm. He turned to see a thin whisp of smoke drifting to the sky from the direction of Darrington Way. The meadow. He walked slowly at first, unwilling to confirm what he suspected, and then began to run.

He reached the gap in the hedge and stared in horror at the damage caused by the lightening. Almost the entire area of the beautiful grassland was gone, replaced by scorched brown earth and in the centre, lay the remains of the Silver birch. All at once the sheer enormity of the tree was apparent. The lightening must have struck one side of the tree for half of its branches were little more than charcoal with not a leaf in evidence, while the other side was still mostly green. A black, ugly stump of a trunk rested on its side, still smoking slightly, with one long root, surrounded by many smaller ones, pointing raggedly up to the sky in accusation. The other half of the birch, despite lying on the ground, could have been mistaken for a tree freshly cut down, if it hadn't been for the roots still embedded beneath the earth on that side. Although Henry could see more deadwood than had previously been apparent when the tree was upright, there was still foliage clinging to fronds that once draped from branches now spread wide on the ground like arms thrown out in despair.

The birch must have burnt fiercely in spite of the rain, dry grass spreading the flames eagerly across the meadow, for the air about it was still thick with heat as Henry approached. He coughed, his eyes stinging, and took out a handkerchief to hold to his nose until he became accustomed to the stench. There was a fairly large hole where roots had been torn from the ground as the tree fell, while the remaining underground roots unable to maintain a strong enough hold on the trunk to keep it upright, bent almost double at the base.

Henry knelt beside the cavity. He'd heard of trees that had been struck by lightning and survived, but this poor specimen, half dead and probably humming with energy from the strange phenomenon, hadn't stood a chance. Almost reverently he touched the beginning of the long root which pointed heavenward. A clump of earth fell away from his hand into the hole and as Henry watched it crumble on impact, he noticed something half hidden in the mud. It looked curiously like a rusty metal bone. He reached down into the hole and using his penknife, attempted to clear some of the mud away from the object. It seemed to be some sort of handle. He looked about him for something better than the little knife with which to dig it out, but there was nothing of any practical use.

Frustrated, he came to the conclusion he would have to go back to the village and borrow a spade. Then he would probably be obliged to explain what he needed it for, unless he lied. For some as yet unknowable reason he wanted to keep this discovery, together with the phenomenon, secret, at least until he had some idea what he was dealing with. Whatever the object in the ground might be, it may well be connected to what had been happening high up in the branches of the tree. There again, it might be nothing. He didn't like lying; he'd learnt early on in life that it generally caused more trouble than it was worth and anyway he was no good at it.

Then, like an answer to prayer, he heard the faint growl of the early bus heading towards the village and inspiration struck. It would be back within half an hour on its return run.

Henry broke off some large clumps of earth and scorched grass from the roots of the dead tree and threw them into the hollowed-out ground to cover up the metal object. It was just a precaution in case any of the local farm workers or villagers took it into their heads to investigate the meadow once they realised where the lightning bolt had found its target. He wasn't too concerned. After all, hadn't the vicar told him people avoided the place? Next, he cleaned himself up as best as he could and set off at a smart pace.

His transport was already in sight by the time he reached the signpost at the crossroads. There were few people on the bus and nobody spoke to him, for which he was relieved. One man in a front seat was reading a newspaper, further along, a middle-aged woman looked him up and down with disapproval as he took a seat nearby, then returned her attention to the front, while the man behind her nodded a greeting to Henry. Henry paid the bus conductor his fare to Chatham then settled back in his seat for the ride.

The bus journey probably took longer than Henry's shopping. He soon found a hardware store and purchased a digging fork and spade which were duly wrapped in brown paper and tied up with string and the store keeper asked if he'd be interested in purchasing some bulbs to plant ready for next spring. Henry counted the money in his wallet before agreeing and chose a dozen tulip bulbs and a dozen daffodils, a decision he was glad he'd made when he got on the bus back to Bushwell and found Ellie sitting near to the front. He'd forgotten this was her day for shopping for supplies and changing her library books. She looked up at him in surprise, watching with interest as he stowed his packages before sitting down beside her.

"Hello, I didn't expect to see you this morning," she said.

"I didn't sleep well after the storm and when I saw the mess it had made of my Landlady's garden, I thought I'd nip out and get a few things to help put it right." He still held the little bag of bulbs and lifted it to show her.

"Oh," she said. "That's nice of you. Doesn't she have garden tools already though?"

"Probably," Henry said. He thought quickly, "But if I asked if I could borrow those it wouldn't be a surprise, would it? Was there any damage at the farm, from the storm?"

"Nothing too terrible. That's a bit extravagant buying tools you might not need, isn't it?" She wasn't going to let it go easily.

"Not really. I shall have my own house one day, with a garden. I thought my fork and spade would be a good investment."

Ellie laughed. "You *are* funny. You'd better be careful about what you go digging up in Miss Noaks' garden though; she's quite particular about her flowers and plants."

"Thanks for the warning. You were telling me how the farm fared during the storm," he reminded her.

"The cows got a bit nervous and Uncle Seth went out to see to them. He stayed in the barn most of the night, concerned if the herd got too upset it might affect the milk supply. I'm still amazed the children slept right through it; the thunder was so loud! Everyone alright in the village?"

"I think so. What are you reading now, then?"

Ellie showed him her books and he encouraged her to chat about literature and music and anything else she wanted to. He was happy just to listen and the journey seemed to pass quickly. Fortunately, nobody else got off at their stop and after walking Ellie to the stile and helping her over, Henry stood and watched as, after waving, she trudged off across the field, pony tail bobbing as she went. Then he turned back towards the lane to his meadow.

The sun felt warm on his back as he crouched down, cutting the string on his packages with his penknife and carefully folding the brown paper so that he could rewrap the tools after using them. He weighted the paper down using the bag of bulbs so that it wouldn't be taken away by a sudden breeze, then he stuck the fork in the ground, removed his jacket and hung it over the handle. He rolled up his shirt sleeves, took up the spade, approached the hole and set to work.

It took rather longer than he had imagined to completely unearth the object, which turned out to be a handle attached to a rather solid box and by the time he was able to heave it out of the hole onto the ground beside him, his shirt clung to his body, drenched in sweat. He lifted his arm to wipe his brow on his shirt sleeve and sat back on his haunches beside what looked to be an old-fashioned iron strong box. It was rectangular in shape, the long sides being just over a foot in length and it was almost as deep as it was long. It had no discernible decoration or markings on the outside and what was most interesting was that, although it had a keyhole, it didn't appear to be locked. With a little help from his penknife, Henry was soon able to persuade the lid to lift. It was stiff with age and he had to push his fingers between the narrow opening to prise the lid open further still until it eventually gave up the fight and opened all the way. At last he was able to inspect the contents.

The first thing he saw was a piece of oilskin, wrapped around a quite lumpy object that just fitted into the top of the box. He lifted it out carefully, thinking it must be an ornament of some kind. It didn't weigh as much as he'd imagined it might. He laid it to one side to inspect any further contents of the box and found pages and pages of handwritten manuscript. The top page was blank but for the name Albert Edward Henry Darrington. This must have been what the dark-eyed man had referred to when Henry had caught the words: *Beneath the Tree* the first time he'd climbed the Silver birch. In Albert's day, the Silver birch wouldn't have been quite so grand, although judging from its appearance before lightning struck, Henry guessed it would have been reasonably tall, even

141

during Albert's time, with perhaps twenty or so years of growth to its credit. It would have been the ideal marker for Albert to dig beneath one of its roots to hide the box.

Henry looked back at the carefully wrapped bundle lying on the ground beside him, curiosity getting the better of him at last, and decided to inspect it before looking more closely at the manuscript. He unwound the oilskin and stared. It wasn't at all what he had expected. It was a baby doll, and not just any baby doll - it was so perfectly made it could almost be mistaken for a real child. Henry carefully wrapped it back in the oilskin, and laid it gently in the box on top of the manuscript. He would take the box back to his lodgings along with the tools which he would rewrap with the brown paper and string as he'd originally planned. That way nobody would know he'd been using them and Mrs. Noaks would just think he'd purchased the strong box (once he'd given it a good wipe with his handkerchief) for his own use.

He stood up. He'd missed two meals now and wasn't prepared to miss his dinner too. It also occurred to him that his landlady might be concerned that he'd been gone for a long time without leaving any message. The box and its contents would have to wait until he was alone in his room this evening.

Chapter Twenty-One

Spring was in the air. The sun was beaming and the birds were singing and Henry was enjoying tidying up the cottage garden for Mrs. Noaks because Ellie was with him. He hadn't seen much of her for the past few weeks, partly because he'd been busy, but also because she'd been sulking with him for being so preoccupied with his work. He still hadn't taken her to see his land or even talked very much about it, although he'd decided after seeing it in all its fresh glory this morning that today would be the day.

He and Ellie had become very close over the past few months, had confessed their growing feelings for one another on Ellie's birthday on bonfire night. They'd been sharing in the village firework celebrations. Christmas had come and gone. They'd exchanged gifts at the wonderfully atmospheric midnight mass service on Christmas Eve. He'd bought Ellie a tiny silver locket in the shape of a heart and she'd given him a smart new fountain pen. As they left the church hand in hand, the air had been frosty and silent. The night was clear, and the sky dark blue velvet sprinkled with stars. They'd parted company at the gate, Ellie to walk with her aunt, and Henry to his lodgings. They had promised to meet for a walk early the following evening.

In the meantime, Henry had enjoyed sharing Christmas dinner with the vicar and Miss Noaks; the two, being old friends, had virtually taken on the role of surrogate parents to him.

Miss Noaks had introduced Henry to her second cousin, a builder and redecorator by trade, Kevin Hardingway. The man spent much of the colder months of the year painting and redecorating in the more affluent areas of the Medway towns. During the warmer weather, he expended more time outside building houses, contracting himself out to work on new offices, flats or even helping out on road construction. Miss Noaks knew he was looking for a labourer to help with the workload as he had so many jobs in hand and Henry was the perfect fit for the post; he was young, keen and hardworking. The extra income enabled Henry to put money by, although it left little time for anything else. Nevertheless, no matter how tired he was when he returned from a day's labouring, he was disciplined enough to spend two hours every evening working on his latest novel.

The story was very different to the one he had originally intended and was influenced heavily by what he'd read in the manuscript, although he'd mentioned Albert's pages to nobody, simply reading them himself then putting them away. In fact, he had never told anybody about his find.

He had gradually come to look forward to sitting down at the typewriter after his evening meal, for the story practically wrote itself. Towards the end, he surprised even himself at how imaginative he could be. The downside of this, though, was that he had not been able to spend much time with Ellie. However, he had promised Ellie he would make it up to her one day, and when a letter came from his publisher in America, suggesting he might introduce himself to a literary agent who had just travelled from America to London, Henry took Ellie with him on the train. Pretending confidence that he far from felt, he left her browsing in a second-hand bookshop while he went to meet the agent, a Mr. Skinner.

The meeting paid off. Henry showed the man the first chapter of his current manuscript and Skinner suggested, rather than presenting it to his present publisher, it should be sent out to several of the major publishing houses in both England and America. If there was enough interest, they could sell to the highest bidder, he told the young writer. In the meantime, his current publisher had hoped the agent would be hired by Henry to set up book signings in various popular bookshops. Henry doubted they had suspected Skinner would encourage him to take his business elsewhere, although he liked the dream of his book becoming an international bestseller, so he agreed and signed Skinner up as his agent.

Business concluded, he had then taken Ellie across London in a big black taxi to the Globe Theatre to see a production of *Much Ado About Nothing* for which he had ordered and paid for tickets weeks in advance as a surprise treat. Ellie had been thrilled and promptly forgave what she saw as his neglect of her, hence her presence with Henry in Miss Noaks' garden the following weekend.

"Your bulbs came up a treat," Ellie nodded towards the bright patches of yellow and red beneath the kitchen window. Henry had cleared a patch of soil for a bonfire on the far side of the garden and was in the process of raking up dry grass and weeds to put on it. He paused in his task and looked over to the tulips and daffodils.

"Not too bad," he said. The flowers had become his landlady's favourite topic of conversation, particularly whenever anyone came to the cottage, such was her delight when the flowers had appeared.

The kitchen window opened now and Miss Noaks poked her head out with one hand waving an envelope.

"Henry, come quickly. It's come. I'm sure it's the letter from your agent!" Ellie looked at Henry and darted for the back door, obviously as excited as his landlady. Henry leaned his rake against the shed, pretending nonchalance, and took his time following her. In truth, he was nervous; supposing nobody wanted the book? What if even his American publisher didn't like it? He took the letter from Miss Noaks and sat at the kitchen table looking at it.

"Well open it then," the two women chorused.

He tore open the envelope and took out the letter and read it. A cheque was pinned to the back. He read the letter twice then looked at the cheque in disbelief.

Ellie snatched the letter from him and mumbling read it quietly to herself. "Jeepers Creepers," she cried. "Henry, you're rich!"

Miss Noaks looked from Ellie to Henry then back again. "Oh my, is it true?" Henry prised the letter from Ellie's excited fingers and handed it over to his landlady. She read it, slowly at first, then her hand flew to her mouth. "Oh my," she said again, shaking her head and handing the letter back to Henry.

"What are you going to do with the money, Henry?" Ellie asked, eyes shining. Henry came out of his shocked trance and jumped to his feet, swinging Ellie around in the small kitchen, almost knocking over the dining chairs. "I'm going to spend it, of course. I'm going to get a car and learn to drive and I'm going to build a house. Yes, that's what I'm going to do. It's just what I was saving for anyway, and I've already mentioned it to Kev. He said we could do it a bit at a time, as and when I had the money, and that I could work with him on it. This will certainly speed things up. Then I'll buy a new typewriter." He stopped talking about his plans then, noticing Ellie had lost her exuberance.

"What's up?" he asked.

Miss Noaks coughed. "I think I'll just put the kettle on," she said, turning away.

"You didn't tell me you wanted to build a house," Ellie said, sounding as petulant as a small child.

"Don't look like that. We need a house of our own to live in and this way we can plan it just the way we want. Come on, I'll show you just where it will stand. It's about time you saw my meadow." He grabbed her hand, but she shook herself free.

"Just you wait a minute Henry Fisherton," she said. "Aren't you making certain assumptions?"

Henry sighed and got down on one knee, glancing sheepishly at Miss Noaks. He took out a small black box from his pocket which contained his mother's engagement ring. He'd been carrying it around all week.

"This isn't where or how I planned to do this," he said, opening the box and taking the ring out to slip onto her finger. "I'd originally intended to take you to see my land and propose to you beneath a lovely old Silver birch tree but it isn't there anymore and besides, it's kind of nice to have Miss Noaks here." He looked up into Ellie's face. "Eleanor Harrison, would you do me the honour of agreeing to be my wife?"

Henry was amused to see Ellie hadn't quite been expecting this. She'd dropped hints that it might be time they took the next step in their relationship, of course, but now it had happened she seemed lost for words. It didn't last long. She threw her arms around Henry's neck, almost causing him to lose balance. "Yes, I'd love to marry you," she said, kissing him. Henry got to his feet and watched as Ellie showed her ring to Miss Noaks, turning her hand this way and that so that the tiny diamond would catch the light from the window and he smiled as the two women admired it. Then Miss Noaks went to a cupboard and fetched out a bottle of sparkling wine she'd been given on her last birthday, announcing that this was the perfect opportunity to open it to celebrate.

"Thank you, Miss Noaks, but do you think you could possibly save it? We'd like to invite Reverend Jacobson and Ellie's family to celebrate with us, if you wouldn't mind."

"Of course, that's a wonderful idea. Would you like me to go to the telephone box in the village and invite everyone around? I could call at the vicarage on my way. I won't tell any of them the reason. Then you can make a proper announcement."

"That would be great," Henry said. "Please do. Ask them to come after tea. In the meantime, I'd like you, Ellie, to come and see my meadow. I've been waiting for it to recover from the storm for you to see it at its best. It really is the prettiest place."

As they walked, Henry told Ellie about the tree and what had happened to it. Miss Noaks' second cousin, the builder and Henry's sometime boss, had proved a good friend. On the run-up to Christmas, when business had been slack, he'd taken the truck up the lane to the meadow on Darrington Way with Henry one morning to look at the land on which Henry wanted to build. Upon seeing the tree, he'd offered to help Henry get rid of the remains.

They'd returned to his workshop in the village to fetch tools, Kevin recounting some of the stories about the land he'd heard during the drive, and Henry telling him on their return journey what Reverend Jacobson had told him.

With a roar of the engine and wheels spinning, Kevin had managed to get the truck onto the meadow and close enough for them to be able to load any wood onto it once it was cut up. Before he got out, however, Kevin had scratched his chin, staring straight ahead to avoid looking at Henry and said, "You sure you want to build here, mate? With all those strange tales about the place?" Henry (who'd had a good idea why such stories had originated, but didn't want to say) later boasted to Ellie how he'd merely insisted he thought it was all a lot of superstitious nonsense. He told her how Kev had nodded then and grinned, and they'd spent the best part of the day clearing away the ruined tree. At dusk, they'd driven back to the village with a truck load of firewood for Miss Noaks to burn on her range and in return she'd made them dinner - steak and kidney pudding and apple pie for dessert.

"I'm glad you made the most of the time you didn't spend with me," Ellie said, no longer even pretending to be annoyed.

They came to the access way to the meadow which had been widened slightly and made more noticeable by the entry of Kev's truck several months previous, although any trace of tyre marks or other evidence of its ever having been there had long since vanished. The grassland and flowers were back, with even a few birds although there was as yet no sign of the butterflies. Henry watched Ellie's face as her eyes swept the meadow and the woods beyond.

"The tree used to stand there," he said, pointing to the centre. "Come on." There was still part of a stump in the ground but the hole had gone. Henry sat down on the fresh, springy grass that had replaced the scorched earth, and patted the place beside him.

"Sit down, the grass isn't damp. There's something I need to talk to you about. I'm going to tell you something which you might find difficult to believe," he said, "although I do have some proof. I don't think anyone should marry with secrets from their partner, do you? It would create an unnecessary barrier."

Ellie nodded slowly, her eyes took on a faraway look for a moment, her mind playing out some remembered scene as Henry watched her. Henry waited for her to sit, cocking his head to one side to gain her attention. At last she caught his eye and, smiling, complied with his request, joining him on the grass.

"What I'm about to disclose is a secret and I need you to promise to keep it for me, agreed?" Ellie, now fully attentive, nodded again, waiting. Henry was silent for a moment, gathering his thoughts, before he began. He told her about his last visit to see his father before he died and how he'd come to Bushwell to look at the land. She listened, transfixed, as he described what had happened the first time he'd climbed the tree. They lay back on the grass as he finished that part and peered up at the sky. Henry told Ellie that if she looked carefully she might even see the patch of strange haze in the air, although they both searched the sky above them, each coming to the conclusion after a while that they could see nothing. She urged him to go on and he continued his story right up to when he had found the box.

"I can show you the pages I found in the box as proof if you'd like." He finally finished.

"It all sounds a bit creepy and unreal," Ellie admitted. "I would like to see the writing, though. Not because I don't believe you, but I think it would be interesting to read." Henry nodded and gave her a kiss on the cheek.

"Perhaps we'll have time before everyone arrives back at the cottage, although Miss Noaks might not like you coming up into my room." He began to get up. Ellie put a hand on his arm.

"Before we go, Henry. I have something to tell you too. It's the real reason why my parents left me with my Aunt. It wasn't just so I could help with my little cousins." She looked a bit uncomfortable and paused for a minute, picking at blades of the new grass. Henry flopped back down beside her, propping himself up on one elbow.

"Go on, then. Remember, no secrets." Henry encouraged her.

"I was a bit young and silly, you see," she mumbled.

"Whereas you're all grown-up now and ready to settle down." Henry grinned. He was relieved that he'd told her everything at last. Nothing she had to tell him could, he was certain, spoil his new-found contentment.

"It's no joking matter," she cried. "It might cause problems when we tell my parents we want to marry." The grin slipped from Henry's face then, although he remained upbeat.

"Come on, out with it. It can't be all that bad."

"You might not say that when you know. You might not want to marry me anymore, but you're right, we shouldn't begin our lives together with secrets between us, so I have to tell you."

Henry put his arm around her. "Ellie, I shall want to marry you no matter what it is," he said. I love you. Please just trust me."

"Okay." She took a deep breath. "When I was only just sixteen, I got involved with an older man, a friend of the family. I suppose it was just a stupid crush, although at the time it felt like the real thing and he confessed to me he felt the same way." She began picking at the grass again. Henry waited. "We were going to run away together, only my mother read my diary and told my dad. I think that was the most horrible day of my life!" She looked at Henry now, tears in her eyes. "I did well at school and was going to train to be a children's nanny, although I lost any chance of doing that with my daft romantic notions." She brushed at her eyes with the back of her hand. "He was in his mid-thirties, you see, and they said he should have known better and it was a breach of their trust. Well, he was old enough to be my father, so you couldn't blame them," she said. "They cut all family contact with him and sent me away and that's the real reason I came to live with my aunt."

Chapter Twenty-Two

During his career as a writer, Henry Fisherton was interviewed many times in order to publicise his novels, first by newspaper and magazine reporters, and then he was invited to speak on the wireless. In the years that followed, he even appeared on television. He was regularly questioned about how he got his ideas, whether he'd always wanted to be an author and, of course, how he got his first publishing break. He quickly realised what most people really wanted to know was how to get their own work published and become rich and famous. However, if he'd been asked more probing questions about the early years, when he was becoming an established author, he would have said that the years 1961 to 1962 had been the busiest and most influential years both in terms of his work and his personal life.

A few weeks after receipt of the first large advance cheque, Henry had a visit from his new literary agent, Godfrey Skinner, who had driven from London in an expensive-looking hire car. He informed Henry that he was still required to supply a second novel to his former publishing house, although he had, with some negotiation, managed to free Henry from any further commitment. Henry was expected to fly out to America to attend a number of pre-arranged book signings and readings for his debut novel, and to deliver his next and final manuscript for that publisher. Skinner had assured him that would be the end of his dealings with them, apart from receiving royalty cheques. Henry was sceptical; wouldn't they need him to promote the new book? Skinner had laughed. Apparently not. The little American publishing house expected to be able to sell the next novel on the back of the much publicised, award-winning novel about to be launched in London.

Henry had six weeks in order to produce the new novel. It didn't worry him too much. He had written most of the story to go with the outline he'd sent off before leaving London to come to Bushwell for the first time. It was nothing like the book he'd just finished, so with a bit of tweaking and some expansion of the story he felt he could be ready for the deadline.

By this time, Henry had convinced Ellie that her confession made no difference to his feelings for her or their plans to marry. He promised her he did not even wish to know any more details of the affair – it was in the past and so long as she loved him and they were honest with each other from that moment on, that was all he cared about. He had wanted to say the past didn't matter, but unfortunately, he was only too aware now that the past shaped the future. However, he wasn't going to allow what had obviously been a schoolgirl infatuation to spoil their happiness now.

With some excitement, they decided Ellie should go with Henry to America. They had written to her parents with their news and asked if Ellie could visit with them while Henry was dealing with business. Her parents had replied by telegram agreeing that Ellie should of course stay with them, but giving no further comment about her proposed marriage. Henry decided they'd deal with any problems once they got there.

As it turned out, he needn't have been concerned. He was to discover later that, without informing him, Ellie's Aunt wrote to Mr. and Mrs. Harrison ahead of the visit enclosing letters from both Miss Noaks and Reverend Jacobson full of praise for the young man their daughter hoped to marry, so they were at least willing to meet him. They met the young couple at the airport and, after Ellie introduced Henry, Mr. Harrison offered him a ride to his hotel. During the drive, he invited Henry to join them for a meal at a nearby restaurant that evening with the intention of them all getting to know one another better.

That was all that was required really for them to give their blessing for the marriage. Ellie's mother had been reassured to learn that Henry was the son of a preacher and Ellie laughingly told Henry later that she had attributed his good manners and charm to his ecclesiastical parent. Her father, on the other hand, was more interested in the content of his books and the fact that he wrote about the future and imaginary technology. They discussed several films and whether or not they were realistic, the ideas feasible. By the end of the evening, Ellie's father told Henry he had decided he would take time off work so he and his wife could show the young couple the sights and discuss preparations for the forthcoming marriage. The Harrisons would definitely be flying home to England to attend their daughter's wedding.

That night, alone in the hotel, Henry thought about the three 'predictions' he had seen and how the third had helped him make some decisions.

Henry remembered he had seen himself standing in what could only have been a laboratory; the room had been large and sterile looking with a variety of strange equipment on view. Electronic panels with blinking lights had taken up one side of the space and two men and three women, all wearing white lab coats, either worked at the instrument panels or with the other equipment about the room. Only the man Henry had come to think of as his Victorian relative had been near the portal to greet him. He had appeared to be in charge.

"No, I am not Albert Darrington," the dark-eyed man had said. "We tried to use the portal to communicate to warn you not to make the same mistakes he made."

"So, where is he?" the other Henry had asked.

"Albert Darrington – the man you learned about in your history - did not actually exist, or at least not in the way you believe. How can I explain? You are now standing in one possible version of your distant future. The portal," he had seemed to indicate the very space through which Henry was spectating, "is like an unstable tear in the fabric of the universe. We call it God's Eye because of what it shows. Not everybody can see through it, only a chosen few. I assume you do know about the Creator?"

"Of course, my father was a man of God,"

"I should hope we are all men and women of God," the scientist said, his face stern.

"I meant he was a priest."

The scientist hadn't commented on that. He went on to explain about the Eye. "For some people, even some of our engineers and scientists, it just doesn't seem to exist."

"So how *does* it exist?"

"We don't really know. When it first appeared, we were experimenting with gravity, in the hope of discovering ways to travel through space without such stringent time constraints as we at present endure. What we noticed was that it seemed to show a number of other realities, generally an average of three for each person looking into it, although one might see each of the three realities more than once."

"God's number," the other Henry had muttered with a small smile.

The scientist frowned, puzzled.

"The Trinity and all that," Henry supplied.

"Hmm. Quite." His host had nodded. "Although one or two of us have been able to see one or more of those three realities again at a later date."

Henry had been able to see his other self as he stared around the laboratory with obvious curiosity. There had appeared to be a platform before the 'hazy, liquid' effect of the portal through which Henry had been watching. The platform had given the impression that the portal wasn't as high up as in his own universe.

"The man you call Albert Darrington was one of our young scientists," the sombre man had continued. "He volunteered to go through the Eye. However, to put it simply, the same cells cannot exist in the same space at the same time. When he tried to enter a dimension in which he already existed, he was thrown back into another reality in your past before he, or any of his other selves, had been born. He created the identity of Albert Darrington, made false records if you like, to fit in and conceal the truth, lest he be thrown into a lunatic asylum."

Henry had sensed the nervous frustration of his other self as he'd paced four or five steps one way then back again before his companion as he listened. He had stopped abruptly and turned to the scientist.

"Created false records? How on earth did he do that?"

"It wasn't as difficult as you might imagine." The scientist had actually smiled. "In this society, we study genealogy and are obliged to memorise our lineage from the first time it was recorded, during our primary education. It also has to be checked with genetic evidence as far back as possible. There are various reasons for this. We have no genetic diseases or disorders, for example, and our social security system is based on extended family financially supporting those who are unable to support themselves, so you see it's necessary to know where we came from and to whom we are related. Our man's real name was Caleb Attlee Fisherton." He had paused to watch the effect of his words on the other Henry.

"In reality he was one of my family descendants?" the other Henry had been aghast. "I've only just got used to the fact that there was no such person as my ancestor, Albert Darrington!"

His companion had sighed and scratched his beard. Henry had been acutely aware of the rasping sound this made. "That isn't quite correct. My colleague from Records will explain." He

156

had pressed a button on his lab coat and had then directed the other Henry to a padded dining seat at a small table in the corner of the laboratory. This had apparently been where the scientists, engineers and technicians took their meal breaks. He had asked the other Henry what he would like to drink and had responded to his laughing request for Assam tea, by approaching a panel in a wall and speaking into it. The other Henry had then been handed a cup of tea which he'd seemed to enjoy immensely. His companion had excused himself and gone back to the control panels near the Eye to speak to a technician.

The other Henry had just been finishing his tea when another man had arrived and introduced himself as the Records Officer. He'd sat down opposite Henry, placed a rectangular object on the table before him and had waved his hand above it.

"Here it is," he'd said, turning to the other Henry who had been staring with astonishment as words had appeared in the air before them. Watching through the portal, Henry had been unable to see anything other than a vague outline of the text in the space before the face of his other self.

"The Darringtons were quite a wealthy family, particularly favoured in the Court of Henry VIII for services to the King. They were not well known by the gentry and elite of that era, so quite what those services were one can only speculate. Whatever the reason, the family were granted certain lands and monies which passed down the family until the Darrington line came to an end." He had waved his hand again to show a rather detailed family tree. "Sir George Alfred Felix Darrington and his wife, Edna Harriet Darrington, together with their six-month-old son, Albert Edward Henry Darrington, died of a fever at the close of 1863."

Henry had felt that the other Henry should really have expressed some sort of regret or sympathy for the lost family.

Instead he had leaned forward excitedly, "So Caleb took the dead baby's identity!"

To affirm this, the Records Officer indicated the family tree. "If you look here, where the text is a different colour, you will see how the family became extended when Caleb altered the records, not only to erase the baby's death, but also to link the Darringtons to the Fishertons. He was careful not to make the link too close otherwise the powers that be in your reality would have realised something was amiss."

"But isn't that illegal or at least immoral?" the other Henry had asked.

The Records Officer had shrugged. "Amoral. If he hadn't done that the land would have most likely reverted to the ownership of the Royal family – although ultimately all land in the country belongs to the Crown anyway –and would probably have been considered common land and been acquired over time by the neighbouring farm, which incidentally eventually came into the possession of a branch of the Fisherton family anyway. He caused no harm and it obviously worked."

Just then the dark-eyed, bearded scientist had returned. "All up-to-date now?" He'd asked the Records Officer. The little man had risen to his feet bowing in acknowledgment. He had tapped the instrument on the table before picking it up and smiling at the other Henry. "I hope I've been of some assistance," he had said, and then he'd left.

"Does that mean Albert or Caleb is dead now? And more to the point, how and when am I going to get back home?" Henry, watching through the portal, could see the stress on the face of his other self.

"That's what we were trying to warn you about – it's a one-way trip," the scientist had told him, his face grave. "Yes, he is probably deceased because he attempted to return. We've worked on a force field to try to prevent anyone else making the mistake of entering the portal from your dimension because obviously, there are other repercussions which I'm not at liberty to go into now. All I will say is that we have been very ignorant and foolish and should have treated the Eye with more respect. Unfortunately, you stepped through before we had time to activate the force-field, although we've done so now."

"Why did you try to get in touch, then? I don't understand," the other Henry had cried, frustrated.

"We tried to communicate with you to ask that you help us to conceal the portal in your universe until such time as we can close it. Now you've come through we will have to create a new identity for you and assist you to fit in with our society."

The other Henry had begun to panic. "But I don't want to fit in with your society. I have a life of my own back home. You have to get me back!"

The man with the beard shook his head, his eyes dark with sorrow. "Your only alternative is instant death." The other Henry had shrunk back in his seat, horrified. The scientist had gone on to explain further. "For a while, perhaps because he'd inadvertently been thrown into your dimension, some of us could see our physicist trying to get back so we realised there must be some slim chance of us communicating. We observed him as he recorded his story and buried it beneath the roots of a tree, that's why I told you to look there. There was nothing we could do to help him, you understand, but then Caleb knew the risks before he entered the Eye. Now all we can do is hope the 'you' in one of the other two dimensions helps us to disguise the portal."

It seemed as if he'd witnessed these events decades ago, although it had only really been a little over a year. Henry now lay in his hotel bed staring at the ceiling. He wasn't really sure he'd understood everything the scientist from the future had told him through his other self, although the man had tried to explain in the most basic terms. What Henry did know was what was required of him and how he could fulfil the promise he made to his father on his deathbed. He would have to conceal the portal.

He had commenced discussions with Kevin, his boss during his time as a manual labourer for the building company, to help build a house. What he planned to do was to himself work on the side of the upper storey where the portal was, to disguise it as a window by placing a frame and glass in front of it. He would ensure the window would never open and there would be several layers of thick glass.

There would be problems, he knew. As he'd been informed through the scientist's explanation to the other Henry, the portal was unstable. It wasn't always visible and not everybody appeared able to see through it. That might make it difficult for him in placing the window, but he didn't think it would be impossible. Further, it could have its advantages for if and when somebody did see through it whilst in the house at some later date, they would probably think they were either dreaming or imagining what they were seeing. Ellie hadn't seemed to be able to see the liquid movement of the portal the day he'd told her about it and they'd gazed upward to where Henry had pointed. Perhaps she would never see it.

When the house was finished, Henry would take the room with the extra window for his study (for he had already decided there would need to be another ordinary window in that room too). That would guard against discovery of the portal to some extent for a while at least.

As his mind slowed and his eyelids grew heavy, Henry turned onto his side and allowed sleep to take him. His last fleeting thoughts were concerned with how his other self must be feeling now, trapped in another reality and knowing that he would never see Ellie again, and probably never marry. He had never seen the tree destroyed or found the box containing

Albert's papers and the doll. His final thought was: why hadn't the other Henry been able to foresee what might happen if he stepped through the portal, known on the other side as 'God's Eye'?

Chapter Twenty-Three
1969 – Whitewood House, Darrington Way

Ellie paused outside Henry's study. The door was shut tight against intrusion and she could hear the click tap-tap of his typewriter keys; he was busy writing his next best-seller. She crept back to their bedroom and went to the wardrobe, taking down a battered suitcase. It had once contained the letters and postcards Henry had written her on trips he'd taken when she hadn't been able to accompany him, along with various other mementos: a small jar containing Melody's first tooth, her first pair of baby shoes, birthday and anniversary cards. These were now packed safely away in a cardboard box in the attic and the old-fashioned brown suitcase, that had always been kept on top of the wardrobe, was now packed with a selection of clothes, shoes and her personal toiletries and cosmetics. She placed it near the door then went one last time to look at her beautiful five-year-old daughter.

Melody always reminded her of a cherub, as she slept, with her head of golden curls, long eyelashes resting on rosy pink chubby cheeks. However, on this occasion the little girl was not sleeping.

"Mummy, cuddles," she said as Ellie approached the bed.

"Hello my angel. Why are you still awake?"

"Bad dream." The child was now sitting up with arms outstretched.

Ellie sat down on the side of the bed and pulled her close, stroking her soft hair. "What was your dream about?" she asked.

"Bad people. In Daddy's office," Melody replied, snuggling into her mother's embrace. Melody had been having this recurring nightmare every other week since she'd caught Ellie standing in Henry's office staring out of the window while he was last away on one of his bookselling tours.

"Now, now, you know there's nobody but Daddy in his office. There's no reason to be frightened. Would you like some milk?"

"No, thank you Mummy. I would like a story please."

Ellie felt her throat tighten as she hugged her daughter closer still. She wouldn't cry. She mustn't.

"Okay, just one. Now let me think. I know. You'll have to wait a moment while I fetch something." She lay Melody back down against her pillows and arranged the blankets about her. "I won't be a minute."

"Not book, Mummy. One of your stories."

"Yes, I know. Give me just a minute. I have a present for you."

Ellie went back to the bedroom and reached up for the iron strong box which had always been stored next to the old suitcase on top of the wardrobe. She placed the box on top of the bed and took out the baby doll then she replaced the box on top of the wardrobe and went back to Melody. She showed the doll to the child then tucked it into the bed beside her.

"This is a very special dolly. Her name is Baby and you must take very good care of her. Do you promise?"

"Is she mine, Mummy?"

Ellie kissed the little girl and smiled. "Yes, she's yours, but you have to keep her safe, because one day when you're all grown up, you will want to give her to another little girl in our family, perhaps your own daughter or grandchild so that the doll can be her Baby."

Melody hugged the doll to her chest tightly. "I'm not going to grow up, Mummy. I'm going to stay little forever and live with you and Daddy always. Can I keep Baby as just mine?"

Ellie chuckled, brushing Melody's hair from her eyes, stroking her forehead.

"You will grow up, my angel. Everybody has to and anyway, you wouldn't like it if you never had another birthday, would you? That's what birthday parties are for – celebrating you growing up. Now, give me your word that you'll take extra special care of Baby because Daddy gave her to me when you were very little, and I would be so sad if she got broken or lost. Promise?"

"I promise, Mummy."

"Don't forget, one day you will pass her to another little girl in the Fisherton family and when she grows up she will do the same."

"Okay, Mummy. But I'm still going to always live with you and Daddy."

"Alright then. Now this is the story of how Daddy first met Mummy and became a famous writer."

Half an hour later Melody was fast asleep, the doll still in her arms. With tears in her eyes, Ellie kissed her one last time and went to fetch her suitcase. She put the suitcase in the hall and walked through to the kitchen to check everything was neat and tidy. The radio was still blaring away on the work top: 'In the year 2525' faded out and Bobby Gentry began 'What do you get when you fall in love?' Ellie switched the radio off with a wry smile. How appropriate, she thought.

Henry did not hear her leave the house. He was still writing. As she walked along the dark lane towards the bus stop she thought about the day she'd given birth to Melody.

Henry had gone to the village to fetch some groceries and post his latest manuscript and she'd been pottering about in the garden. The sun had been shining and all had seemed right in the world. They had a wonderful house, designed and partly built by her adoring husband, in wonderful surroundings. She had knelt down to deadhead some marigolds, listening to the birdsong from the meadow beyond the garden, when pain had suddenly ripped through her. She felt herself beginning to tremble and the world about her spin until she sank to the ground in darkness.

164

She awoke in hospital feeling dazed, her abdomen sore. She had undergone an emergency Caesarean section, they told her, and she was then presented with her gorgeous baby girl. Apparently, she'd had some sort of fit, triggered by the last stages of her pregnancy, something to do with her blood not being compatible to that of the baby's.

Henry told her that it was fortunate one of her young cousins had been sent by her aunt to visit and had found her and raised the alarm. Henry had gone to a lot of trouble and expense to have a telephone installed in the house before she came home from the hospital. He told her he needed one to keep in touch with his agent, and that it would be handy for calling her when he was away on business, but she knew his main motive had been that they should have a means of getting help quickly in future in case of an emergency.

As she nursed the child for the first time, Henry had asked Ellie what she'd like to call their daughter, since they hadn't managed to come to an agreement beforehand. She thought about the birds singing in the meadows and, gazing with adoration at the tiny baby in her arms, had said, "Melody, Melody-Aria." To her joy, Henry had agreed instantly, but then he'd already known what the doctors would be telling her later that day. She'd never quite forgiven him for not breaking the news to her himself, although she supposed he'd had his own shock and grief to deal with.

There would be no more babies, they told her. For her to attempt to carry another child would surely end in death for both her and the unborn child.

At first it hadn't seemed so terrible to her. She had Melody who was the most perfect, charming infant in the world. It wasn't until Melody was two that she began to feel broody again. She talked to Henry but he was adamant. The doctors had warned them of the probable result of any further pregnancy and he was not prepared to take any risks. They'd argued and she'd cried for days until she realised Melody was unhappy, sensing something wrong. She called a truce and Henry had given into her care the doll, Baby.

She had never found the time to read Albert's manuscript, so that evening she took time to do just that. The story it told made her realise just how precious the doll was. This was the reason she'd given Baby to Melody before leaving. She also left a letter to Henry on his pillow for when he eventually left off writing and went to bed. By then she would be long gone.

The bus journey took little over an hour. When she stepped down onto the pavement at the corner of a narrow street, it was raining hard and cold. Few people were about and she felt this was a good omen. She found the house easily enough, a 1930s semi-detached with a small front garden. Houses of a similar age and style stretched along the street ahead for as far as she could see in the dim light of the street lamps. She checked the house number then opened the gate, walked up to the door and rang the bell.

A man in his forties opened the door. He looked at her with a bemused expression on his face.

"Eleanor, is it really you?" he asked.

She tucked a strand of wet hair behind her ear as she looked back at him, shivering slightly. She was drenched through.

"Hello John. May I come in?" she asked.

"Yes, of course." He moved aside and as she stepped into his tiny hall she saw him looking at the suitcase she was carrying. He made no comment about it, just closed the front door on the cold autumn night, took the suitcase from her and led her through to the front room, seating her in the armchair he'd obviously just vacated. He placed the suitcase on the floor beside her chair then put another log on the fire, using the poker to push it down so the flames licked at it hungrily, creating a good blaze.

"Would you like a cup of tea?" he asked, turning back to Ellie.

"Could I possibly have some warmed milk?" she asked. He smiled and with a slight bow left the room. Picking up the paperback from the little side table beneath his reading lamp, she called through the adjoining door to him.

"Ian Fleming? You still like James Bond, then. I'm glad to see you haven't changed much."

She listened as he poured milk into a pan and lit the gas beneath it. "No, in some ways I haven't changed at all," he said. "How did you find me?" He waited for her answer. She imagined him standing very still in his kitchen, watching the milk.

"I went back to Gravesend and met Gale, the receptionist from your old firm, for lunch. She managed to get a forwarding address for you and told me you'd moved to Cartwright, Harpers in town." Ellie said.

She heard him opening and closing a cupboard, then a kitchen drawer, before he came back into the living room with a mug of warmed milk which he handed to her. He sat down in the chair opposite her and watched as she sipped her drink.

He said, "I didn't know where you'd gone. I thought it was time I moved on. I hadn't realised you live nearby."

Ellie laughed. "Oh, come on John, do you expect me to believe that?"

He glanced at the fire before replying. When his eyes met hers again they were, like his voice, full of hurt. "I didn't meddle in your life, did I? I just wanted to be close by, know that I was breathing the same air as you, is that so difficult to understand?" She shook her head. Then he said quietly, "Why are you here, Eleanor?"

"I'm here because I know you still love me and I need your help," she said, her heart sinking as she saw the spark of hope in his eyes. "I love Henry, John. He's my husband. I also have a lovely little girl called Melody." For a split second his demeanour made her think of how a badly neglected dog must look, still sidling up to its master, hoping for kindness, after it had just been given a beating. Then he sat up straighter and his eyes took on a new look of pride and perhaps a kind of defiance.

"What do you need from me, then? Are you hoping to make me the new family solicitor because your parents refused to employ me in future? You really didn't have to come out on a night like this to find me. You could have made an appointment at Messrs. Cartwright, Harper and Green. I assure you, I would have treated you like any other client."

Ellie pressed her lips together until they became a thin line. Then she said, "I shouldn't have come. This was a mistake." She put her mug down on the side table and stood up.

"No!" the Solicitor cried, springing to his feet. "I'm sorry. Please sit back down and tell me how I can help. You're obviously desperate if you've come to me. Please."

Ellie shook her head and sat back down. "I came, John, because I hoped you'd be a friend to me. I thought I might trust you because I believe you really do care for me."

"I do. Please, Eleanor, tell me how I can be of assistance."

"I need complete discretion," she warned.

"Absolutely. I'm a solicitor. I'm good at keeping confidences."

"Yes, I know that, but what I'm asking will be difficult for you and may cause you problems," she said.

He bent to retrieve and hand her the mug of half-finished milk, by way of reply, then sat back down in his own chair, giving her his full attention.

"First of all, I'm going to need a place to stay for the foreseeable future. I've left my husband and I don't want him to find me. It breaks my heart to leave my little girl, but it's for the best. Henry doesn't deserve to lose her too."

"That can easily be arranged, I've room enough here."

"I don't want a relationship with you, John. Just a place to stay. I'll be your housekeeper if you wish, in recompense for my lodgings, but please don't expect or hope for anything else. You do realise, I need to live here in complete secrecy?"

"I understand."

"I left a letter for Henry telling him I was lonely at home."

"Lonely?"

"Yes. Our house is in the middle of fields and woodland, so our nearest neighbours are at least a couple of miles away. Although I regularly visited with my aunt and cousins on the farm, and I went to the village at least once a week, Henry was often away promoting his books, so it meant sometimes I was alone with a young child for days at a time."

"Did you ever discuss this with your husband before you left?"

Ellie glared at him, immediately defensive. "Not really. I used to nag him sometimes about being away so much. Listen, I didn't come here for marriage counselling. Loneliness was the only excuse I could come up with for leaving," she said, sounding for the moment like a mutinous teenager.

"You needed an excuse to leave? Forgive me for saying this. You aren't making a great deal of sense, Eleanor, and I doubt very much your husband will be deceived by the reason you gave for leaving. I'm certainly not." He folded his arms as if to underline his point.

"That's why I came to you. I need you to convince him for me. I want him to believe I'm out of reach. Perhaps you could say I've gone back to America because I wanted to go to some of the music festivals we've heard about. Have you heard about Woodstock? Or you could say I joined one of those peace movements, and that I'm living in a commune with lots of other young people, if you like."

"You want me to lie for you?"

"Yes. It isn't breaking the law. Would you do that for me?"

He gave no answer, so she went on, "I've told him I've been so deeply unhappy I didn't think it was healthy for Melody to be around me and I needed time to find myself. In a way that's sort of true too. I've said I will keep in touch with him through my solicitor."

"Wouldn't that make him think you were considering divorce?"

"No. I've told him in my letter that he's my one true love and I will be home as soon as I'm ready. I also requested, if he feels able, to send me money to live on through my solicitor."

"I see. And I'm to be that solicitor."

"I told him a long time ago, before we married, that I'd become involved with an older man when I was a teenager, but he doesn't know it was you. I also promised I would never lie to him, so it will have to be you that throws him off the scent."

Ellie looked at the man she had once believed she adored. She could see from the way he was looking at her that he really did still care and she was aware she was being both selfish and unfair. She also knew she had to tell him the truth because he'd learn soon enough anyway.

"I'm pregnant," she said before he could ask about her true motives, "and Henry would never allow me to go through with it. Once my child is born I will go back home."

He was studying her intently now, saying nothing. She found herself blathering on, her nerves as taut as violin strings. "If the baby's a boy I'll call him Christian because Henry's father was a vicar. I'll call a baby girl Harmony because she will bring peace and contentment to our family and it seems right that Melody's sister should also have a musical name. Henry will look at our new baby and will immediately forgive me," Ellie's eyes danced as she spoke of her dreams. "We both wanted more than one child, you know. He just didn't want me to risk my life having another, but I know everything will be alright. I've seen him greeting me and the new baby with such delight, in a vision."

"A vision?"

"Yes, I know it sounds crazy, but I looked out a window one day and I saw it all happening before me. I think it was God showing me the future."

"You believe you had some sort of religious experience?"

Ellie lowered her eyes. "Yes, I do," she said, her voice barely audible. The solicitor sighed and stood up, then picked up her suitcase. "Follow me," he said. "I will show you to your room."

Henry had been sitting in the waiting room at Messrs. Cartwright, Harper and Green for twenty minutes before he was called by a young woman in a white polo-neck jumper, miniskirt and boots standing at the waiting room door. She told him to follow her and took him up the stairs he'd come to know so well, two flights, to a door with a plaque that read 'J. Tumber, Esq.' and beneath that 'Solicitor'. The young woman knocked, put her head through the door and announced Mr. Fisherton.

Mr. Tumber, unlike his colleagues, never seemed to greet his clients at the door with a handshake, choosing instead to wait behind his desk. Henry thanked the retreating back of the secretary and pushed the door open to enter the office.

John Tumber had a stack of files on one corner of his desk and was bent over some papers, busily writing even as Henry took his seat. After several minutes of sitting in silence, waiting, Henry coughed to gain Tumber's attention. The man looked up, a look of irritation on his face. "I won't keep you a moment, Mr. Fisherton," he said, then continued writing. Not for the first time, Henry had the distinct impression Tumber didn't approve of him, though for the life of him he couldn't imagine why. The letters he received from Ellie, via the solicitor, were loving if somewhat brief, and even if the man had somehow managed to read them (which Henry sincerely doubted) there was nothing that would give rise to disdain. Henry didn't believe for one moment that Ellie had told the solicitor anything unkind or untrue about him.

At last Tumber paused in his work for a moment and opened the drawer to his desk. He took out a pale envelope and passed it to Henry with a tight-lipped smile, then went back to scanning his paperwork. Henry did not take offence easily. He said, "Thank you," to the patch of thinning hair on the top of the man's head, then carefully prised open the envelope. There were only a few lines in Ellie's neat handwriting, thanking him for his last letter and the money, requesting more news of Melody and finally declaring her love, asking for his patience, and saying that she hoped to be home soon. That was all. Disappointed, Henry turned the paper over to see if anything had been written on the back. Nothing. He opened the envelope again and peered inside. It was empty.

"Is this all?" He asked. Tumber exhaled noisily and put the cap back on his fountain pen, placing it on the desk next to the paper on which he'd been writing.

"That is all that my client instructed me to give you," he said.

"Did you send her my last letter? I told her I've given permission for four other houses to be built on the meadow. We'll have neighbours. She won't be alone anymore. I was sure she'd agree to come home, if I told her that."

"I did, indeed, forward your previous correspondence to my client, Mr. Fisherton. I can only guess that she wrote that," he nodded towards the envelope in Henry's hand, "before she received your letter. Overseas mail takes time, you know."

"I gave you my letter months ago, man. Surely she must have received it by now!" Exasperated, Henry leapt to his feet. He noticed that the solicitor cringed as if he expected Henry to strike him. Feeling a little ashamed, he said, his voice now quiet and reasonable, "I have a little girl, Mr. Tumber, desperate for her mother to be back next week for her sixth birthday. Melody's a wonderful child and I know her mother adored her." He ran his hand through his hair. "I can't believe Ellie's been gone seven long months, traipsing around the world, as you say, living in some hippy community, while her husband and child need her at home. She's not that sort of woman."

"I'm sorry, Mr. Fisherton. I have nothing more for you."

Henry's sigh was heartfelt. "I'm sorry too. It's not your fault. You're just doing your job."

"Indeed."

"You'll call me if you have any further news? Immediately?"

"Yes, I will."

Henry felt inside his jacket pocket and brought out a photograph, taken using one of the new self-developing Polaroid cameras. "This is the last picture I took of Ellie. I was thinking of hiring a private investigator to try to find her, but you say she doesn't want to be found?"

Tumber took the Polaroid snapshot and glanced at it. "I should wait another couple of months, Mr. Fisherton, and see what transpires. As you intimate, it wouldn't do to disrespect Mrs. Fisherton's wishes. I'm certain once your wife reads about the new housing she'll be in touch."

Henry shrugged. "Thanks. I guess you're probably right. I hope so, anyway. I look forward to hearing from you soon, then." With that he left, head low, dejected.

Tumber returned his gaze to the picture of Ellie that Henry had forgotten to take back. It was a good likeness, although the pregnancy had filled her face out somewhat. He reached for the new leather notebook she'd given him as a present for Henry that morning and slid the photograph inside. Then he placed the book in his desk drawer, pushing it to the back where he could easily forget about it. The man she'd married, who had so easily taken his place in her affections, didn't deserve gifts from Eleanor, he thought. She hadn't told Tumber that her husband had promised to have further houses built on his beloved meadow, just so she could have neighbours and not be lonely anymore. Perhaps she thought it as ludicrous an idea as Tumber himself did. Still, it meant she hadn't confided something that could be quite important to her decision to return. The idea of intercepting Henry's letters

174

once again slid into his mind and once again he pushed the notion away. He was quite comfortable in deceiving Henry Fisherton, but not so much the trusting, beautiful Eleanor, the woman he still loved. How he envied Henry her fidelity. It was becoming more difficult with each passing day to conceal his jealousy of her husband from her.

That evening John Tumber arrived home a little later than usual. His train had been delayed. He called through to the kitchen as he hung up his coat, but there was no reply. He walked through the house, looking for Ellie. There was no evening meal cooking on the stove and the table had not been set. Feeling uneasy he called up the stairs and upon hearing a faint cry, took the steps two at a time. He tapped on her bedroom door and heard another strangled cry. He twisted the doorknob and went inside. Ellie lay on the bed, cheeks flushed, eyes wild, trembling violently. With two strides, he crossed the room and took her hand. "Eleanor?" he said. She seemed completely oblivious to his presence. He touched her forehead. It was clammy. He looked down at her rounded belly as she groaned, and for the first time since he'd entered the room, noticed the dark stain on the bedclothes, slowly spreading beneath her.

He dropped her hand and ran down the stairs, grabbing the handpiece of the telephone in the hall to ring for assistance. His finger kept slipping as he tried to dial, the slow return movement of the round dialling mechanism intensifying his feeling of panic. When he finally got through he was assured the ambulance would be on its way shortly. Feeling helpless, he threw open his front door and darted up the path and out onto the pavement to look for it.

A middle-aged woman wearing a nurse's uniform was pushing a bicycle up the road towards him and he shouted to her for help. He explained there was a pregnant woman in trouble inside his home and she abandoned her bike in his front garden and hurried inside and up the stairs.

"What's your wife's name?" she asked Tumber.

"She's not …" Tumber hesitated, then said, "Eleanor, Ellie." He watched as the nurse leaned over Ellie, looking into her eyes and telling her she was here to help. After a brief examination, she told Tumber that she'd delivered babies before, but on this occasion, was very concerned. Then she quickly set about her business, flapping her hands at him to dismiss him from the room after he'd provided hot water and towels. The ambulance seemed to be taking forever. Ten minutes later the nurse had called Tumber into the room to break the news.

"I'm dreadfully sorry your wife didn't make it," she said, wiping her hands on a towel.

It was the second time she'd assumed they were married and again he didn't correct her. He stared at the lifeless form on the bed, not quite believing this was really happening. The nurse had wrapped the tiny lifeless form of the baby in a towel and had tucked it into the bed beside the woman – how could such a tiny scrap of innocence have been responsible for the death of a woman who had loved life so very much?

Tumber bent to kiss his beloved Eleanor's forehead. Her face was cooling, though her skin was still shiny with sweat, and as he tasted the trace of salt on his lips, something inside him shattered. He crumpled to his knees, head on his arms on the bed, hands snatching at the sheet, as he sobbed. The nurse allowed him a little time for his grief while she tidied the room. Where was the ambulance? As soon as he'd cried himself out, she went over to him and stretched out a tentative hand to pat his shoulder.

"The baby that died was a boy – but you still have a daughter," she said. "His twin sister is still alive. Let her be some consolation." He raised his head in bewilderment and she handed the little bundle to him. He slowly got to his feet, clasping the child tightly yet gently in his arms, mesmerised at the tiny, screwed up face. He couldn't speak.

Seeing this, the nurse became at once business-like again. "I've finished here and I've written up a report," she said. "I'd stay and wait for the ambulance, but I've another mother to attend to in the next street over. Would you give this to the ambulance driver when they take your little one to be checked over? It's a miracle she survived delivery." She handed him the papers. "I've written my contact details on the top in case there are any questions, ahh, what's your surname?" She took back the report and scribbled Tumber next to Ellie's name on the top sheet. "I don't suppose I'll hear anything further, though. It's obvious she'd already haemorrhaged and lost too much blood before anyone could have done anything to save her. It must have been a dreadful shock to find her like that. I am so sorry for your loss," she said again as she returned the papers to him and pulled on her coat.

"Thank you. I'm sure you did all that you could," Tumber managed, his voice little more than a croak. He showed her out, the small bundle still in the crook of his arm. As he closed the door behind her the baby began to squirm and cry. It was such a little, inadequate squeak. Tumber went back up the stairs and the motion soothed the child. Casting one last look at Ellie, pale and still as a waxwork model on the bed in her room, the other tiny bundle just as silent beside her, he carried the living child to his own room. He laid the infant on the middle of his bed then emptied his underwear out of the top drawer of his chest of drawers. He fetched a spare blanket from the airing cupboard and used it to line and pad out the bottom of the drawer then he laid the baby gently inside, covering her little body with a couple of pillow slips. She promptly fell asleep. He got onto his knees then and placed the drawer with the baby inside under the bed. After that he hurried back to Ellie's room to retrieve the midwife's report. He took it downstairs to the living room, glanced through it briefly then threw it on the fire, prodding it with the poker to ensure it burned thoroughly. He could hear the faraway sound of a siren.

A few minutes later the ambulance arrived, the driver apologising for the delay caused by a major road traffic accident. Tumber took the medics upstairs and showed them into Ellie's room. Worried that they might hear the living baby cry, Tumber felt the tension build in his body as the two men inspected the corpses and he began to talk to fill the quiet. The woman had been a friend, he told them, staying for a short while. She must have gone into labour early for when he found her she was barely conscious. There had been so much blood and he hadn't known what to do. He had immediately telephoned for an ambulance, then run out onto the street and pleaded with a woman passing by for help. She'd said she was a nurse and she had done her best to help deliver the baby, although mother and child had died shortly afterwards.

The medics asked for the nurse's name and he lied, telling them he'd been in such a state of shock he'd forgotten to ask and she hadn't offered it. They told him not to worry, that it couldn't be helped and probably wouldn't matter anyway. The medics left shortly afterwards, satisfied that there was no further need of their assistance. They informed the necessary authorities of the tragedy by radio and agreed with Tumber he could contact the next of kin if he wished. They told him a coroner's vehicle would be sent to collect the bodies in the morning.

After they'd gone, Tumber went to check on the baby hidden in his own bedroom. The child was still sleeping, her tiny chest rising and falling rhythmically. The trauma of birth had left the poor little soul exhausted, he thought. A wave of tenderness held the solicitor spellbound for several seconds.

Then he very gently kissed the soft, downy hair on the infant's head and murmured, "Don't worry, little one, I will take care of you. You shall be my daughter, Harmony, and I shall register you as such. I'll pay for the best care possible for you. You shall want for nothing, my darling little girl." He nodded to himself. That upstart, Fisherton, may have stolen Eleanor from him, but he would never know about the surviving child. Tumber had his revenge at last, and with it came the unexpected consolation prize of becoming a parent.

Chapter Twenty-Five

Later that evening John Tumber locked up his house and drove with the new child, snuggled in the wooden drawer, to Broadstairs, where he owned a large house on the sea front which had been converted to apartments.

He had stopped briefly at a chemist store on the way, having wrapped the child in a white lacy cardigan that had belonged to her mother and now served as a shawl, to purchase baby bottles, formula and nappies. He'd been relieved that the shop assistant, who rang up his purchases, had been distracted by an argument with her boyfriend earlier in the day, and was more interested in telling her colleague all about it than in showing any curiosity as to why a middle-aged man should have a new-born baby with him. He'd rehearsed what he'd say if he had been challenged or any interest shown. However, he doubted, as he left the store, that the shop girl would even remember him.

By the time he drew up at the parking area near the flats, the baby was howling. She needed changing and feeding. He picked her up from the drawer and cradled her in one arm, while retrieving the three bulky bags containing his purchases. It was a struggle to lock the car and let himself into the building, and then he knew as he pressed the light switch at the bottom of the stairs, that it was on a time-delay. He didn't have long to get to the second floor and unlock his flat before being plunged into darkness again, yet he managed somehow, although the child was still screaming. He dumped the bags just inside the door and threw the light switch, while awkwardly transferring the baby to his chest and patting her back. With a final sob, she quietened at last. He closed the door behind them with his foot and stood for a while, surveying the lounge and thinking what to do next.

The building housed three flats, each on a different level. The top and bottom floor flats had been rented out to provide him with extra income. The second-floor apartment in which he now stood he'd kept for himself, originally as a holiday retreat. It had two bedrooms so that he had extra accommodation if he wished to invite guests to stay. This had been the flat to which he had intended bringing the young Ellie when she'd agreed to run away with him, before her parents had intervened. He had therefore taken some pains to make it as comfortable as possible, paying extra for good quality carpeting, fitting the kitchen out with the best appliances and adding an en-suite bathroom to the master bedroom. The bottom and top floor occupants had no such luxury and shared the main bathroom on the landing just below his flat.

Now that she had quietened, he lowered Harmony back into the crook of his arm and looked down at her. She looked back with a solemn, other-worldly gaze.

"We're going to sort out some milk for you first – I'll have to boil your bottles to sterilise them. Then we'll bath and change you, by which time your milk should be cool enough for you to take." He felt slightly ridiculous talking to the baby, as if he was really talking to himself. He'd have to get used to it, he thought, making his way to the kitchen.

Once she'd been bathed, he took one of the nappies from the dozen he'd bought and then he realised he'd forgotten to buy safety pins. The fluffy, snowy white square of the nappy seemed big enough to completely envelop the tiny baby and he had absolutely no idea how to go about putting it onto the bottom half of her. However, after several attempts, he settled on folding it in half and, although it still looked huge, it was much preferable to the old hand towel he had wrapped about her beneath Ellie's white cardigan for the journey here. He tied the nappy at the corners, feeling clumsy as the baby wriggled, and then secured it with a little pair of rubber pants which he'd bought as a pack of three. Satisfied that this would keep her dry for a while, he topped this with a little cotton nightdress and by the time he'd finished she seemed happier. Harmony took her milk surprisingly easily, although it had taken a few attempts to encourage her to take the teat into her mouth. Before the bottle was empty she was sleeping and Tumber laid her back in the drawer which he'd utilised as a makeshift cot and placed this on the floor beside his bed. Tomorrow he would buy a little pram that could also be used as a carrycot.

Once he was satisfied the baby was content, Tumber left the bedroom with the door open so he would hear the baby if she awoke. He made himself a coffee and drew up a chair near to the small table on which the telephone sat. He was glad now that he'd decided to have it installed when he'd refurbished the flat, so that he could be reached by the solicitors at work whenever he stayed here. He telephoned the office now and left a message on the machine to ask his secretary to cancel any morning appointments as he would not be in until the afternoon.

Next, he rang Mrs. Nettle, the woman who cleaned his flat and kept the food cupboards well-stocked, to ask if she would be available to babysit between 1pm and 6pm the following day. He had always been generous to her, occasionally topping up her already reasonable wages with the odd bonus, and he knew he could rely on her discretion. There would be time enough to invent a story of a quiet wedding and wife's illness and, after an appropriate passage of time, subsequent death.

After that, he rang his housing agent at his home. Having the man's private number was a privilege few clients could boast. Anthony Collins was an old friend who'd attended the same public school as Tumber and now enjoyed a good working relationship with him. Tumber put work his way whenever possible and was now calling in a favour. He explained that a visitor had died in one of his properties and the authorities would be collecting the body the following day, so he would need somebody to open up the house early and wait until they arrived. He also asked that Collins arrange a deep clean of the property and that it be immediately advertised as a furnished house for rent. Tumber had decided to load his clothes into his car, together with anything else he wanted or needed from the house, after work the following evening. They talked for some time then Collins agreed to all that Tumber had requested.

As he replaced the receiver, the solicitor realised he was hungry. His first thought was that he fancied fish and chips. However, he couldn't leave the baby and didn't want to disturb her while she slept, so he made do with a baked potato and tinned tuna.

After he'd eaten, he made further plans. He decided he would spend the afternoon at work next day informing Henry Fisherton of his wife's death and reading her Will to him. Hopefully, even if Fisherton did discover where Eleanor had been staying, he would not now realise the house belonged to Tumber. The solicitor would see that her personal effects were returned to her husband and, if necessary, he would even help with funeral arrangements. He'd ensure that his other client files were up to date and easily accessible by one of the other solicitors in the event of any problems, then he would speak to his senior partner and request a leave of absence.

He would need to equip the flat better for the child and organise more permanent, professional childcare so that when he went back to work he would not have to worry. Perhaps he could hire a live-in nanny, instead of relying on daytime care. He would telephone the local agencies and set up some interviews. Of course, once the child was four or five he would send her off to one of the best private schools available to ensure she had the best possible education available. By that time, he envisioned having found a proper house in Broadstairs. He didn't mind the long drive to work each day and he could even commute come to that, if it meant his secret was safe. However, they couldn't live in the holiday flat forever. Harmony would need more space and a garden to play in.

The child would make such a difference to the dull and lonely existence he'd endured before. There was so much to look forward to now. He treated himself to a whiskey, made up a bottle of formula for the baby's night feed, then took himself off to bed. It had been an exhausting day, and even though his heart had been broken by Eleanor's death, he had managed to keep his wits about him.

Tumber decided he would worry about how to go about registering the child later. After all, he had six weeks to sort something out. He was sure he could find a way, although he knew he'd be breaking the law. He already felt he loved the little girl enough to risk his career as a solicitor, and probable imprisonment, just to keep her as his own. She was Eleanor's child, after all. An idea was beginning to form. Could that be the answer? Just for the sake of official requirements, perhaps on paper she could be another woman's child, with Tumber named as the father. It might be difficult, but not impossible with the right kind of financial inducement, to find a suitable woman willing to perjure herself. Later, of course, the 'mother' would abandon both child and common-law husband, leaving him as the sole legal guardian. He switched off the bedside lamp ready to sleep.

Chapter Twenty-Six

The funeral was held in St. Luke's church, Bushwell and was well-attended. The day was appropriately overcast and damp, despite the time of year. Henry stood, uncomfortable in a black suit and tie, hand in hand with his small, unnaturally quiet daughter, and he was trying not to cry. All he could think about was how Ellie had always loved the spring: the fresh scent of new grass, plants and trees coming back to life, birds and other wildlife seeking out mates after the long dark days of winter. How could Ellie be dead?

He looked over at Tumber standing slightly apart from the other mourners. Their eyes met and held for long seconds. The solicitor wore a serious expression on his face, conveying something between sympathy and professional civility. Henry hated him in a way he had hated no other person in his entire life. How could that appalling man use the excuse of client confidentiality to explain why he'd kept Ellie's presence in England and her pregnancy a secret? Even now the man refused to reveal where she'd been staying. He continued to stare long and hard at the solicitor, willing him to show some small sign of remorse. There was none. The man must be a sociopath, Henry decided, and was glad to see him look away and retreat from sight, melting into the crowd of villagers, when Ellie's parents joined Henry and his daughter at the graveside.

Henry's mother-in-law was openly weeping and her husband had his arm about her as they looked down into the grave. When the vicar had finished the burial ceremony and the crowds had begun to disperse, Ellie's mother turned on Henry

"How could you not have known she was pregnant? How could you have let her die?" she cried.

"Please, Honey, think of Melody. That's not going to help," her husband took her arm and, sending a look of sheer misery at Henry, led the distressed woman away.

"I just want to know," she wailed, her voice drifting back to Henry. Beside him, Melody clasped Baby more tightly to her chest and looked up at her father. Henry tried to smile, blinking away tears.

"Grandma doesn't mean it, Darling," he said pulling her closer to him. "She knows Daddy would have done anything to keep Mummy with us. Mummy just wanted to surprise us with another little one like you, but it wasn't meant to be. They're in Heaven now."

Melody said nothing. She didn't even cry. Clinging to her doll she allowed Henry to take her back to the car and he drove them home in silence.

As the car turned off the lane towards their house Melody suddenly said, "Daddy, what are those men doing?"

Henry had already seen the workmen ahead, working with a theodolite and he muttered an expletive. As soon as he'd killed the engine, he leapt from the car, calling out to them. He hurried over, leaving Melody behind, watching from the car window, while he talked the men into leaving the meadow for the time being. He explained that he'd just lost his wife and that he and his child needed some privacy. He promised them he'd call their boss immediately.

With Ellie gone, he realised he didn't want any more houses to be built on the land. In fact, he never had really wanted it, he'd just been trying to please his wife, prove his love for her with a futile grand gesture. He guessed he'd always had the idea in the back of his mind that once they were reconciled he could convince her they didn't need other houses nearby. He wanted the meadow to be left just as it was. There would be other ways for her to enjoy companionship. He'd stay home more often. Now it was too late, for she was gone and he'd waited too long to renege on the contract. He hoped the wealthy owner of the construction company from the city would be sympathetic.

Henry walked back to the car and got into the driver seat. He looked back over his shoulder at Melody and gave her what he hoped was a reassuring smile. "It's going to be alright," he told her, before starting the engine and driving the short distance to their house. "Daddy needs to use the telephone, sweetheart," he said.

He let himself and Melody into their home and took the stairs two at a time, barely registering that his small daughter was climbing the stairs after him, still clutching her doll. He went straight to his study, throwing his keys down onto the desk and rifling through his desk drawer to find a small card. He lifted the hand piece of the telephone and, looking at the card, dialled the number. He turned to face the door and his child, who stood, with her thumb in her mouth, watching him as he listened to the ringtone and waited for the call to connect.

However, once he got through to the man in charge of the project, it took less than five minutes to realise his fears were grounded. If Henry seriously wanted to stop the building work he would have a fight on his hands – a long, expensive legal battle that he might well lose.

At about the same time John Tumber was visiting and assessing possible boarding schools for the four-year-old Harmony to attend once she was five, Henry Fisherton was busily erecting an internal wall in his house in what had once been his study. He had begun by removing his desk and chair and bookcases – carefully packing his collection of fiction and reference books into labelled boxes – before his ten-year-old daughter had even been awake. Most of the contents of his study would be collected later that morning by a storage company. Meanwhile, he had stripped back the carpet and carried up the materials and equipment he needed for the wall. After much preparation, he began to work approximately four feet in front of the window to the side of the house. He was about half-way through when Melody padded in with bare feet, still wearing her pyjamas, her hair ruffled from sleep. She was holding a cereal bowl, spooning cornflakes into her mouth as she watched him.

"Dad, what are you doing?" she asked.

Henry scraped away the excess cement from the brick he'd just placed and sat back on his hunches.

"What does it look like?"

"Building a brick wall? Why are you building a wall in front of your office window?" The spoon clattered in her empty bowl and she wiped the milk from her mouth with the back of her hand.

"It isn't going to be my office anymore; I'm making the room into a bedroom. We don't need two windows in here," he pointed to the other window through which sunlight streamed, "and more wardrobe space would be useful. So, I am going to put up a wall here, plaster and paint it then a man's coming in to fit a wide walk-in closet."

"O-k-a-y," Melody said, drawing out the word, obviously puzzled. "So where are you going to do your writing without being disturbed?"

Henry picked up another brick. "I'll talk to you about that later. For now, I have to get on. I've got someone coming to measure up for the new carpet and to talk about new bedroom furniture this afternoon. I want to be ready. Isn't your friend, Hayley, coming over this morning?"

"Yup. I'd better get ready. We're catching the bus into town with her mum because Hayley needs some new shoes, and we thought we'd stop by the record shop. D-a-d …?"

Henry sat back on his heels again, dusting his hands on the thighs of his jeans before pulling his wallet from his pocket. He handed a couple of notes to Melody. "Don't ask for another advance on your pocket money for the rest of this month," he said. Melody snatched at the money and kissed his cheek.

"Thanks, Dad. I'll be back lunchtime."

"You be careful and do as Mrs. Hunter says. I know what you two girls can be like when you're out together."

By this time his daughter was in the bathroom. "I will," she called back, her mouth full of toothpaste. "I promise."

The wall was at knee height by the time he heard her come out of the bathroom. The record player went on in her room and Donny Osmond began singing that he'd still be loving until the 'twelfth of never'. Henry got to his feet, stepped over the brickwork and went to the window for one last look out before he sealed the window away from the rest of the world behind the new wall.

He saw her, his beautiful wife, immediately. She was standing looking up at the window. Her hair was longer than it had ever been since the first time he'd met her, but to keep it from falling in her face, she'd plaited the front locks and pulled them round past her ears to secure them at the back of her head, forming a kind of headband. As for her clothes, they were bright and flamboyant, for she was dressed as a hippy. Most startling of all, she held the hands of two beautiful children, a fair-haired little girl dressed in a pink dress on one side and a dark-haired boy of the same age and height, dressed in dungarees on the other. Ellie released her hold on the little girl momentarily and raised her hand to wave, as if she could see Henry looking down at her, and numerous bangles jiggled about on her wrist. The flood of longing for her was almost intolerable and the impulse to try to get through the window somehow, to join her in whatever dimension she was still alive was so intense that he forced himself to turn away. She didn't need him, she was already happy with more children. She was waving, he liked to believe, to one of his other selves.

Henry knew, without the tiniest flicker of doubt, that he was one of the rare people described by the scientist with the solemn eyes as being gifted at seeing through the portal whenever he looked rather than just the three times usually experienced by others. Fighting back tears he glanced back out the window and found he could barely see the lawn and road because there were now branches of a tree in full leaf obscuring the view. He smiled to himself.

"Dad, why isn't there very much of that stuff around the bricks near the bottom right-hand corner?" He hadn't heard Melody come back into the room. She stood now, dressed in a green polo neck sweater, bell-bottomed jeans and trainers, her pretty face perplexed. She looked so much like her mother. He ran a hand through his hair and stepped back over the brickwork to look where she was pointing.

"Well, it's just an idea I had that if I ever wanted to take the wall down again it might help to have a 'weak spot' that I can start at and that seemed the most obvious place. If I didn't do it there, when the plaster covers it up, the place would be too difficult to find."

"O-k-a-y." She often spoke as if she thought him completely mad. He thought she was going to ask why he was putting the wall up in the first place if he was already considering a time when he might want to pull it down again and he wasn't sure how he'd answer her. Instead she said, laying her head for a moment against his arm, "Daddy, you aren't going to make me change bedrooms, are you? I mean I know this room is bigger but I really prefer the room I have now."

"No," he laughed, kissing her head.

"Good," she said, grinning up at him, "because no offence, Dad, but this room has always given me the creeps. I'm not surprised you don't want it for an office anymore. I bet it's haunted or something."

"Don't be silly, Ellie. I helped design and build this house and we're the only ones to have ever lived here, remember?"

He hadn't even realised he'd called her by her mother's name until she said, "Melody, Dad. My name's Melody. I wouldn't mind if it was haunted by Mum, though. It would be nice to see her again." She drifted towards the door, then stopped and looked back at him, a bright smile pasted on her face. "Got to go, Dad. See you later. Don't work too hard!" She blew him a kiss and skipped away, off down the stairs and out of the front door.

At half past one Henry finished his work and had a quick wash before going down to the kitchen to make some sandwiches. He read the morning newspaper, sitting at the kitchen table, and drank a cup of tea. By two o'clock there was still no sign of Melody, so he started in on the plate of sandwiches he'd prepared, determined not to worry. Mrs. Hunter had probably treated the girls to burgers and milk shakes.

After he'd finished eating, he took his cup and plate to the sink, took an apple from the fruit bowl and collected the morning's post, taking it through to the lounge to read. He could relax for a while and wait for the carpet and furniture reps. The brickwork was finished. He would wait a couple of days before plastering the wall and then leave it to dry out. He didn't need to paint it until after the wardrobe frame had been fitted, before the doors were attached. He bit into his apple, holding it by his teeth while he leafed through the letters. There were a couple of junk mail leaflets, a letter with the local estate agent's stamp on the front and one which was obviously from his solicitor. These were the two letters he'd been waiting for before he could discuss his decision with Melody.

He found himself staring at the unopened solicitor's envelope in his hand while reflecting on all that had happened over the past four years. He'd worked hard to earn the cash to fight his legal battle and it had been a protracted and arduous campaign, although it might well have been prolonged even further if he hadn't finally settled out of court on the advice of his solicitor.

The deal was that four more houses could be built on the meadow and no more. They would have to be in the style of his house and there would be a private road to the small estate which would be named after this house. It would be called Whitewood Close. The rest of the meadow, the woodland and surrounding fields of Darrington Way were to remain untouched and protected. It was the best he could do; hopefully much of the wildlife, and in particular the pretty white butterflies for which he'd named his house, would remain with most of their habitat untouched and secure.

The letter from the Estate Agents would be about the Tenancy agreement he'd had drawn up. His house would be let out on short term leases for the foreseeable future. No tenant would have permission to alter the house and garden in any way and the agents would see to the general upkeep and any repairs. He'd left strict instructions that the window at the top side of the house should be left untouched. He had told the agents he'd left the window on the outside of the house for purely decorative purposes. Inside it had been bricked up to provide more cupboard space. It had been the only way he could think of to deal with the problem of the portal and the unique capacity of the window while he was away. For he intended to leave behind the heart-breaking reminders his house continually provided, to take his daughter to be educated in, and enjoy the benefits of America. His only worry now was that she would rebel and hate him for taking her away from her friends and the life she knew, but he felt the time was right as she'd just finished junior school.

The doorbell rang, interrupting his thoughts. It was a man and woman who'd come to give quotes for the carpets and furniture, and to talk through his requirements. They'd brought several catalogues with them which they looked through together and discussed before they went to take their measurements.

Henry was standing at the bedroom door watching them work with their tape measure when he heard the front door slam and Melody hurried up the stairs, clutching a couple of carrier bags. With a quick, "Hi Dad," she pushed past him to use the bathroom, then hurried straight to her room to play her new records. The woman looked up from the notebook on which she'd been jotting down figures and Henry grinned and shrugged. "Kids!" he said. She smiled then went back to her calculations.

By the time the reps had finished, shaken Henry by the hand, and left, the now familiar strains of the record 'Tiger Feet' by the pop group Mud was blaring out from Melody's bedroom. Henry grinned, tapping lightly on her door, knowing that when he opened it he would find her with her thumbs hooked into the top of the pockets of her jeans, shaking her feet in time to the music and leaning forward and back as she attempted to follow the popular dance moves. He sat on the edge of her bed, watching until the record finished. Then he patted the space on the bed next to him and she came to sit down, panting slightly from her exertions.

"There's something I need to talk to you about," he began.

"Oh Dad, if you're going to tell me about the birds and bees and the female curse, please don't bother. I already know all about it," she cut in.

"Do you now?" he said, amused. "No, it's not about that, although perhaps we should have a little chat about just exactly what you do think you know later. I was thinking about how you said that you wished you could see more of Gran and Grandpa Harrison. How would you feel about moving out to the States for a while?"

It hadn't been how he'd intended to say it, blurting it out in a nervous rush, but he was relieved to be getting it over with. Surprisingly she didn't look too upset. She seemed to be thinking about something. He needed to be cautious. "Only I've been offered a pretty good publishing contract out there, but I'd need to be in New York quite a lot for research, rewrites and book promotions and it just makes sense to live there for a while. What do you think?" Silly to ask really. It didn't much matter what his daughter thought, the decision had already been made; he'd been planning this move for almost a year now.

"I think I'd like it," she said. "Donny Osmond and all his brothers, you know, the Osmonds, live in America."

"You do know that you'd be extremely unlikely to meet your favourite pop stars," Henry warned.

"Oh, I know. You'd be more likely to take me to a concert to see Donny perform, though, for a birthday treat or something. Dad," she got up and began pulling at his arm, "Can we have tea in front of the telly tonight? I want to watch *The Tomorrow People* — it's getting really good."

Pleased that their chat had gone so well, he laughed. "Okay, but on one condition," She paused, waiting by the door and he knew she was expecting him to say she'd have to help with the dishes afterwards. Instead he said, "Tomorrow you'll come with me to buy something."

"Okay. That all?"

"No. I want to get a sapling, a special young tree called a Silver Birch. I'm going to plant it at the side of the house to replace an old tree that once grew quite near the spot on which this house was built, and I want you to help me."

Melody slipped the letter she had written into her pocket and joined her husband, Roger, in the car. Without a word or as much as a glance in her direction, he revved the car engine, pulling away from the drive and out onto the lane, accelerating so that she was pushed back into her seat. They were headed for London, Harley Street, and the therapist Henry's money was paying for her to see.

She missed her father. It was her own fault because she'd made his life so difficult after he'd married his second wife, the inscrutable Siobhan Kerry, an Irish-American with a passion for writing murder mysteries. Siobhan had made every effort to befriend her step-daughter, taking an interest in her artwork, offering to take her to exhibitions during vacations, buying her clothes and make-up. Still Melody resented the woman and because of her attitude and behaviour, Siobhan had eventually given up trying to befriend her step-daughter.

Too late, Melody had realised that her father hadn't forgotten her mother; he had simply been lonely and wished to get on with his life. He had wanted to free himself from the tragedy that had seemed to colour his every waking thought for so many years. However, by that time Melody had already decided not to go back to college, and had on impulse married a man twenty-two years her senior that she knew Henry despised.

Surprisingly, Henry's reaction, when they told him about the marriage and their intention to return to England, was to sign over the deeds for the house he had built in Whitewood Close. Melody realised sometime later that this had been his way of ensuring Melody would begin her married life with some sort of security. Being the fool she was, she'd immediately had the house put into their joint names, as a final act of defiance.

Now, Roger parked the car and opened the passenger door to help Melody out. He took her arm as they climbed the steps to the elegant building, but she shrugged him off. Once inside the receptionist directed Roger, with a glassy smile, to a waiting area and then took Melody to meet Dr. Greaves-Hamilton, the man Melody very much hoped would be able to help her.

As it turned out, Dr. Greaves-Hamilton was a woman. She rose to shake hands with Melody across the expanse of a highly polished mahogany desk, and then re-seated herself in order to refer to the computer monitor on her desk. The receptionist left the room, closing the door with a quiet click behind her. Melody looked about the room with interest. Unconsciously she had wrapped her arms about herself as if cold.

"Do I need to lie on that couch?" she asked at last.

The therapist smiled. "Only if you wish to," she said. "Most of my clients prefer the armchair." Melody perched on the edge of the chair, fighting the impulse to nibble on a thumb nail to relieve her nerves.

"Now, Melody – or would you prefer me to call you Mrs. Stockman?" The woman looked over the top of the computer monitor at her and Melody shook her head. "Melody, then. Let's get the preliminaries out of the way; your full name is Mrs. Melody Aria Stockman – your maiden name being Fisherton. You're twenty-six years old, born in Canterbury on 28th April, 1964." She looked up and Melody nodded, "That's correct."

"You are a housewife …"

"I'm an artist. I paint landscapes, real and imaginary, and the owner of a local gallery sells them for me. I just haven't worked for a while," Melody interrupted.

"Noted. You previously lived in the States until 1984 and you currently reside at 3 Whitewood Close, Darrington Way, Bushwell, near Rainham in Kent."

Melody nodded again.

"Can you give me your postcode, please?"

Melody did so.

"Thank you." The doctor clicked the mouse to close the file on her computer and rose from her seat to come around the desk to sit in the armchair opposite Melody. "Your husband has spoken to me at some length on the telephone as to how he feels I can be of assistance, but now I need to talk to you about how you believe I can help you. How are you feeling today?"

Melody eyed the woman, with her sleek, shoulder-length hair and perfectly made-up face. She was watching her, grey eyes peering through gold-rimmed spectacles. She sat comfortably in her chair, one leg crossed over the other, pen poised above the notebook on her knee. She had an open file on the little table next to her which Melody assumed contained her medical records.

"Miserable," Melody said, then blurted out. "I'm bloody furious."

"Good." Dr. Greaves-Hamilton jotted something on her notebook. "Can you explain why that is?"

"Well, for a start my husband is trying to get me put away."

"I understand you tried to harm yourself. Twice."

"No, once. It was when I first discovered my father had died of a heart attack."

"I just need to clarify: that was about three years ago?" The therapist leafed through the papers in the file on the table.

"Yes, 1987. I overdosed on painkillers. What happened more recently was an accident. I slipped while crossing a stream and hit my head, knocking myself out. The water level was high due to heavy rain and I nearly drowned as a result."

"Ah, yes. Your husband said that you ran from the house and that you were hysterical. He followed you, he said, because he was afraid you meant to harm yourself."

"Huh, that's a joke!" Melody's eyes flashed in anger. "He wouldn't care if I had killed myself. In fact, it would probably suit him. He doesn't care at all about my feelings. Did he also tell you that despite knowing that I wanted children he lied to me and went ahead and had a vasectomy without telling me?"

"He did not. Is that why you were upset?"

"No," Melody shuffled back further into the well-upholstered seat, ready to relax. "He tried to steal the doll my mother gave me. He thinks it's valuable, but whether it is or not, I've had it since I was five and it's very precious to me." She realised she sounded childish, particularly when Dr. Greaves-Hamilton looked at her over her spectacles and said, "That's interesting."

"It was the last time I ever saw my mother, when she gave it to me," Melody quickly added. "I wouldn't sell it for the world and Roger knows that."

"So, you argued about it and then you ran away?"

"Yes, and I slipped and fell into the rush of water. It was an accident that happened *because* he was chasing me, not because I wished to hurt myself."

"I understand he found you and took you to hospital."

"Not because he wanted to save me. He wanted the doll."

The doctor made a note on her pad. "Then when you were released from hospital you ran away again."

"I left my husband, yes. I didn't run."

"Yet according to him you left in the middle of the night and gave no explanation, and no indication as to where you were going or might be staying. He said that you had been behaving irrationally during the day leading up to your departure. Was that something to do with the doll again?"

"No!" she paused. "Well, I suppose so, Yes. Let me explain. I told Roger I wanted a divorce and he refused to let me leave. He locked me in the spare bedroom and went off out in the car. When he got back he said that I could go if I gave him my doll. I told him I no longer had it and he wouldn't believe me. He searched me, as if he thought I could hide it in my clothes! Then he turned out the bags I'd packed. After that he went through the whole house, upending furniture and turning cupboards out. I followed him about and watched. In the end, he shouted in my face that I'd be sorry and shook me by my shoulders before storming out again. He drove off in the car and I repacked my bags. I left then and yes, it was quite late and, no, I didn't tell him where I was going. Unfortunately, he caught me walking along the lane. He had a man I didn't know with him and they dragged me back to the car, kicking and screaming. I didn't know the other man was the new village GP. He gave me an injection, some sort of sedative, and put me to bed. I think Roger told him it was me who had wrecked the house."

The therapist, who had been listening in silent concentration, now closed her notebook and placed it on top of the file on the table. She leaned forward, clasping her hands together around one knee.

"Melody, do you understand that both your GP and the Mental Health Psychologist from the hospital agree with your husband that your mental state requires formal assessment?"

Melody began to bite her thumb nail, no longer caring if she looked afraid.

"That means you will need to go before a panel of specialists. They will talk to you and you will have the opportunity to speak up for yourself, but ultimately, they will decide whether you should be committed to a secure mental health facility for treatment, until such time as you are considered well enough to leave. They can do this under certain sections of the 1983 Mental Health Act. That's why it's known as being sectioned. Now, your step-mother has provided funds for me to try to help you."

Melody removed the thumb nail from her mouth and mumbled, "I'm very grateful."

Dr. Greaves-Hamilton smiled, although her eyes remained serious. "What I need you to do now, Melody, is to be as open and honest with me as you possibly can. I want you to tell me everything, right from the time when you first began to feel depressed. It doesn't matter how long it takes. Are you prepared to do that?"

Melody nodded. After answering several further questions, she settled back in her chair and then she began her tale.

Chapter Twenty-Nine

You asked me about my childhood, so it seems as good a place as any to begin. In my opinion, people always assume that if you suffer from severe depression, it must have a root cause in your childhood, especially once they learn you lost someone close to you. My mother died just before my sixth birthday and I remember feeling very sad that I wasn't going to see her anymore. However, I was lucky enough to have the best father in the world. He brought me up single-handed, but made sure I always had family and friends around and that I wanted for nothing. We were very close.

I think I was ten or eleven when we moved to the States to be nearer by maternal grandparents. Dad was a writer and he then also became a major shareholder in a publishing company which he helped manage. That was where I met Roger when I was nineteen.

I had just arrived home on vacation from Art College and Dad had promised to take me out to lunch so we could catch up properly. He'd said he had something important to tell me, so I arrived early and was waiting in the reception area near his office when this man introduced himself to me. Once he discovered I was Melody Fisherton, he told me he was hoping my father would be publishing a book he'd written about antique toys. He was one of those people who travelled the country looking through old junk for items that could be restored and resold as antiques or collectors' items. After a few years on the road he had decided to concentrate on toys and had written a book about his work and how to value different items.

My Dad called him into his office at that point, and after a while he came back out and left without speaking to me again. My Dad told me they'd had to turn down his book because a lot of it had been plagiarised. I commented that I'd got the impression he'd taken the news badly. However, my Dad was never one to criticise anyone and brushed aside my questions, asking how I'd been enjoying college. Over lunch he told me he was getting married again. I was devastated and jealous – pathetic really for a woman of almost twenty.

Although his fiancé was kind and patient with me, I wasn't very nice to her. I'm ashamed to admit I took every opportunity to pick a fight with her, after which I'd run to Dad and complain about her, trying to undermine their relationship. It caused no end of problems between them. One day, Dad took me aside and suggested that once I finished college he would help me to find me my own apartment so I could move out of their home. His wedding went ahead and I pretended I was fine with that, although I secretly wrote to my college informing them I wouldn't be returning to finish my course.

There was a period of peace in the house for a while. Dad took us to the Winter Ball in New York. It's a charity affair and a lot of writers and people who work in the publishing industry, and of course their families, attend. All authors working with Dad's company automatically received courtesy invitations. Anyway, Roger Stockman was there (I guess the invites were sent out before they turned his book down) and he asked me to dance. When we got back to our table Dad waited for my dance partner to be out of earshot – I think he'd gone to get me a drink or something – and told me he didn't like or trust the man and he advised me not to encourage his attentions. I was still smarting from Dad's apparent rejection of me in favour of his new wife, so when Roger later asked if he could see me again I agreed.

We dated without Dad's knowledge for six weeks. When Roger proposed, I accepted, smugly thinking it would punish Dad; he'd married someone I didn't like so I would do likewise. Roger organised the special licence and that was that. He told me he wanted to go to the UK and set up a business buying, restoring and selling antique dolls. He'd seen my doll by then and had told me he was certain there wasn't another like it in existence, but he didn't suggest selling it at that point. I think he was biding his time. Anyway, my head was full of romantic notions and we made all sorts of plans before confronting Dad.

It still hurts when I remember the day we went to his office and presented him with the fait accompli - we were married and there was nothing he could do about it. Dad looked at me with such sorrow, not even disappointment, just sadness and love. I'd anticipated a huge scene, but instead he congratulated us, shook Roger's hand and invited him – us – over to dinner that evening. He said he had in mind a wedding gift for us. That was when he gave me the house where I'd spent the best part of my childhood. He'd already sent the deeds to his solicitor for my title to be registered and he handed me the key just before we sat down to eat.

I'm not sure if I was ever really in love with Roger. I certainly believed I was and must have been terribly infatuated with him and perhaps in love with the idea of being in love. Once we were in England and settled into the house, Roger began his work collecting and restoring dolls, buying spare parts during occasional trips away. Sometimes I went with him, but most often I stayed home. Then he'd spend many hours carefully cleaning, sewing, gluing and painting to restore the dolls he'd found. It was intricate work and he was good at it. Whenever I saw a finished project, it never failed to fill me with admiration. He made a fair living restoring and selling dolls at auctions or to antique shops. It wouldn't be long, he would tell me, before he had his own shop and then he'd be able to advertise his restoration services to other dealers. The future seemed bright and I thought we were happy.

We'd been in England some three years when Siobhan called me to tell me my father had suffered a massive heart attack. I took the first flight back to the States. Roger agreed I should go, although he didn't offer to come with me. It didn't occur to me at the time that he ought to have been more supportive. I never dreamed I would lose my lovely Dad so soon; he was only forty-eight. I knew I'd behaved badly towards him. I'd always believed I would have time to make it right, you see. I used to fantasise about taking his first new-born grandchild to see him and then, of course, we'd talk and sort things out. He was such a wonderful, special person, so very kind and wise and I wanted to make him proud of me again.

On the aeroplane, I regretted that I'd waited. I thought how I'd let him down and I planned to apologise to both Dad and Siobhan, maybe stay a while once he was out of hospital to spend time with them.

However, it was already too late. When I arrived at the hospital I discovered he had already passed away. I was distraught when they told me, and crying hysterically, I ran out of the building, onto the street. I kept on running along the sidewalks, across roads, through darkened parks, until I came to a cemetery. I sat on a bench, head bowed in pain, no tears left. After an hour or so, I walked to a late-night drug store and purchased a bottle of water and pain killers for my headache, probably caused by the combination of dehydration and too many tears. My stepmother, the woman I'd treated with such disdain, had been searching for me all this time. She finally found me unconscious on the cemetery bench, having overdosed on the pills. She managed to get me back to the hospital, stayed by my bedside until I'd recovered then took me home and cared for me.

In all that time, almost three weeks, Roger never once tried to contact me. In the end, Siobhan rang him and explained what had happened, told him she'd booked a flight for him to join us and that he should come and take me home.

In the meantime, Siobhan reassured me that Dad knew I loved him and she insisted he wouldn't want me to remember him with sorrow and regret. She told me he'd had a few personal items stored for me and when I felt stronger I was to let her know and she'd arrange for them to be sent to me. She told me she would always be there for me whenever I needed her and that she considered me her daughter.

When Dad's Will was read, he'd left everything to Siobhan apart from our home, which he'd already given to me, and the rest of the land known as Darrington Way which he passed to a cousin, as he wanted it to remain in the Fisherton family name.

Roger was beside himself with anger when he found out, and raged that I'd been cheated of my inheritance, but I felt relieved. I didn't want all the worries that would have come if I'd inherited shares in his publishing company, and I knew my stepmother deserved and would appreciate having them more than me. As for the land around the house, I knew a condition of the Will was that there should be no further attempt at building on Darington Way and that was good enough for me; it's a place of great natural beauty with fields, woods and even, as you know, a stream running through it. I believe it has some sort of preservation order on it so was legally protected anyway.

I returned home and life went on much as it had before. I kept in touch with my step-mother and tried not to be too sad when I thought about Dad. I'll admit deep down I felt melancholy a lot of the time, but I told myself there was so much to look forward to in the future.

After yet another couple of years had passed and I hadn't become pregnant, I began to fret. Roger didn't seem overly concerned. He suggested I start painting again to take my mind off things. Once I relaxed, he said, I would probably conceive without any trouble. Of course, by then he'd already had the vasectomy, booking himself into a private clinic while I thought he was away on a trip to find new stock. Then his business began to fail and he suggested we sell my doll. I refused, telling him I was keeping it to give to our first child. (I was always convinced our first would be a girl.) That was when it all came out about the vasectomy; he said that he'd never wanted children, didn't even like them. He'd just agreed with me about having a family so I would marry him. He'd been interested in Dad's money, you see. Perhaps Dad had sensed it all along.

I remember when Roger first told me, I couldn't believe he could be so cruel as to deprive me of the chance to have children. I began to see him in a different light. It's a bit unnatural, if you think about it, that a man can be so obsessed with dolls, yet not like children. I think that's when I first admitted to myself that my depression was a little more serious than a passing mood. Roger wouldn't talk about it. We never argued; he had this passive aggressive thing going on where he could hurt me with his silence. He thought I'd give in and let him sell my doll – after all, I had nobody to give it to anymore.

About a month after the vasectomy confession he went away again. He hadn't sold anything for a while and he said he was going to another auction in the West Country and would travel about a bit while he was there, looking for prospective customers. We were practically living separate lives by then and no longer made love, though we still slept in the same bed. We were also beginning to have very real financial problems as my paintings weren't selling either. The owner of the little gallery in town that had generously shown my work, had asked me to stop taking paintings in for the time being until they had more space available. I therefore agreed with my husband that he should go; I believed it would be a good idea for us to have a break from each other for a week or so and there was a chance he might make some money buying and reselling at the auction.

Thinking back, it's strange how things happen. By chance, it was the day after he'd left that I came home from buying groceries in the village to find a woman sitting on my doorstep. She was a little younger than me and had a small child, about three or four years old, with her. She introduced herself as Harmony Tumber and said that she thought we might be related. We laughed about the coincidence of our musical names. "My mother was a bit of a hippy," I'd said and she'd replied, "Yeah, mine too." I was charmed by the way she spoke and enchanted by her little girl, so I invited them in.

It was late afternoon by the time she'd finished talking to me; I'd given the little girl some pens and paper to amuse herself drawing, and having tired of that, she had climbed up onto her mother's lap and fallen asleep, as we drank cup after cup of tea.

Harmony told me her home had been in Broadstairs for most of her life, although she'd attended boarding school. When she was fourteen she had been given a history homework assignment for the summer holidays, the task being to collect together photographs and any other items of interest about her family and put together a family tree, as detailed and extensive as possible. That was, she explained, how she came to discover the family link and she would, she said, get to that later. Anyhow, she said her father had been reluctant to provide much in the way of information, when she first mentioned the homework assignment, although he gave her a copy of her birth certificate and told her a few stories. She showed me the birth certificate and from the date I could see she was about six years younger than me.

Harmony had thought nothing about her father's reticence at the time, believing he didn't like discussing her mother who had abandoned them when she was just a baby.

Then, while he was at work one day, (he was a solicitor and caught the train early every morning) she hit on the idea of trying to find her mother. The housekeeper suggested she ask at the local library for help and Harmony made the woman promise to keep her secret from her father as she didn't want to upset him further.

The birth certificate gave her mother's name as Amy Carling and, although it took a few weeks, she did manage to track her down. Then she became bolder still and decided to go to see her. She looked up bus timetables and planned her visit.

The woman had married and was living on the outskirts of Gillingham. She was not happy to see Harmony when she answered the door, but agreed to meet her at the Strand to talk for half an hour. Harmony went to the water front to wait. She listened to the cries of children playing in the outdoor pool as she sat on a bench overlooking the water and fed the gulls some sandwiches the housekeeper had packed for her lunch. She'd felt unable to eat because she was so nervous about the meeting.

However, when the woman, Amy, arrived she launched into a confession about having posed as Harmony's mother to register the birth. She'd been paid a great deal of money to do this and had no idea who Harmony's real mother was. She said that if the police were told what she'd done, Harmony's father would get into a great deal of trouble, and with that she had left the girl sitting on a park bench and hurried back to her own home and life.

I was entranced by her story. "What did you do next?" I asked her, having relieved her of the sleeping child and taken the little girl into the lounge to lay her gently on the sofa. Harmony had followed me and taken a seat near the child's feet.

"Well, you can imagine how shocked I was. All the way home I thought about how I would confront my father. I decided it would be best to wait until after tea when the housekeeper had gone to her room. My appetite still hadn't returned and I couldn't eat a thing because I was so upset. My father kept frowning at me, puzzled because he could hear my stomach rumbling."

Then Harmony told me how, when she'd confronted her father with what she'd discovered, he had broken down and actually cried. Then he told Harmony the name of her real mother: Eleanor Fisherton.

Chapter Thirty

I liked Harmony from the moment we'd laughed about our names together, yet when she'd said my mother's name, I wanted to slap her.

"I'm sorry," she said, seeing the look on my face. "I wasn't sure how else to tell you. I think I'm your half-sister. My father told me he had an affair with our mother. He was her solicitor, you know."

Something wasn't adding up. I could still vaguely recollect the night my mother had given me the doll, although by then it seemed unreal, like a dream. She had come into my bedroom and kissed me and I could recall feeling a bit worried because she looked like she had been crying. Then she had smiled and stroked my hair and told me a lovely story until I drifted off to sleep. The next day I was told she had gone away.

I remember missing her for a very long time before being told she had died. Was it possible that she'd really thought herself in love with someone other than my father, Henry, left home to be with her lover and had a child by him? Had she then been willing to sacrifice being involved with that child, Harmony, because she realised she still wanted to be with my father and me after all? Could she have been secretly meeting up with Henry to plan her return, got pregnant and died giving birth to yet another child? It seemed incredible that my mother could have been such a selfish, capricious person, although my father had always told me she was very much her own person.

I remember studying Harmony, noting our similar hair and eye colour, and that we shared the same slim build. I wanted desperately to talk to my father, but he was no longer on the end of a telephone line. Therefore, I did the only thing I could think of; I invited Harmony to stay for a while.

I'd planned to put the little girl in my old bedroom, but when we took her upstairs she cried and insisted on sleeping with her mother in the middle room. I took her into our double bedroom to find a t shirt she could use as a nightdress and she saw the doll sitting on my dressing table. She picked it up, holding and rocking it as though it were a real baby. I thought I might give it to her since she was probably my niece and I was unlikely to ever have children of my own; it would teach Roger a lesson.

Once little Alicia was in bed, for that was her name, Harmony and I went back downstairs to wash the dishes and talk. I asked her about the child's father.

"I rather went off the rails after my father's revelation," Harmony said. "I don't know why, really. It was one thing to know your mother has left you and run off because she doesn't want the responsibility of bringing up a child, but quite another to discover your mother is actually dead."

I remember pausing with my hands in the soapy water, to watch as she dried the plate she was holding and put it into the cupboard.

"I'd always had this dream about finding the mother who had abandoned me and listening to her tell me how much she'd regretted doing it and how she'd been sorry she'd missed seeing me grow up," Harmony went on. "I suppose I thought I would one day have a real mother/daughter relationship and with my father's revelation the chance of that had been snatched away." She picked up a mug and wiped it with the tea towel. "Then there was the fact that my father had lied to me, although he did explain he'd done it because he hadn't wanted to disgrace my real mother's memory as she was married to somebody else. Anyway, I started playing truant from school. I met my baby's father at a fairground, believe it or not. He was responsible for running the bumper cars. Of course, by the time I realised I was in trouble the fair was long gone. I was just fifteen. I kept my pregnancy secret for as long as I could and when they found out at school, I got expelled. The Head teacher summoned my father and he took me home. He never once suggested I get rid of the baby, I'll give him that. He supported me in my decision to have the child."

I presumed then that Harmony had waited some time before attempting to find out more about her mother. She hadn't wanted to distress John Tumber any further than was necessary. I was wrong about that though, because she told me next that she'd left home shortly after her baby was born and had gone looking for the child's father. She'd earned enough for herself and the baby to live on by fruit picking and working on market stalls. By the time she'd caught up with the fair and been rejected by her former boyfriend, it was too late to go back home. John Tumber had made good on his threat to disown her if she left, and he'd ignored her attempts to contact him by telephone or letter. Harmony hadn't seen John Tumber since and little Alicia had never had the opportunity to get to know him either. It was a sad tale and we were silent for some moments, each thinking about Harmony's past.

Harmony asked me about my life then, and I told her about my childhood and our grandparents in the States. My grandma died before I married and grandpa was, at that time, in a care home, suffering from Alzheimers. I told her about my beloved father and how gifted he was at writing. I didn't tell her much about Roger, only a little about his work and that he was away on business at present. I wasn't yet ready to admit to myself that my marriage was over and certainly didn't feel able to confide my fears to anyone else.

The days sped by. I got used to having Harmony and little Alicia around; looking back, they were some of the happiest days of my adult life. We pottered about the garden and house, talking about how she could get a job and rent a small house somewhere nearby, perhaps in the village. She did say she'd have to return to the place she'd been renting in Faversham, just to tie up a few loose ends of her old life. However, she promised to be back with my neice before I'd had chance to miss them.

Then Roger came home. He wasn't best pleased when I introduced Harmony and Alicia, and was coldly polite. I put it down to his not liking children and thought no more of it until two days later when he arrived home, having been to town, and asked, no demanded, that Harmony leave. He told me he'd been looking into her story and he placed a copy of my mother's death certificate on the kitchen table in front of me. He pointed to the date of death and announced that Eleanor Fisherton had died giving birth exactly seven months after leaving her husband. She must have been aware she was pregnant before she left Henry, he insisted. Since there was no evidence of problems in the marriage and, he reminded me, she had sent letters to Henry promising to return home, the baby must have been his.

"That woman," he said, nodding towards Harmony who had come into the kitchen to find out why he was shouting at me, "is an imposter. Your mother's baby died at birth. It was a boy - there's a notice of the funeral of your father's wife *and son* in the newspaper archives. I want her," he pointed at Harmony, "out of this house now, and she should take that brat with her!"

Little Alicia had witnessed the whole episode and now hid behind her mother, trembling. I felt mortified that he should behave so brutally. Of course, I begged him not to be so hasty, pleading that there must be some explanation. I should have stood up to him better, but that's never been my style. He wouldn't listen to anything I said, and Harmony quietly turned away, taking her daughter's hand to collect together their few possessions. I whispered to her to write to me as she hugged me goodbye and I kissed little Alicia. However, I haven't seen or heard from them since, although that night I lay awake thinking about the evidence my husband had provided to discredit Harmony. Suddenly the truth hit me and I sat up in bed and began to shake Roger awake.

"What now?" he pulled himself into a sitting position. "You've been grizzling all evening. Can't you just get over the fact that you were duped? The woman was a liar and a fraud. I proved it to you."

"No, you didn't. I've just realised what it is that's been bothering me. The date on my mother's death certificate is the same as the date on Harmony's birth certificate. She showed it to me. She's more than my half-sister, she's my dead baby brother's twin and therefore my Dad's daughter! Don't you see? Rather than proving her a fraud you've shown that in fact she's my sister!"

It was then that I realised just how malicious my husband could be. "Too bad you won't be able to tell her," he said. "She's long gone by now."

I'd lay a bet you're thinking I gave my doll to the child, Alicia, and that she took it with her when they left. She was a gorgeous little girl and I did in fact, give Baby to her the day after she'd first seen the doll. However, she woke one night and called to us while Harmony and I were still downstairs, talking. It was before Roger got back from his trip. I asked Harmony if I could go and see what was wrong with my niece and she agreed. I found Alicia sitting up in bed, eyes wide with terror, clutching Baby. She told me she'd had a dream that if she took the doll she would never see me again. I tried to comfort her, saying that it was just a silly nightmare, but she gave the doll back to me there and then. It was still warm where it had been clutched tight to her small body in bed.

"There's a horrid man wants to take her, Aunty Mel. Don't let him. Hide her and keep her safe."

Her words sent a chill through me, so I took the doll and put it back in my room. I returned to settle my little niece again in her bed and calm her. I found she was already asleep.

After my husband tried to steal the doll from me a week or so ago, I remembered my niece's words. I secretly made a few preparations and then I waited for the day he would need to leave the house for several hours. He had a long drive to see a customer in Leeds. That's when I hid the doll and he will never find it.

I'm pretty sure you, as a doctor, must be bound by some sort of Hippocratic oath, and that you are required to respect patient confidentiality, so I will tell you what I did and trust you'll never tell.

Before my father took me to the States as a child, he built an internal wall in one of the bedrooms to cover up a window and make space for built-in closets. I saw him do it and he showed me where he'd left a small 'weak point' at the bottom of the wall which he said would make life easier if he should ever decide to take the wall down again at some future date.

I bought and hid a small tub of quick dry paste that could be used to repair plaster, and a little pot of magnolia paint. I bought a small hammer, a chisel and a smoothing tool for the paste. I found the weak point, chiselled out the plaster and cement, removed a couple of bricks, and placed the doll behind the wall. I'd already parcelled her up in brown paper to protect her. Then I repaired the wall again, repainted it, closed the closet doors and put my tools and materials in an old carrier bag which I hid at the bottom of the trash can outside, underneath the dust from the vacuum cleaner.

I put a bowl of pot pourri in the room to cover up the smell of the paint and fortunately it was dry when I checked it later, before Roger arrived home. I was terrified the whole time I worked that he'd come back and catch me before I'd finished, but I took care to do a good job. I've inspected it since and I'm quite confident nobody would ever be able to tell where the wall has been repaired.

The story took most of the day to tell. Alicia told how, once her aunt Melody went back to the States to live, her stepmother had given her Henry's trunk which had been stored with instructions that his daughter should have it after his death. It contained various papers, family photographs – including those handed down from his father, Nathan – first editions of Henry's novels, the manuscript found with the doll and, perhaps most important of all in helping her to piece together the story with the help of her sister and stepmother, Henry's personal journals. Some of the details of the story, Alicia admitted, were pure conjecture, although based on what they did know. Such details were, therefore, merely a filling in of blanks.

Imogen showed Alicia the notebook which she'd found in Tumber's desk drawer, explaining where she worked and how she'd come by it. Then she gave her the snapshot that had slipped out from inside of the book. Alicia studied it and said the girl in the picture was most certainly her grandmother, Henry's wife, as she'd seen other photographs of Eleanor from the trunk. Imogen and Dawn huddled closer to look over Alicia's shoulder at the photograph, which had been snapped in the 1960s, and they all marvelled at the remarkable likeness to Alicia.

"I'd just about convinced myself I'd imagined you, or that you were part of a dream, after you disappeared that night, because I discovered I'd left my key on the inside of the front door. I was certain nobody could have got in without breaking in, unless I opened the door to them. Then when I found the photograph I began to believe you must be a ghost!" Imogen said. She turned to Dawn, "You can understand why, can't you?" She turned her head to look back to Alicia. "Then your little girl kept appearing in my back garden while the side gate was locked from the inside, and I couldn't find how she got in or where she disappeared to either…"

"Because you didn't know about the hidden gate. It was very cleverly concealed. I feel bad now for having caused you so much concern," Alicia said.

"I'm just relieved that it all makes some sort of sense now," Imogen assured her.

They decided they should take a break, then. Dawn helped Imogen to make sandwiches, and they cut up a sponge cake and raided the fridge for salad and fruit to enjoy as a picnic in the garden. Afterwards, they spread a rug under the trees and vacated the garden furniture. Alicia helped little Echo, to make a daisy chain while Dawn drew up a simple nature trail to keep the child further occupied for when they went back to their discussion.

"Where's your little boy?" Imogen asked, as they waited for Dawn to re-join them.

"Lee? My friend, Tamsin, kindly offered to take him swimming. We'd never have been able to sit and talk like this if he'd been around, but it wouldn't have been fair to land her with both children for the whole day."

"Twins must run in your family, then, I mean your mother, Harmony was a twin to the baby boy that died. It must have been really strange for her to discover that her dad wasn't her biological father."

"I agree. I think she coped well, though. I've always admired her for her strength." She looked across the garden at Echo who was kneeling picking daisies and talking to herself. "I'm so lucky I had no problems when my twins were born. I guess medical science has moved on. Apparently my great-grandma was also a twin. Once she was sure of the truth, my Ma, Harmony, went to a great deal of trouble to get her name changed to Fisherton which is why I kept the surname and hyphenated my married name."

Dawn re-joined them, taking her place on the picnic rug out of the heat of the bright sunshine. They had been lucky with the weather recently. Dawn picked a blade of grass and, holding it taut between her thumbs, blew on it to make a wheezing whistling sound. Echo glanced over and smiled, then went back to her nature trail.

"Where did Harmony take you after Roger Stockman demanded you both leave Melody's house?" Imogen asked, adding as an afterthought, "This house."

"Oh, she took me back to Broadstairs for a while. She had hoped she'd be reconciled with John Tumber, but he had moved away to be nearer his place of work again. Fortunately, he hadn't sold the house in Broadstairs and had continued to employ the housekeeper Ma had grown up with to take care of the place. The housekeeper gave Harmony, a large padded envelope he'd made the poor woman promise to keep and give to her if she ever returned. Ma said that the old girl was glad to be relieved of it," Alicia smiled.

"Inside was a wad of cash and a letter, not detailing the amount of money enclosed, but admitting everything. He said that he had changed his Will and she was no longer a beneficiary, so he felt he should give her something. He asked only that she allowed him to live out his remaining days in peace. He didn't want her to contact him and they remained estranged to the day he died, by which time she'd used the letter to apply to have her surname changed and it did help – the letter, I mean."

"I don't blame her for changing her name. What a dreadful thing to do – steal a baby, I mean. Poor Henry never got to know of Harmony's existence, let alone you, his grandchild," Dawn said. "I bet he left the money because he felt guilty."

"I guess, although I think it's rather more complicated than that. Ma told me he had always been a truly affectionate 'father' and she'd never wanted for anything. He wrote in the letter he felt she had betrayed him, by leaving. Don't forget, he really suffered when Eleanor left him as a girl. What to her had been an infatuation he'd obviously felt was true love. Also, you have to remember my Ma might really have struggled if he hadn't provided that bundle of cash for her."

"He died in December of 2002. I know because it was the year I stopped working for the solicitors," Imogen said.

"I guess he might have had a change of heart towards the end of his life, we like to think so, but didn't have the opportunity to do anything about it. Or maybe it was simply his stubborn pride – who knows? It didn't matter, we'd settled in America by then," Alicia said. She sat up straight, gathering the strands of her long, blonde hair at the back of her neck and pulling it forward, so that it fell over the front of her right shoulder.

"You know, I was told there were rumours at the solicitors' office that John Tumber had an illegitimate daughter!" Imogen exclaimed. "When the partners tried to trace her, though, it was as if she had never existed. That must be because Harmony changed her surname!"

Dawn had been silent for some time, watching Alicia and Imogen as they conversed. Now she slowly nodded in agreement. "It does seem likely," she said. "I'm now beginning to wonder, though, if perhaps the cash was a sort of 'pay off' because he didn't want the world to know he'd abducted a client's child. I mean, why else would he insist Harmony shouldn't ever bother him again? I think he must have been quite callous."

"I didn't know him well, of course, because he kept himself pretty much to himself when I worked for the solicitors previously," Imogen admitted. "He always seemed harmless enough to me and he had impeccable manners. I believe at the time I thought he was quite a sweet old man."

Alicia made no comment about that. She said, "A few months after we'd been back to Broadstairs, Ma, Harmony, decided to try tracking down her great aunt and cousins. That's who owned the farm near Bushwell which was turned into the animal sanctuary. Milltop Farm, it was called. They invited us to stay awhile and she hoped she might be able to get in touch with her Melody again."

"So, what happened to poor Melody?" Dawn asked. "That's what I want to know."

"That was quite sad," Alicia said, taking up her story again. "Fortunately, she'd written to her step-mother, the woman I know as my grandma. She lives in Boston now. Fortunately, she'd already managed to telephone, explaining what had been going on with Roger, and that's why Grandma intervened by paying for my aunt to see a therapist. However, Melody knew that Roger had been in contact with the therapist before she was taken for her first appointment, so she decided to write about her fears. She gave the letter to the receptionist on the way in to see the psychiatrist and the woman promised to post it. Just as well really, since the woman's boss (Dr. Greaves-Hamilton) agreed with Roger Stockman that Melody should be put into a mental hospital."

"Nooo," Dawn and Imogen cried in unison.

"Sure did," Alicia said. "She said Melody was suffering from paranoid delusions and was likely to harm herself, as she had in the past, or hurt somebody else if she wasn't sectioned. She said that Melody had an unhealthy obsession with a doll which the patient felt was very valuable. Mr. Stockman had shown the doctor the doll and it was a cheap reproduction antique, worth no more than a few dollars, sorry, pounds I should say. It obviously wasn't Baby because Melody had hidden her, but the therapist chose to ignore what my aunt had told her about that. Melody was therefore taken before the panel and put away. That's when Grandma stepped in.

As soon as she received Melody's letter, she flew to England and took legal advice. The case ended up in court, but she managed to get Melody free, albeit into her guardianship. One of the provisions was that my aunt would receive further treatment in a facility in the States, where Gran took her back to live. It didn't take long for Melody to convince the new psychiatrists and doctors that she was perfectly sane. She divorced Stockman, but it meant she lost the house."

"I met him when we came to look at this house and I never did really like him," Imogen said. "We only saw him a couple of times, of course, but I always thought him a bit sinister, rather odd. I was sorry he had cancer and all that, and admired him for wanting to make the most of what little time he had left by travelling. Now it seems like karma that he became ill. That's an awful thing to say, yet hearing what he did to Melody makes my blood boil."

The chimes of an ice cream van sounded and Imogen went to fetch them all ice creams, taking Echo with her. Dawn and Alicia took the cups and plates they'd used for lunch inside the house to load the dishwasher.

"Tell me, how did you finish up living in the States after your mother found the relatives at the animal sanctuary?" Dawn asked as they worked. She knew she should be waiting for Imogen to re-join them but her curiosity was getting the better of her.

"After Harmony, had introduced herself to the family at the farm and they'd welcomed us and invited us to stay, she enquired after Melody and was told she had gone and they didn't know her whereabouts. Ma asked for information in the village but to no avail – even the people in the Close knew nothing of what had happened. Stockman was very crafty," Alicia said. "He managed to keep the whole affair quiet."

Imogen and Echo returned carrying enough ice cream cornets for them all and they sat down at the kitchen table to eat them.

"I was just telling Dawn," Alicia said, wiping her sticky fingers on a tissue, once she'd finished her ice cream. "When my Ma, discovered Aunt Melody had gone, she made arrangements to travel to New York. Melody had told her about Grandma being a writer, Siobhan Kerry – she's quite a celebrity in the States – and had given her a copy of one of her paperbacks to read. Harmony went to the publishers and contacted her through them." Alicia paused to give permission to Echo to go back out into the garden to play. All three women watched as the child skipped off out of the house, then she continued.

"It took a few weeks, but Grandma and Ma finally met. That's how we eventually caught up with Aunt Melody again." She sighed and stood up. "I'm afraid the rest is going to have to wait until next time, I've already stayed longer than I planned. Now, where did I put my bag?"

Imogen retrieved it from where it had been hanging on the back of her chair, a generous-sized, brightly patterned, soft canvas affair with a flap like a satchel, a large silver buckle to keep it closed and a shoulder strap. She passed it over. Dawn eyed it enviously.

"That would be terrific for carrying papers and files for school," she said. "Would you mind telling me where you bought it?"

Dawn tried not to look peeved when Alicia shook her head. Alicia undid the buckle of the bag and pulled open the flap, taking out an A4 manila envelope, her purse, some keys and a mobile phone. She used the phone to call for a taxi then handed the envelope to Imogen.

"That contains a Photostat copy of the manuscript written by Albert Darrington, otherwise known as Caleb Attlee

Fisherton. He's one of Henry's distant cousins. I'd like you to read it before we next meet. I've made plans with my friend for tomorrow, so can't see you then. Do you think we could meet at the pub in the village for lunch the day after, say 1 pm? I'll ask Tamsin to have the twins for the afternoon. She'll probably take them to help out at the animal sanctuary."

"Certainly, I look forward to it," Imogen said, hugging the bulky envelope to her chest.

"Me too," Dawn grinned, "I'm really intrigued as to how the story ends."

"That's for you, since you like it so much," Alicia passed the empty bag to Dawn. "Please take it, I'm afraid you won't find another like it in the shops, it's one of the designs my husband worked on for months and then rejected."

"Really?" Dawn reached for the bag then stopped herself, putting her hands to her mouth. "No, I couldn't, that's an original designer bag... Okay, I will, if you're sure!" she grabbed the bag. "Thanks."

All three women stood smiling at each other for a few awkward seconds then the little girl ran back into the house from the garden, and tugged at her mother's hand.

"It's been a pleasure meeting you at last, Echo." Imogen knelt down to speak to the child, who gave a toothy grin and stuck out a grubby hand as if she were an adult. Imogen shook hands with her.

The insistent beep of a taxi horn sounded outside. "I'll see you to the door," Dawn offered, leaving Imogen at the table, already removing the pages from the envelope to read.

From where she sat in the kitchen, Imogen clearly heard the front door being opened and then a male voice and Dawn's exclamation.

"Oh!" Dawn said. "How did you find out where I was? You didn't call ..."

"Dawn! It's good to see you," the voice replied, before greeting Alicia and Echo with a friendly "Hello."

Dawn remembered her manners and in turn said, to the woman and child, "Bye then. See you soon." Imogen pictured her waving to their departing guests before turning back to the man.

"Eli?" Dawn said. There were a few seconds of embarrassed silence then Imogen heard Eli's response.

"Actually, I didn't know you were here. I came to see the house owner, Mrs. Imogen Miles. Is she home?"

Chapter Thirty-Two

Imogen looked up from the photocopied manuscript as Dawn came back into the kitchen, closely followed by Eli Croft.

"Imogen, you have a visitor. I'll be upstairs getting ready to leave, if you'll excuse me."

Imogen stuffed the papers back into the envelope. "Er, Hi," she said, standing up and offering a hand to shake. "Aren't you…"

"Elijah Croft, Managing Director of the Jaxen Foundation, yes."

"I was going to say her boyfriend," she said, staring at Dawn's retreating back.

"Uh yes, I guess I am, although I don't think she's very pleased with me at the moment, because I told her I was here on business." He grinned, his green eyes full of mischief. Imogen liked him immediately.

"How can I help you?" Imogen said, motioning for him to sit down before reseating herself.

"I understand this house is on the market and I'd like to make a formal offer, on behalf of the Foundation. Whatever your other prospective buyers are prepared to offer, I will pay you five thousand pounds more."

Imogen laughed. "You'd be going up against Dawn, then, except I've decided not to sell for the time being after all."

"Dawn was going to buy *this* house? I thought she was moving into a village."

"Bushwell's only a couple of miles away," she made a dismissive gesture with a hand to show his assumption wasn't that far from the truth. "What does the Foundation want with my house?"

"Not just your house, Mrs. Miles, the whole Close."

"Call me Imogen. May I ask what you intend to do with the five houses, should the owners decide to sell?"

"Take them down and build one small complex of laboratories in the middle, for scientific research, engineering and new technology. We're already in communication with the owner of Darrington Way. This is a piece of breathtakingly stunning countryside and the shareholders of the Foundation are keen to keep it that way. Good for the natural environment. Perfect for public image. Everyone wins."

"I believe the land hereabouts already has some sort of preservation order on it," Imogen said.

"That is correct," he said. "However, since at least some of the work we undertake will be of a sensitive nature, this relatively small area, the ground on which Whitewood Close is built, would be strictly off-limit to the general public. That can only be an advantage to the wildlife and flora."

"I thought the Jaxen Foundation was concerned with Mental Health," Imogen commented.

"You're well informed, although we're also involved in innovative scientific research. Joseph Jaxen was, of course, a scientist himself, worthy in my opinion of the Nobel Peace Prize," he shook his head as if to rid himself of some unpleasant memory. "Yes, a lot of our work is related to mental wellbeing. That's how we came to know about the Close, and in particular this house," he said, his eyes serious.

"Really?"

"Yes. My partner, Kathy Seton, is a trained psychologist and heads up the branch of the Foundation that deals with mental health issues."

"Your partner?"

"In business. We were once an item, romantically involved, but it didn't pan out. We're still great friends though. She's engaged to a brain surgeon now who works for the NHS and I'll most likely be the best man at their wedding."

"Does Dawn know ... about Kathy?"

"We haven't had the talk about previous relationships yet. I expect she's still wondering whether I'm the sort of guy she needs in her life. Don't worry, I've a few ideas I'm sure might help convince her, and there's always my considerable charm to fall back on," he said grinning. "I digress. Where were we? Ah yes, Kathy recently flew over to the States to interview applicants to run Art Therapy sessions in our American branch. She gave the position to Melody Fisherton, nee Stockman. She was a former patient at the Foundation years ago, though not for long, and she's been working for us part- time as a volunteer ever since. One of our success stories."

They were so engrossed in their conversation, neither of them realised Dawn had returned to the kitchen until she spoke.

"Did you know the woman who just left?"

"The sexy blonde with the kid? Er, yes, I might have met her once or twice. Why?"

"That was Melody's niece," Imogen supplied.

"Yes, I know. She seems a nice enough woman, though I haven't really had an opportunity to have much of a conversation with her."

"What did Melody tell you or your people about this place, then?" Dawn asked, joining them at the table.

"Just that it was isolated enough to be inconspicuous if we wished to restrict public access, and that it had a lot of positive natural energy. That can be interpreted in a number of ways. We hired a Private Investigator to discover as much information as possible about Darrington Way. I think his report was pretty thorough. There isn't much we don't know about the place or its history."

"Oh, I think you'd be surprised," Dawn said. Imogen shot her a meaningful look, wondering if she could get away with a swift kick under the table. Instead she said, "Have you got a card you can leave me? Telephone number, email address?

Then if I change my mind I can get back to you." Eli handed her a card and she stood up. "It's been nice meeting you Mr. Croft, Eli," she corrected herself. "If you'll excuse me I have some reading to do. I'm sure Dawn won't mind seeing you out, when she's ready."

She left the kitchen, taking the thick manila envelope with her, and made for her bedroom. As she climbed the stairs she smiled at the scrap of conversation she heard between Eli and Dawn.

"I've got my motorbike outside. How do you feel about breaking the law and riding pillion along the lane through Darrington Way?"

"How would we be breaking the law – going too fast?"

"I can go fast if you'd like. No, I was thinking of a nice romantic ride to enjoy the scenery, you with your arms about me, wind through my hair," he sounded wistful until, "Of Course you'd be wearing my crash helmet, so I'd be the law-breaker. I'm not risking your pretty head ..."

Imogen closed her bedroom door behind her and sat on the edgeof the bed, taking the manuscript back out of the envelope. The pages had been photocopied using a colour photocopier. The paper of the original manuscript was obviously creased and yellowing with age and had been handwritten. After squinting in frustration at the spidery scrawl for some minutes, Imogen flicked through the photocopied pages. Henry must have found it as difficult to decipher the handwriting as Imogen now did, for she discovered, when looking at the last few pages, that he had provided a typewritten transcript.

The typewriting was poor, the words faded in places, although far easier to read. The very first page was blank but for a name typed in capital letters: Albert Edward Henry Darrington. Imogen plumped up the pillows on her bed and sat with her back against them. She put the title page to one side, along with the photocopied handwritten sheets, took up the next typewritten page and began to read.

Chapter Thirty-Three

On this the 12th day of July in the year 1893, I am about to attempt a treacherous journey. I am aware that the likelihood of my success is negligible, for this is no ordinary excursion, but another step for me into the unknown. I therefore feel compelled to record my story to the best of my ability, and if my attempt should fail, I put my faith in God that these words will one day be discovered, and that they will serve both as a warning and an instruction to the reader.

To begin I must confess that Albert Edward Henry Darrington is a pseudonym. I took the identity of a deceased infant and have gone to some considerable trouble to alter the records to give my identity substance. This was no easy matter as I also had to make a link between Darrington and Jonathan Edward Fisherton so that he could inherit, inventing a marriage between Albert's great grand-aunt who had died a spinster, and my great grandfather, a widower with a young son whose real mother had died in childbirth, conveniently leaving no other family behind. Needless to say, all record of my great-grandfather's first marriage had to be eradicated for the link to Darrington to work. That having been done, I have in effect become my own ancestor! I will not elucidate as to how I went about all of this, only to say it involved me ingratiating myself with certain people and the exchange of a substantial sum of money which I first had to earn. However, I then inherited the meadow, on which I shall conceal this testimony. I also inherited the surrounding lands, which I presume would otherwise have reverted to being property of the Crown and become common land. For this reason, and because I shall gain no monetary benefit from such inheritance, my conscience is reasonably easy in that regard.

My real name is Caleb Attlee Fisherton and I am a scientist, a physicist, who has inadvertently travelled from the future, the year 2026, to the past, not in a time machine but through a hole, a kind of doorway without a door, that connects to other dimensions of reality. I now believe the doorway, named the Eye of God by the scientists in my own time, to be a tear in the very fabric of the universe as we know it. The Eye occurred as the result of experiments and research into the nature of gravity. Although many of my colleagues could see a number of dimensions through the Eye, perceptions varied and we soon discovered no two people ever experienced the same view, and that each person generally saw about three different realities, sometimes more but never less. Various hypotheses were put forward to explain this and I believe the people in my own time are still working on a number of theories.

At the laboratory where I worked, I was asked if, having been granted certain privileges, I would be willing to volunteer to step through the Eye into another dimension and, knowing the dangers involved, but excited by the prospect of gaining untold knowledge, I agreed. The experience was not a pleasant one. I felt I was being tugged, thrown and spun through light and dark without relief for what seemed a very long time, until I thought I must perish. Then there was a flash, like a small explosion and I found myself falling some twelve to fifteen feet through the branches of a young tree until I reached the ground. It did not take me long to discover I was in a meadow and on further exploration I found the village of Bushwell and soon realised I had arrived in the past, in the nineteenth century.

I enacted the role of Albert Darrington, Victorian, gentleman scientist, with extreme care. I have managed to avoid romantic entanglements and, that being said, I have some pride in the way I have managed to fit in with this society without raising suspicion, for who would wish to alter history without understanding the possible consequences?

My greatest regret and reason for wishing to return to my own time is that I left behind my beautiful and wise six-year-old daughter, Alamea. She was and continues to be the very reason for my continued interest in life. She sensed, rather than understood, that my next project at work involved some sort of danger. I tried to reassure her and told her I'd be gone just a couple of days – for that was the time allocated for me to investigate one of the other realities. She refused to be comforted until I agreed to take her doll with me.

Alamea's doll is very special to her because it was a gift from me shortly after her birth and she cannot remember a time when she didn't have it with her. She calls the doll Baby and it is actually quite unique because it is made partly from a new material which has the look and feel of fine porcelain, while retaining the durability and flexibility of the toughest plastic. The doll was produced as a prototype at a laboratory annexed to a textile company for which I worked for a couple of years to gain experience as a physicist, just after I finished my PhD. I was due to become a father two weeks before I left the place. My wife and I had decided against knowing the sex of the child and my boss gave me the doll as a parting gift, teasing me that the baby would be a girl. They had no further need of the prototype since, to my disappointment, the formula for producing the material from which it was made was to be discarded. The material was never officially marketed as it was extremely expensive and complicated to make and was not considered financially viable.

I kept the doll thinking it would be a wonderful gift if we did have a daughter. However, our first child was a son and, in my joy, I forgot about the doll until Alamea came along later. The first time I held her in my arms, I was immediately entranced by the perfection of my baby daughter, and now that she has grown, I swear a brighter, more loving, sweet-natured child you could not hope to find.

When she handed Baby to me, Alamea made me promise I would keep the doll with me at all times and give it back to her on my return; that was her way of ensuring I'd be safe. For this reason, I need to hide it here with this account in the hope that one of my relatives will one day find it and pass it down through the family until it reaches Alamea again. I dare not risk taking the doll back through the Eye with me for fear that it might be lost with me. This way, if I fail to return, perhaps my child will take some comfort from the return of her doll.

Two long years have passed since my arrival and I have managed to visit the meadow and look up through the branches of the tree to watch for the Eye to open again. It seems almost fluid in its appearance and if it were not for the tree it would be difficult to discern against the sky. The tree has grown relatively quickly and is now approximately five meters tall; the branches look strong enough, at the height of the Eye, to take my weight.

Tomorrow, at first light, I shall put these pages and Baby in an iron box and will bury the box deep beneath one of the roots of the tree. After that I shall climb up and take my chance throwing myself back through the mysterious doorway. If I can choose the correct moment when the dimension from which I came appears, I will arrive safely back in my own time and be able to assist in closing this dangerous enigma, the Eye, although I will not have the doll and I hate the thought of my child's disappointment. Please, if you find these words, do everything possible to get Baby back to Alamea and, in the event that I didn't make it back, tell her I love her and I'm sorry that I couldn't keep my promise to return.

May God, the Creator of all things, bless you, friend, and keep you in peace, granting you the grace to fulfil the obligation for which I have charged you in returning the doll to my daughter, and also the wisdom to protect the secret of the Eye until such time as it can be permanently closed.

In His Name
Caleb Attlee Fisherton, Aka Albert Edward Henry Darrington.

Chapter Thirty-Four

Imogen put the copy manuscript back into its envelope, satisfied that the mystery of the doll had been solved, although something continued to bother her tired mind about the story that she couldn't quite fathom.

She went to her closet to take down from the shelf the box that contained the doll, Baby, and placed it on the bed beside her. She removed the lid and felt among the tissue paper within until she found the doll and took it out. If her understanding was correct, somewhere in the year 2026 a little girl was mourning the loss of her father, without even the comfort of her beloved doll. Imogen wondered about the child's mother. Caleb hadn't mentioned his wife again after the birth of his daughter, even when describing his decision to go through the eye. He hadn't mentioned his son again, either. Imogen speculated about that, giving her imagination free reign. Had his wife left him, taking his son with her and abandoning their daughter? Or had they been involved in some sort of accident and been killed? That made Imogen even sadder because she imagined Alamea being treated as an orphan when the scientist had failed to return.

She gently touched the intricate lace of the doll's gown. If there was some way she could help to ensure Baby was returned to her true owner, she was more than willing to assist. She thought about Roger Stockman and what might have happened if Melody hadn't managed to hide the doll and she shuddered as she imagined it being auctioned to the highest bidder. Caleb's efforts would have all been for nothing.

She smiled, holding the doll to her shoulder and patting its back as if it were a real baby; Caleb must have been (or could someday be) a wonderful father, going to all that effort, struggling and risking his life to falsify an identity and inherit land, just so that he could have somewhere to hide his child's favourite toy until such time as it could be reunited with her a hundred and twenty-nine years or so in the future. She lay back on her pillows, still clutching the doll, confident now that it could not easily be broken, and drifted off to sleep.

Next morning Imogen padded into the kitchen, after her shower, to find a note propped up by the coffee-maker informing her that Dawn had gone back to London, but would return in plenty of time for the meeting the following day. She made fresh coffee and sat down at the table, yawning. It was a cold, grey morning and the garden looked forlorn. She had no intention of selling the house now and, as she looked at the tall conifers, she made a decision that she would apply to the local authority before next spring for permission to have the conifers cut down. The garage was slightly to the side, behind the Silver birch, so she would be able to replace the conifers with a low fence, opening up the rear of the property to the wonderful view of the meadow and woodland beyond.

Just as the rain started, the doorbell rang and she opened the front door to find Tilly holding a newspaper over her head to keep off the first heavy drops of water. Imogen took her to the kitchen and poured more coffee. Tilly had only left the morning before, yet it now seemed like an age ago; so much had happened. They settled down to exchange news. Tilly began first.

"Imogen, I'm so glad I had those odd dreams when I stayed over. I went in to find Adrian and Neil sitting at breakfast together, neither of them talking. I thought at least it was a start and I felt chuffed that my plan to leave them to it had at least placed them in the same room together."

Imogen noted the worry lines had disappeared from Tilly's forehead and her eyes were bright with hope. There was obviously more to come.

"I helped myself to some muesli, poured myself a cup of tea and sat down. Neil didn't ask where I'd been. He knew I'd not been best pleased with him for going off to play golf when he should have been waiting in for his son." She couldn't keep herself from smiling. "Halfway through eating my breakfast, I very casually asked Adrian whether his mum was well and how he was getting on with her partner. Neil looked at me grumpily and Adrian looked from one of us to the other, then suddenly the truth came spilling out. You should have seen his father's face! I could see him beginning to sit up straight as he listened and when Adrian got to the part about how he'd been treated by that awful man with whom his mother lives, well! Neil stood up, got his jacket and told Adrian and me to stay where we were. Then he left."

"Weren't you worried?"

"Not really. I figured that bully was going to get what was coming to him and I was right. A couple of hours passed, then I had a phone call and Adrian and I went down to the police station to pick Neil up. The police had arrested Neil for assault. Once they knew the circumstances and that all he'd done was threaten violence if Adrian was abused again, they advised charges be dropped and Neil was free to leave. The three of us went out for a meal and Neil and Adrian had a long talk. Adrian's going to get a place of his own. We talked about helping him with rent for a flat and Neil's even going to put up the money for his business idea. I think everything's going to be alright from now on."

"That's great, Tilly. I'm so pleased." Imogen leaned forward, her arms resting on the table. Her face was wreathed in smiles. "Well done you!"

"What about you? Have you had more strange dreams?"

"Hmmm." Imogen took up her cup to finish her coffee, then pushed the empty cup away so she could fold her arms and lean forward on the table again. "Can you keep a secret?"

It was almost midday before she'd finished telling Tilly everything.

239

"I had enough trouble believing in a window that could help you make decisions by predicting the future, but time travel? It seems crazy. So why has this Alicia come back now?" Tilly asked.

"I'm not sure, that's one of the reasons I'm looking forward to meeting her for lunch, to find out. I think it's probably a combination of factors. The Jaxen Foundation have been in talks to purchase Darrington Way and that might have prompted the Fisherton women into action, particularly if they heard from Eli Croft that my house was on the market too." She sighed. "I know I'm probably being a sentimental idiot but I really do want to help get that doll back to the little girl and I'm hoping they feel the same way."

"Well, the whole story sounds incredible to me. You will let me know how you get on, won't you? I'd better go and let you get ready to go out. At least it looks like the rain's stopped." Tilly pointed to the window, got to her feet and then said, "Imogen, what do you think would happen if the powers that be found out about that window?"

"I don't want to even think about it. That's why I asked you to keep it all a secret."

***

The Wheatsheaf was an Elizabethan building positioned between the village butcher shop and a privately-owned Edwardian house in the centre of Bushwell. Imogen watched as Dawn parked her car in a designated space across the road and waited for her friend to join her. They pushed open the pub door and stepped down a narrow step immediately into the public bar.

The interior was dimly lit by wall lamps all around the room, compensating for the lack of natural daylight through the small windows. The walls were whitewashed, hung with framed old photographs of village scenes in times gone by, the low whitewashed ceiling supported by dark oak beams. There were padded corner seats, upholstered in red and fronted by long wooden tables with matching chairs. The bar was well lit, the polished wood framing the counter adorned with gleaming brass ornaments. There were no fruit machines, no flat screen television on the wall. It was almost as though they had stepped back in time. The landlord stood behind the bar, shirtsleeves rolled up, polishing a wine glass with a white cloth. They appeared to be the only customers at present. Dawn took a seat in the far corner away from the entrance door, while Imogen asked for two pints of bitter shandy. The landlord served the drinks then went through the little door to the adjoining bar in the saloon. The women heard low voices and a sudden burst of laughter, then all was quiet.

Imogen had just finished telling Dawn what the manuscript had revealed when the outside door rattled open again, the little bell above it jingling the arrival of the next customer who turned out to be Alicia, closely followed by Eli. Imogen glanced at Dawn who had noticeably tensed and Imogen bit her lip in an attempt to hide her amusement; Dawn was jealous! Eli followed Alicia to their table and after a brief greeting to Imogen and Dawn, pulled out the chair for Alicia to sit down, asking her what she'd like to drink.

"Can I get you two ladies anything else?" he asked.

"No, thank you," Dawn said glaring at him.

"You could ask the landlord for a menu," Imogen suggested. "They do great scampi and chips, or jacket potatoes with a variety of fillings, and they also have a special meal of the day." She knew she was babbling. She stopped.

Eli went off to the bar and Alicia rummaged in her bag, this one a black knitted affair. Flicking back her long hair in a now familiar gesture, she laid a thick paperback novel on the table. She looked up at the girls and smiled. "I hope you don't mind that I invited Mr. Croft along, only Ma suggested it when I rang her last night. I've had to tell him everything, I'm afraid, but I think he might be able to help."

Imogen picked up the book, reading the title aloud. She looked up at Alicia, startled, having read the author's name. The book was entitled *The Lonely Traveller* and was a science fiction novel written by Henry Fisherton.

Chapter Thirty-Five

Alicia promised to explain why she'd brought the book with her after they'd eaten. Eli returned with the menu and they made small talk while they waited for and then ate their meals. Afterwards, Eli fetched more drinks and they took them out into the beer garden where they would have complete privacy. All evidence of the rain, which had stopped mid-morning, had evaporated and now it promised to be a pleasant bright afternoon, if a little chilly.

"I've read the manuscript and have told Dawn about it. Thank you for allowing me to see it," Imogen said. "I have to ask, how come you never came to find the doll before? I mean, the house hasn't been in the Fisherton family for years. Weren't you afraid someone might knock down the wall and discover the doll, and for that matter the strange properties of the window? And why didn't your Aunt Melody come herself instead of sending you, no offence intended," she added.

"None taken," Alicia smiled. "Let me tell you about my aunt and my Mama first. Aunt Melody makes her living selling art and, as you know, has just accepted an appointment as Principal Art Therapist with the Jaxen Foundation.

"I've also told you that once she was back in the States, Grandma handed to her a locked trunk which her father had left for her. Among the items inside, were several of his personal journals and there was also a letter from Henry explaining how he'd discovered the portal and subsequently found the manuscript and doll. He confirmed my aunt's suspicion that he'd bequeathed Darrington Way to his cousin as he felt it should be passed down the male line of the Fisherton family because of what the manuscript revealed, and he said that he hoped his daughter would understand this decision and see to it that the doll also remained within the Fisherton family. He said that Caleb's account of the little girl,

Alamea, had caught his imagination probably because of the love he had for his own daughter and he therefore fervently hoped the doll would one day be returned to its true owner.

"He directed Melody to look at one of the paperbacks he'd written – this one here. Certain parts had been highlighted for her attention. She and Grandma apparently discussed it at some length and decided to do nothing for the time being, since the house had been given to Roger Stockman in the divorce. Strangely he'd never noticed the extra window outside, so they hoped he never would."

"Not so strange really," Eli said. There's a theory that certain people can become virtually invisible, not because they can't be physically seen, but because nobody bothers to notice them. Perhaps the window's like that and most people just don't see it."

"Yeah, I've heard about that theory," Dawn said, glancing around at everyone except Eli. "It's been written about too. I think they used it for an episode of *The X files*. Terry Pratchett used it as well in his *Disc world* novels to explain away why none of the characters could see the death character until it was time for them to die."

"I suppose it's a bit like people who long for babies suddenly noticing prams everywhere, only in reverse," Imogen added. "After all, the same people didn't particularly think about all the prams and pushchairs everywhere until they wanted children themselves."

From the way in which Alicia was looking at her, eyes full of sympathy, Imogen realised she may have inadvertently disclosed her own longings. She shrugged uncomfortably.

"Anyhow," Alicia said, shifting the attention away from Imogen, "by the time Stockman sold the house, Aunt Melody had made a life for herself and had no desire whatsoever to return to England."

"She must have a lot of painful memories about the place," Imogen said.

"Grandma was convinced that if the window was discovered we'd learn about it through the news and media," Alicia continued.

"Ma said she'd never noticed the extra window the whole time she was staying with Melody, and that's why she didn't think anyone else would either, so they left it at that. They decided they'd wait until 2025 before deciding what to do the following year. That was until the Jaxen Foundation contacted the family and entered into talks about buying Darrington Way."

Dawn asked, "So how long was it, after finding your Grandmother, before your mum met up with Melody again? They must have been so pleased to see each other."

"I don't really know. It seemed a long time to me. I'd attended primary school in Broadstairs before she managed to trace the relatives at Milltop Farm near Bushwell and then it was a while after that before she discovered where Melody was and had saved enough cash for our flights.

"She made a good life for us in America. She took waitressing jobs for a while to save to go to night school. She refused to allow Grandma to help her financially, although she would have been more than happy to contribute. We did live with Grandma for a while because Ma needed someone to keep an eye on me while she was working and Grandma insisted that it would have been what Henry wanted if he'd known of his second daughter.

"Eventually she went to college and she's now a lawyer, although she works for people on low income, so she doesn't make a great deal of money."

"Very commendable," Dawn said with obvious admiration.

Eli was watching Dawn again, Imogen noted. He had barely taken his eyes off her since they'd come into the garden. Dawn on the other hand had been treating him with polite indifference, despite several attempts by him during their meal to engage her attention. Dawn had ignored him, smiling and chatting with Alicia instead, sharing jokes and asking about the twins while they ate. Eli now turned to Imogen, a rueful expression on his face.

"I'd quite like to see this window I've heard so much about later, if you wouldn't mind," he said.

Imogen nodded. "Of course, but first I'd like to know about the book and how you think we can help, Alicia. Obviously, we need to make sure Alamea gets her doll back."

Dawn said, "According to the manuscript the chap reckoned he came from the year 2026, that's only ten years from now. If he was, or should I say will be, in his early thirties then, surely, he shouldn't be too difficult to find now. He'd be, what? Twenty-two, twenty-three at most."

"Yeah, well that bothers me a little," Eli interrupted. "Harmony faxed me through a copy of Henry's letter explaining about his third 'vision' and describing the laboratory he saw and some of the technology. I suppose there's a faint possibility that science will have advanced to that extent within ten years, but it seems highly unlikely."

"As much as I hate to admit it, I agree," Dawn said.

"And what about the society he talked about, where social security depends on family connections. I can't see that happening in such a short period of time. Then there are the deep, unchallenged religious convictions of the people with only one religion, the whole culture seems alien!" Eli said.

"That's why I thought you might be able to help," Alicia said. "Take a look at the highlighted sections of this book." She passed the novel over, pages opened at the appropriate point, and Eli took it, eyes skimming the coloured lines. The women waited, watching him. He read the sections indicated twice, then smiled and looked up.

"We're forgetting that the portal isn't simply a time corridor. It's a passage between different realities," he said.

"Then we can't return the doll! It's a different reality!" Imogen said. She leaned her elbows on the table and put her head in her hands.

"Listen," Eli read: *"The different realities shown are linked. They have exactly the same people. The only distinction is that they each respond differently to the same set of circumstances or problems, and that affects the outcome."*

Imogen looked up. Eli let his eyes travel from person to person around the table.

"So?" Dawn said.

"The reality in which Henry saw the laboratory was a *different* reality with the same problem. He was even watching a different Henry. In our universe society and technology have evolved in a completely different way, probably because of different solutions to problems in the past."

"I'm sorry, I still don't get it. I get about it being a different reality, of course, but the doll is in this reality." Alicia shook her head.

"Exactly!" Eli said his eyes alight with triumph.

Imogen began to smile. "I think I know what you're getting at, and what Henry was trying to show us! The same problem occurred and the doll existed in all of the realities. Caleb in the future of *this* reality may well not have the same technology for showing family trees, for example, or a society that insists he knows the genealogy of his family. What's to say he's not a Born Again Christian in this reality, who studied the history of the Fisherton family as a hobby?"

"I see, Yes! Once he found himself in the past, all he'd have to do is research Albert Darrington's family tree to see how he could forge a link!" Alicia said, beaming. "It would be quite a challenging task, though, with no computers to help but it is plausible."

"Talking of computers, let's go back to my house and see if we can get onto the internet and find out a bit about this Caleb in the present day," Imogen suggested. "Then we can show Eli, and Alicia the window and the doll."

Chapter Thirty-Six

The window was a great disappointment to both Eli and Alicia for all either of them could see were the branches and leaves of the Silver birch that Henry and Melody had planted so many years ago, and the ground below. Nobody appeared to be about outside on the Close. Imogen couldn't see anything untoward either. Dawn gazed through the window for some minutes and then turned away, just shrugging her shoulders and shaking her head.

Imogen went to her own bedroom and fetched the doll. Eli took it first, examining it closely. "It's certainly unlike any material I've ever seen," he said and gave the doll to Alicia to look at. She held the doll differently to Eli, fingering the linen dress with its lace trim, and then holding it to her shoulder as Imogen had done the night before, as if it was a real baby.

"It looks so lifelike," she said. "It's just as I remember it." Imogen put an arm round her shoulders when she saw tears start in the young woman's eyes. "It must have been the window behind the concealed wall that made me dream of the horrid man stealing the doll, the man I immediately recognised to be Stockman when he returned from his business trip all those years ago. He was so bad-tempered and aggressive the last time I saw him. He really frightened me."

"Come on," Dawn said, making for the door. "Let's go research Caleb."

They all trooped back down the stairs and into the kitchen. Dawn made hot drinks and rummaged through the cupboard for biscuits while Imogen fetched and opened up her laptop. Alicia and Eli looked over her shoulder as she logged onto the best known social media web sites. After half an hour of frustration, she tried one of the sites that linked business and professional people together and typed in Caleb's full name.

"Bingo!" Eli said. "Send him a message."

"What shall I say?" Imogen asked.

"I think we should arrange a meeting," Eli said. "We can give him the doll and maybe talk him out of going through the portal."

"I agree," Imogen said. "Hopefully we can prevent the little girl losing her father as well as helping her to keep her beloved doll."

"Absolutely," Dawn approved. "We have to at least try."

"He lives in Manchester!" Alicia said. "That's a bit of a way to travel and I'm due back in the States the day after tomorrow. It could be a problem."

"Imogen and I could go, save you the trouble," Dawn said, putting mugs on the worktop.

"Let's not get ahead of ourselves. We need to contact him before we start worrying about that, see if he's up for a meeting with us," Eli advised.

Imogen thought for a moment then typed: *I am writing on behalf of the Jaxen Foundation and would like to speak to you urgently concerning a business proposition.* She typed in her telephone number and asked that he call.

"He'll think it's about a job," Eli said. "Good idea, Imogen."

"Supposing he doesn't ring," Alicia said.

"He will," Dawn said, handing her a mug of coffee. "He wouldn't be on that website if he wasn't interested in at least looking at new career prospects."

After they'd finished their drinks, Eli said that he needed to get back to work. He smiled at Imogen, and attempted to give Dawn a peck on the cheek. She turned her face away from him. Apparently oblivious of the tension between Eli and Dawn, Alicia also excused herself saying she needed to rescue her friend from the twins. She shook hands with Eli and when he'd gone, hugged the two women, promising to be in touch before leaving for America.

Once they were alone, Imogen said to Dawn, "You were quick to volunteer to go to with me. How are you going to manage with school? It will take the best part of a day to get to and from Manchester."

Dawn sighed. "I like Alicia, I honestly do, but I don't want to encourage her to stay. Eli is far too interested in her."

Imogen burst out laughing. She couldn't help herself. "You've no cause to feel threatened. She's already spoken for, married with children!"

"She's far too pretty. She makes me feel dowdy and plain."

Imogen raised her eyebrows and pulled a face. "Yeah, I felt like that the first time I set eyes on her and believed she was Sean's mistress."

Dawn shook her head. "Imogen, when I looked out of the window I saw them together. She was in his arms."

"What Eli and Alicia? No way." Imogen stood up. "Come on," she said. "Let's go and have another look. You saw us going to the barbecue, which helped you to decide to move in. Perhaps the window will have something else to show you."

They went back upstairs and without hesitation Dawn went to the window and looked out. After a few seconds, she turned back to Imogen, her face shining with delight. "I've just seen myself in a bridal gown! I never thought I could look that elegant," she said.

"What do you think now, then?"

Imogen noticed the effort it took Dawn to reign in her enthusiasm. "I don't know about marriage. I've imagined myself with a long-term partner, even eventually living together if I found the right man, but actual legal, matrimonial commitment? She pulled a face. "I do really like Eli, though," she admitted at last. "I've been rather foolish. I allowed the green-eyed monster to colour my perception, didn't I?"

"Perhaps a little." Imogen smiled. "At least you've sorted out any reservations you had about whether Eli's boyfriend material!"

"It's not like me to feel worried about another woman, especially one I like. He was probably comforting her or she was thanking him or something. It's bound to have been entirely innocent and anyway it wasn't our Eli and Alicia, if you think about it. It was in a different universe!"

"Call him and arrange another date. You could invite him over and cook a meal. I can make myself scarce," Imogen suggested.

They were still making plans and discussing why Eli might have been holding Alicia in such an intimate embrace when the telephone rang. The answering machine clicked on and the two women stood still, waiting and listening. It was Caleb Fisherton. His voice, though youthful, was confident. He said that he would be available to meet a representative of the Jaxen Foundation at just after five the following evening and gave the name of a restaurant bar in the city centre. He said he would immediately email, via the business website, a map and directions and a photograph of himself so that he could be recognised.

They waited for the email and when it came Imogen printed off the map and photograph. They studied the image of Caleb Attlee Fisherton with interest.

"He's little more than a school kid!" Dawn said, "There's a vague resemblance to Alicia going on here," she added. "It must be the Fisherton genes. It hadn't occurred to me before - he's related to her."

"I expected him to look young. I can see what you mean about the likeness, though. It's his colouring and the shape of his eyes. We should ring her and ask if she's certain she can't postpone going home so she can meet him."

It was then they realised they didn't have contact details for Alicia, and had been relying on her to get in touch with them.

"You'll have to ring Eli," Imogen said. "He might have her mobile number. You were going to ring him anyway."

The phone rang again. This time Imogen picked up the receiver. It was Alicia. Imogen talked for a while, telling her the news and then listened to what Alicia had to say. After she'd replaced the receiver she said to Dawn, "I'm sure you could tell from that there's a problem. She has to go back to the States tonight because her grandmother has had a stroke. We're going to have to deliver the doll ourselves after all."

Dawn looked up from staring at her own mobile. "Imogen, I'm really sorry, I can't come with you either. I've got to arrange an emergency meeting of Governors and staff first thing in the morning. I've just received a call that's been diverted from my office at the school. OFSTED are coming in tomorrow."

Imogen shrugged. "Oh well, never mind. You can't help it. I'll manage."

"Do you think you could reschedule with Caleb?"

Imogen shook her head. "I don't think so. He might just decide not to bother after all. I can't risk it. Don't worry about it. I can catch the train and then find a taxi. I'll be fine. You need to concentrate on work," she said.

Dawn hesitated, a look of uncertainty on her face.

"I mean it, go! I'll be fine."

Dawn hugged her and grabbed her coat, heading out to the car to drive to school. Imogen went back online to book a return ticket to Manchester for the following day, then she emailed Caleb again, this time to say she would be keeping the suggested appointment with him. She wondered how he would react when he realised she wasn't from the Jaxen Foundation and couldn't offer him a job. Then there was the whole story of the doll. How was she going to manage to explain all that without him walking away in disgust, thinking she was some sort of crackpot?

She decided to put her worries on the backburner for when she was heading for Manchester on the train – there would be plenty of time to think about it then.

Chapter Thirty-Seven

A Sandwich box with cheese and ham sandwiches inside, an apple and a muesli bar, a bottle of water –these were the first things Imogen put into her rucksack. Next, she added the copy manuscript and the box with the doll in it. Finally, she printed off the documents she needed for her journey and placed them, with the map and picture Caleb had sent, into the side pocket of the rucksack together with her purse. She glanced at her wristwatch and grabbed her coat, stuffing her mobile telephone into the pocket before leaving the house. She pulled the front door closed behind her with a slam and began a brisk walk to the bus-stop. Hopefully she'd be at Rainham train station with time to spare.

The early morning train to London Victoria was jammed tight with commuters and there were no seats available. The carriage felt stuffy and Imogen was grateful when the train finally reached its destination and she was able to disembark. She had to wait for her connection so she bought herself a coffee and stood, among the crowd of fellow travellers, gazing at the electronic board overhead showing the destinations and departures of all the different trains. Every now and then it clicked and changed as another train arrived or was ready to depart and the crowd would thin out temporarily, then increase in size again as other travellers arrived to inspect the board.

At last Imogen's connection was announced and she found the train and the seat with the number she'd been given when she'd booked. She sat down and looked out the window, relieved. Within five minutes the train was pulling out of the station and she was on her way.

Briefly she wondered how the other Imogens in the different dimensions she'd seen through the portal had dealt with the problem. One of them might have decided to give the doll to Alicia and tell her she couldn't help. She imagined Alicia taking Baby back to America and the family waiting until 2026 before trying to locate Caleb. Another Imogen might have tried to reschedule the meeting and then Caleb was offered another job and wasn't interested in keeping the appointment; What if he decided to move abroad before they could contact him again? That would mean travelling even further afield! Perhaps she should have gone up and looked from the extraordinary window in her house before she'd booked her ticket, yet she instinctively knew this wouldn't have been necessary and she was confident in her decision. Any number of things could have happened to prevent the doll finding its way back to Alamea, still might in fact. There were a variety of possible reasons to keep Caleb from turning up or even to detain Imogen causing her to miss the meeting: she might get lost, for example, or the train or taxi might even crash! She decided she just had to have faith that everything would turn out fine.

It was a long journey and she was glad to get off the train at last and stretch her legs when she arrived in Manchester. She found a taxi without too much trouble and asked to be taken to the restaurant. As the taxi drew close to her destination, she noted there were a number of tables on the pavement outside the restaurant bar. She paid the driver, giving him a generous tip and got out of the cab, looking along the restaurant front. She soon saw him; Caleb was sitting alone near the corner of the building, coffee cup on the table before him, he was staring at the traffic flowing by. She was pretty sure he hadn't noticed her yet. She approached, rehearsing her introduction.

"Mr. Fisherton?" she asked. He sat up straight before answering, a keen look of interest on his face. She obviously wasn't what he'd been expecting.

"My name's Imogen Miles. I arranged the meeting with you," she said, avoiding any mention of the Jaxen Foundation.

"Pleased to meet you," he said, rising. They shook hands and sat down.

"I want you to look at something," Imogen said. She unzipped her rucksack and pulled out the box with the doll inside. She pushed the box towards him.

"Please inspect the contents of the box and give me your opinion."

Caleb took the lid off the box and pulled the doll out. He examined it, then glanced up at Imogen. "Why am I looking at this? Is it something to do with the position the Jaxen Foundation are offering, or just some sort of a prank?"

It took every ounce of courage Imogen had not to excuse herself and leave right then. Caleb didn't look particularly impressed and she hadn't been ready for him to be quite so forthright. She bit her lip, feeling sick. It was now or never.

"The textile company you're working for are developing that material. It's a special kind of plastic. They're going to make a doll just like that and they'll give it to you when you leave; they'll abandon production of the new material because it isn't cost effective." There. She'd said it.

He replaced the doll in the box. "I think you've got the wrong person. I do work in the research lab at a textile company at present, but we aren't developing anything like this. Besides, why would they give it to me and how do you know all of this, anyway?" His voice was irritable as he tried to return the doll to her. When she didn't offer to take the box, he pushed it to the middle of the table between them.

"The doll is from the past but also the future. It's one of a kind. It's really important you listen to me," Imogen leaned forward, her voice urgent.

Caleb gazed at her for a long time with an unreadable expression on his face. At last he stirred himself and spoke in a low, controlled voice.

"I came here to discuss prospective employment with the Jaxen Foundation because I've heard a lot of good things about their work and I need a decent career." Caleb said. "I guess that isn't on the cards after all." He got to his feet again.

"The doll belongs to your daughter, Alamea." Imogen waited for the words to take effect. He glared at her. "Do I look like I have children," he said, raising his arms slightly, hands open.

"You will have. A little girl. I know she hasn't been born yet, but when she is you'll give her this doll, or one exactly like it, and when she's six she'll ask you to take it with you when you participate in an experiment. Please Mr. Fisherton, Caleb ..." she caught hold of the sleeve of his jacket as he began to push his chair in to leave. "If you don't want to listen to me, at least read this," Imogen pleaded, pulling the copy manuscript from her rucksack and placing it next to the box with the doll inside. Please. You'll be an excellent father. Just don't make the mistake of working with gravity and definitely don't volunteer to explore any strange phenomena that might occur as a result of your research, for the sake of Alamea."

Imogen picked up her bag. "I'm leaving now. All I'm asking is that you think about the information I've given you and all that I've said." She stood up, put her rucksack strap over her shoulder, turned and walked away. She resisted the urge to look back to see if he'd take the doll and the copy manuscript.

The bag felt strangely light, and she wondered whether she'd managed to alter the course of her own destiny in trying to convince Caleb to change his. Perhaps, even as she walked, history was busy reorganising itself to fit in with a completely new future. In theory, she considered, her intervention in events might even help to close the portal, although she had to admit it seemed doubtful from the way he'd reacted. Still, it was a thought. Feeling bolder than she had in a very long time, she decided to find a bus stop to see if she could get back to the train station without the expense of another taxi cab.

Caleb stared at the strange woman as she walked away. She didn't look back and he felt so angry he thought he might embarrass himself and cry, right there in front of the restaurant. How dare she let him think there was a possibility of a decent job, when all she had wanted was to tell him some stupid story about a toy! She'd raised his hopes and wasted his time. He should have listened to Samera – she'd said it sounded too good to be true. He really needed that break. The textile company didn't pay well and Samera had just told him she suspected she might be pregnant.

Her family were good people but they were strict Muslims and, although initially sympathetic about the couple's evident feelings for one another, had nevertheless banned Samera from seeing Caleb again once he'd left university, in the hope that she would marry someone from within their own cultural community. Samera had wept, when she told Caleb, explaining how frightened she was that her family would disown her when they discovered she was going to have a baby. She'd be disgraced.

Caleb remembered how he'd comforted her and promised her he'd make a life for them both, for the three of them if it turned out she was indeed pregnant. Although he didn't expect it to be easy, he felt sure he would eventually persuade her family to accept him if he proved to be a good husband and provider. He'd even gone as far as to promise Samera she would have the chance to finish her study once their child was born. What was he going to do now?

He slumped back down into his seat and picked the doll up out of the box. It was really rather neat, he thought, looking at it. Perhaps he'd keep it, on the off-chance that they did have a little girl, if not now sometime in the future.

Then he saw the envelope containing the copy manuscript and pulled it across the table towards him. A waiter approached his table and he ordered another coffee. He'd just about be able to afford that. Caleb took out the pages of the manuscript and began to read.

Epilogue

Elijah Croft finished perusing the report and leaned back in his chair, nodding his satisfaction to Clive Acton who sat opposite him.

"This seems fairly comprehensive," he said. "My PA will transfer the fee we agreed to your business account this afternoon. The two men rose to their feet and shook hands across the desk.

"It's been a pleasure doing business with you, Sir," Acton said with a slight bow, before snapping his briefcase shut and retrieving his raincoat from the back of the chair he'd been sitting in. Eli saw him to the door and watched from the window of his office as Acton got into his car and drove away.

It had been money well spent; Eli decided, sitting back behind his desk and taking up the report once more. The Private Investigator had done a thorough job, even going to the trouble of providing photographs, not that it had been necessary for him to do that, for Eli knew the place well. In fact, the lane to Darrington Way was just a short distance from his home. It was a wonderful piece of countryside boasting a beautiful, ancient meadow, set amid farmland with woodland beyond. It was secluded, situated at least a couple of miles from anywhere, the village of Bushwell being the nearest area of extensive housing. The meadow had one tree, an old Silver birch which stood virtually in the centre of the field. He and his wife had, on numerous occasions, picnicked there, enjoying the shade of its branches. It had been a favourite haunt of theirs since before they'd been married, a respite from the stress and strain derived from their busy careers.

He glanced at the framed photograph of his wife, Dawn, and smiled fondly. She was the Headmistress of the village primary school, which was becoming increasingly popular due to its recent hard won OFSTED grade of Outstanding. That was down to her hard work and determination, he thought with pride. Prospective parents from the Medway towns were competing for housing in the village in the hope of gaining a place for their children at the school and there were rumours of further building work and development in the area to meet the demand for new homes. However, no part of Darrington Way had ever been built upon and Eli intended to ensure the land remained as unchanged as possible, with one slight exception.

He looked back down at the file before him with a tiny pang of guilt. Darrington Way had been considered common land since the Darrington line died out in the nineteenth century. A local family, who'd farmed much of the surrounding area, had gradually acquired most of Darrington Way by cultivating it for agricultural use, even occasionally grazing sheep in the old meadow to keep the grass down. In this way, they had retained rights of use over the land down through the decades until such time as their main holding, Hilltop Farm, had become an animal shelter sometime during the late 1980s, all agricultural work having ceased with the death of the last of the farmers. Some of the farmland had been sold but Darrington Way had reverted to common land and had fallen into the ownership of the local council.

The legal team of the Jaxen Foundation had already commenced talks with the local authority who had given every indication that they were willing to sell, on the understanding that Darrington Way retained its status as common land. Eli believed, once the land was in the possession of the Jaxen Foundation, he had enough information now ready to put forward a strong application to build a small science complex on the meadow. It would be an ideal location, taking up a mere third of the space, yet he remained uncertain about the morality of such a decision. Regardless of his intention to ensure all remaining land would be protected by law from further building development indefinitely, he was worried whether it would really be enough to safeguard the natural beauty of the place for future generations.

He closed the file and opened another, skimming the list of new proposals for possible scientific work to be funded by the Foundation. Most involved ideas for the improvement of mental health which was the predominant reason for the existence of the organisation. However, it had always been the remit of the Jaxen Foundation to provide funds for other branches of scientific investigation too. He came to an item proposing research into the nature and effects of gravity and he sighed. His assistant had informed him earlier that day that the kid they'd been watching since he'd got his PhD in physics, had turned down the opportunity to work on this project. His name was Caleb Attlee Fisherton, a distant relative of the Bushwell Fishertons. Eli had been interested in Caleb because he showed such promise – might even be considered to be a bit of a genius. It was just so disappointing. They could look for another candidate to take his place, of course, but on impulse, Eli crossed the item through. Someone else, somewhere else in the world, could study gravity. The Jaxen Foundation would be funding something entirely different in its place.

Eli glanced at his watch. It was almost lunchtime and he remembered that Dawn had organised a special celebration party in the pub at Bushwell for their friends, Imogen and Sean Miles because they'd just discovered, after many months of IVF treatment, that they were expecting their first child. Eli grinned to himself, certain that he and Dawn would be asked to be godparents when the time came. Eli stood up again, gazing out of his office window for a while, remembering how Sean had once confided to him over a pint, the difficulty he'd had trying to remain positive during the treatment, and how he'd been tempted and almost succumbed to the charms of another woman at a time when even his business seemed to be failing. He'd remained faithful, though, and their marriage had survived the strain. Eli was glad. Imogen was one of those exceptional women, a successful and attractive business woman who championed loyalty and integrity above all other considerations; she had stood by her husband through tough times and, in Eli's opinion, deserved his fidelity. Besides, they were excellent friends and he and Dawn spent a lot of time socialising with them.

Dawn had insisted on inviting other friends to the celebration, including the Fisherton family: Melody, Harmony and Christian, together with their partners. Their father had come to visit old Reverend Jacobson back in the sixties to tell him of his father's death (as the two vicars were old friends), and had stayed. Henry, now a well-known Science Fiction writer, had met and fallen in love with a local girl, by the name of Eleanor Harrison, during the bus journey to the village. Henry had stayed with the Reverend for a while and eventually felt the calling to become a priest. He answered the call and took over at the vicarage after Reverend Jacobson died.

Henry's writing was a hobby – one at which he was incredibly successful, although his novels had raised a few eyebrows in his congregation at first. However, Henry believed God, the Author of all creation, wasn't offended and in the end the villagers became some of Henry's most ardent fans. After all, if anyone was interested in tales of scandalous behaviour and sin they need look no further than the Bible, they said to one another.

Sadly, Henry's wife had died in childbirth when the twins, Harmony and Christian, had been born. The villagers had rallied round, giving Henry their full support and, despite his grief, he had stayed in Bushwell and remained the resident vicar.

Eleanor would have been so proud of her children, all successful in their own rights and all happily married and producing grandchildren. Reverend Henry Fisherton had always been considered a dear friend, and in Eli's opinion, the man's successful novels made him a hero. He hoped the Rev would turn up at the celebration too this afternoon – he'd certainly been invited.

Enough musing. Eli grabbed his jacket and left the house. He'd been working from home, a converted oast house next to the animal sanctuary that had once been Milltop Farm – the very place he'd been thinking about as he'd considered the report on Darrington Way. He walked across the field and climbed the stile, stepping down onto the lane the other side, opposite the old signpost and bus stop. A BMW drew up beside him.

"Hey Mister, want a lift?" Dawn called through the driver window. He grinned and walked over to the car, bending down, with one arm on the roof, to kiss her through the opened window. Imogen Miles was seated in the passenger seat, and she smiled and lifted a hand in greeting.

"Actually, I was thinking of taking a walk to the old meadow first," he said.

Imogen leaned forward, touching Dawn's arm. "Oh Dawn, that sounds like a lovely idea!" To Eli she said, "Would you mind if we joined you?"

Dawn parked the car and Imogen lead the way down the narrow lane to the hidden gap in the hedge. Dawn and Eli followed behind, strolling hand in hand in companionable silence. They came to the opening and made their way through the long grass at the edge of the meadow, pausing to look at and enjoy the view. The sky was intensely blue.

"Heavenly," Imogen sighed. "I hope it always remains this way."

"Mmm, me to," Eli said after a moment, mentally destroying the file containing the planning application for the research laboratory, suddenly determined to actually do just that when he next returned to his office. The Jaxen Foundation would keep Darrington Way as a nature reserve.

Eli shielded his eyes with one hand and peered up, pointing at the branches of the Silver birch. "Look!" he said.

There appeared to be a patch of shimmering haze which hung for some seconds, mid-air between the branches of the Silver birch, then seemed to suddenly explode into tiny stars with a faint pop, before vanishing completely. Eli blinked, rubbing his eyes. "Did you see?" he asked, bemused.

"See what?" Dawn said, squinting in an attempt to see where her husband had been pointing.

"Nothing," Eli said. Perhaps his eyes had been playing tricks, yet he had the oddest sensation that something extremely important had just occurred, something that he should somehow be able to remember yet couldn't. He shook his head and sighed.

The three adults stood for a while longer, gazing about them. The sun was warm on their faces but there was a cooling breeze which whispered through the grass and caused the leaves on the old Silver birch to shiver. It was a comforting sound. Here and there in the grass, wild flowers could be seen and flitting about above them, as if to complement their brilliant colours, the lively Whitewood butterflies enjoyed the peace of an undisturbed habitat.

Enjoy this book?
For more like it, please visit:
www.efictiongroup.com

21492168R00157

Printed in Great Britain
by Amazon